Ruby gave him a look filled with appreciation. "Thank you for putting aside your resentment and giving me a chance."

"Don't thank me yet." Nash took a step back. "Goodnight, Ruby."

She offered him a soft smile. "Goodnight."

He locked the kitchen door and went up to his room. Thanks to Ruby he had his children back under his roof and could rest easy about that. Her presence here wasn't conducive to sleep, however.

He thought of her traveling the country with her theater friends and riding that horse all the way to Nebraska on her own. In a way it bothered him, but on the other hand she impressed him beyond measure. He couldn't think of another woman who would be so independent or daring. Few females would have packed a bag, saddled a horse and ridden alone for weeks and weeks.

Ruby was not like other women.

And those differences kept him awake at night.

Author of more than fifty romances, **Cheryl St. John**'s stories have earned RITA® nominations, *Romantic Times* awards, and are published in a dozen languages. In describing her stories of second chances, readers use words like 'emotional punch, believable characters and real-life situations'. Visit her at www.cherylstjohn.net

Books by Cheryl St. John

Mills & Boon® Historical Romance

Wed Under Western Skies
Almost a Bride
The Tenderfoot Bride
A Western Winter Wonderland
Christmas Day Family
Prairie Wife
His Secondhand Wife
The Magic of Christmas
A Baby Blue Christmas
The Lawman's Bride
Western Winter Wedding Bells
Christmas in Red Willow
Sequins and Spurs

**Visit the author profile page
at millsandboon.co.uk for more titles**

SEQUINS
AND SPURS

Cheryl St. John

Published in Great Britain 2015
by Mills & Boon, an imprint of Harlequin (UK) Limited,
Eton House, 18-24 Paradise Road, Richmond, Surrey, TW9 1SR

© 2015 Cheryl Ludwigs

ISBN: 978-0-263-24800-5

Printed and bound in Spain
by CPI, Barcelona

SEQUINS
AND SPURS

"Forgiveness is not an occasional act,
it is a constant attitude."
—Martin Luther King, Jr.

Chapter One

Crosby, Nebraska, 1883

The screen door barely squeaked, but the familiar sound made Ruby's heart leap. She'd never tiptoed all the way across the porch without Mama hearing that hinge and ordering her back to finish chores. *Ruby Gail! Stop right there, missy.*

Apprehension and uncertainty rising, she pushed open the unlocked interior door and entered the front room. In the remaining light of day it took a minute for her eyes to adjust enough for her to tell the furniture had been arranged differently, and the curtains at the windows were unfamiliar. The farmhouse sat eerily silent. No cooking smells met her senses; in fact, she wrinkled her nose at a faint antiseptic scent mingled with lingering lemon wax.

She hung her hat on a doorknob, lit the lantern sitting on a nearby table, and held it high to investigate. In the golden glow, she noted a light film of dust covering the wood furniture. Ruby frowned. Her mother dusted this room every day.

Stifling her unease, Ruby tiptoed across the dining room and through the open door into the nearly dark kitchen. Half a dozen dirty coffee cups sat on the sink board, but other than those, there was no sign of occupancy.

"Mama?" Ruby called. Striding to the back door, she flung it open and studied the dooryard. Chickens squawked from inside a wire enclosure. The plot where her mother always grew a vegetable garden was overgrown with weeds and a scattering of volunteer beans. Concern grew to a heavy weight in Ruby's chest.

Lighting lamps as she went, she searched each room. Finding no one downstairs, she headed up the worn front staircase.

"Mama?" Ruby's voice echoed throughout the upper hallway, and her unease rolled over into trepidation.

All the doors were closed. She went to her mother's straightaway, a flicker of panic pumping her blood faster as she stood with her hand on the faceted glass knob. "Mama?" she called, more softly this time.

The bed was neatly made with a plain wool blanket, instead of the quilt she remembered. On the dresser sat an ivory-handled comb and brush set Ruby recognized. She picked up the comb and ran her thumbnail across the teeth. On the surface of the bureau remained a clean outline where the comb had lain. Her heart skipped a beat. She placed the comb back where it had been.

In the mirror over the bureau, a worried face—a face that had seen too much sun this past week—stared back at her. She looked down. Opening a few drawers revealed neat stacks of clean stockings and underclothing. The scent of lavender offered a small measure of reassurance. Dozens of memories washed over her, some of them good. In the armoire, Laura Dearing's dresses and cotton shirtwaists hung in neat order. Ruby caressed a sleeve and drew it to her cheek. Where was her mother?

From the doorway, she peered into her sister's room. It, too, seemed unused. Pearl had undoubtedly married and moved to town or to another farm. Perhaps she lived a far distance and her mother had gone visiting. If that was so, however, Mama would have taken her comb and brush.

After finding the other two bedrooms unoccupied as well, Ruby at last entered her old room. Pink-and-white flowered wallpaper had been added. Lace curtains replaced the faded checkered cotton of her girlhood days. She didn't recognize the doll on the bed. Another child had apparently stayed here.

Opening drawers and checking the wardrobe, Ruby found nothing familiar—nothing at all. The few pieces of clothing she discovered belonged to a small girl, which was puzzling. It was as though Ruby had never been here. But of course, what had she expected? She hadn't been home for eight years. Any clothing she'd left behind wouldn't fit her fuller figure now, anyway.

Back on the main floor she did a closer inspection. There were staples in the pantry: coffee, flour, beans. The bin beside the stove held chunks of firewood, but even the stove was coated with a layer of dirt.

Ruby headed out the way she'd entered. She untied her bundle of belongings from the saddle, set it inside the door and then led the Duchess to the barn. "Hopefully, there's something tasty for your supper, girl," she said to the horse. "You deserve a treat and a nice long rest."

As she approached the structure in the near dark, she spotted a building she hadn't seen before. Farther to the west and bordered by rows of cottonwoods stretched a long low stable.

She led the horse to the trough first, then unsaddled her and walked her indoors. The three nearest stalls were occupied by very pregnant mares. Ruby spoke to each of them and rubbed their bony foreheads. "Who's taking care of you ladies?"

The oats in the bin were fresh, so she scooped a pail, set it inside a stall in the back corner and led in the Duchess. The impeccable neatness of the barn contrasted with the evident neglect in the house.

Her mother's absence grew more troubling, and Ruby didn't like the growing feeling of dread. Heading back to the house, she found supplies in the pantry, lit the stove and made herself a pan of biscuits. She'd hoped for something more than what she'd been eating on the trail, but this was quick and filling.

She prepared coffee, washed all the dirty cups and then filled a pail with sudsy water and wiped every surface in the kitchen, changing the water twice. Wherever her mother was, she'd be mortified if she knew how much dirt had settled in her house. Speculation spun in Ruby's mind. Someone was taking good care of those horses out there.

It was foolish to leave all the lanterns burning, so she moved through the rooms, turning down the wicks. Back in the kitchen, she was so tired she could barely think. She'd figure out things tomorrow and do more investigating when it was light.

She'd pour one more cup of coffee and then go up to sleep. Ruby settled herself at the table.

A sound woke her.

Disoriented, Ruby sat up with a crick in her neck and groaned. She'd fallen asleep with her head on the kitchen table. It was full dark, and someone was outside. Perhaps her mother was returning!

Ruby jumped up and peered out between the panels of the curtain. In the moonlight, a tall, broad figure moved toward the house. Certainly not her mother and definitely not anyone she knew.

She held her breath, waiting for the man to pound on the door. Instead of a knock, the doorknob turned and he entered the house uninvited. The hair on the back of her neck rose and her heart rate accelerated.

She shrank back against the still-warm stove, her hand coming in contact with the skillet she'd set there to dry. As silently as possible, she picked up the heavy pan and got a two-fisted grip on the handle.

The stranger fumbled in the dark, most likely

looking for a match. He groped along the shelf beside the door, coming closer to where she stood. If he found the matches and lit the lamp, he'd see her standing there.

She was trapped in the kitchen with an intruder.

She stood in the moonlight that arrowed through the slit in the curtains. He stopped short.

He'd spotted her.

Shooting into action, Ruby lunged forward with the skillet.

Moving with more agility than she'd expected, the intruder ducked, and the pan whacked him on the back of the head. With an "oomph," he crumpled sideways, striking a chair and knocking it over. As though fighting for consciousness, he groped for the table, but fell forward directly onto it and lay unmoving.

Heart pounding, Ruby reached for the matches and lit the wall lamp as well as the lantern.

The man sprawled across her mother's kitchen table wore dusty dungarees and boots, and the sleeves of his shirt were rolled back over corded forearms. He groaned and his hat fell away, revealing midnight-black hair and a jaw with a day's growth of beard. He was a dangerous-looking fellow, one she'd never seen before in her life. He'd probably come looking to rob the place while her mother was gone.

"Now what do I do with him?" Realizing she still gripped the heavy skillet, Ruby rested the impromptu weapon back on the stove with a clang. This fellow was a lot bigger and stronger looking than she. If he came to, she wouldn't have much chance of fighting or subduing him.

She cast her gaze about the room, wildly grasping for a solution. Noting the cotton square of toweling she'd hung to dry, she jerked open a cabinet to find a stack of embroidered towels.

Nash's head throbbed and red blotches swam behind his eyelids. Attempting to round his shoulders and move his neck, he emitted a groan. A wave of shock racked him. He couldn't move.

He blinked against harsh light, and the memory of finding someone standing in the dark kitchen swept over him. Something or someone had come toward him, and he hadn't been fast enough to escape the blow to the back of his neck.

Was he paralyzed? Genuinely panicked now, he tried to raise his hands, move his feet. He could feel them. But why couldn't he move his limbs more than a fraction of an inch?

Squinting, he opened his eyes against the

painful glare. He was sitting in a kitchen chair, his arms behind him.

A figure moved into his line of vision. A woman in boots, a riding skirt and an unbecoming loose shirt. Some member of an outlaw gang hiding out here? Who else was nearby? He'd seen no one and nothing out of the ordinary when he'd come to the house.

She stood in front of him, and he raised his aching head to discover a startling halo of wild, curly golden hair. A jolt ran through his befuddled mind, but after the first initial stab of pain, relief settled over him.

He was dreaming.

It was the most realistic dream he'd ever had, though he couldn't recall going to bed. The last thing he remembered was heading into the house. He'd never made it across the kitchen.

He studied the realistic vision standing before him. What on God's green earth had his wife done to her hair?

She was a little more slender than he remembered, but it was hard to tell with that baggy shirt. In real life Pearl would never have been caught dead in a getup like that. She'd ironed even the dresses she wore to do laundry and cook and work in the garden, and all her clothing had been made in feminine colors, with collars and ruffles and pleats.

Hard to tell at that moment if his head or his heart was hurting more. He closed his eyes and made a concerted effort to wake up. Doing so, he felt lonelier than ever, but at least awake he had control over his memories.

"Who are you?" she asked.

That wasn't Pearl's voice. Pearl's tone had always been soft and lilting. The dream woman's gravelly voice sounded as though she'd been screaming for a week. He opened his eyes and frowned.

"I said who are you? What did you come looking for?"

"Coffee, I think."

"Come morning I'm going for the marshal," she said. "And you're going to jail."

"If Marcus Styles puts anyone in jail, it'll be you." Nash frowned again. "But then dream people can't go to jail, can they?"

"Are you touched in the head, mister?"

"I wasn't until...." He scanned the room as it slowly came into focus, taking note of the cup and saucer on the table, the cast-iron skillet on the stove. A very heavy skillet, as he recalled. "Is that what you hit me with?"

No wonder he was still seeing stars! He tested

his hands once again, finding them securely bound behind his back. His feet, too, were firmly tied to the legs of the chair.

"Sit still or I'll clobber you again," she threatened, dropping onto a chair.

Now that she sat directly in front of him and he didn't have to squint upward, he had a better view. Her shiny hair was wilder than Pearl's, flaxen ringlets curling in haphazard disarray. Her face and hands weren't pale as Pearl's had been. But her features were delicate and feminine, her nose slim, albeit freckled. She had eyes as blue as his wife's, but with dark lashes that belied her pale hair.

And her mouth… It was wider, her lips more full… She had a mouth that would keep a man tied in knots.

Something about her reminded him of Pearl's mother, Laura, as well. Perhaps her eyes. Perhaps the stare that seemed to look into a person's soul, and required accountability.

He wasn't dreaming.

He knew exactly who this woman was. "The question is what are *you* doing here?"

"This is my home," she declared.

"I don't think so."

"And what does a robber know about me?"

"I'm not a robber. Untie me."

"So you can tie me up? Or perhaps kill me and steal everything in the house?"

"There's nothin' in this house that amounts to much," he told her. "If I was going to rob someone I'd find a more prosperous rancher. And I know everything I need to know about you." Then he added, "Ruby."

Chapter Two

Her eyes widened in surprise and she straightened on her chair. Her gaze darted aside for a moment and then narrowed on his face again. "How do you know my name?"

"You look just like your sister. Well, not *just* like her. You're not as pretty."

His insult didn't seem to faze her. "You know my sister?"

Anger and remorse carved a new pain in his chest. He swallowed before saying, "Yes."

"Who are you?" she asked again.

"Nash Sommerton."

Her expression revealed no recognition. She gave her head a half shake.

"Her husband," he clarified.

Ruby's confusion was plain, but oddly, it seemed tempered with relief. She cast him a skeptical glance. "How do I know you're telling the truth?"

"Why would I lie?"

"Where is she?"

"Untie me."

"Where is she?"

"Untie me."

They sat like that for a full minute, staring at each other, hobbled in a battle of control. He knew a stalemate when he encountered one. He'd learned most of what he knew about this woman from his wife and mother-in-law, women who didn't speak evil of anyone and who always expected the best. The rest he'd learned from what they hadn't said—from the hurt on their faces and the silence that yawned when her name came up.

"Your sister is dead," he said finally. It made him angry to say it like that. To be helpless to escape the fact.

"You're lying." Ruby narrowed her eyes and gave him an accusatory glare. "I don't know why you'd say such a cruel thing, but you're lying."

"I might be a lot of things," he replied. "But I'm not a liar."

Her doubt was easy to read.

"Look around," he suggested. "She's not here. Hasn't been here for nearly two years."

"She's probably somewhere else. If you're her husband, she's at your place."

"This *is* my place."

Ruby's mouth opened and shut before she asked, "What are you talking about?"

"The Lazy S is my ranch now."

"This is the Dearing farm."

"It's not a farm. Only crops out there are grains to feed the horses. Did you not notice that on your way in?"

She'd noticed. He saw it on her face.

"Two years?" she questioned, as though just grasping the information. "How could she be dead?" She shook her head. "I mean—how? How did it happen?"

"She was driving back from town with supplies. A storm came up and the wagon overturned in Little Wolf Creek. She was trapped under it. She drowned."

Ruby didn't want to believe him. "Where's my mother?"

"You'd have known all this if you'd have been here."

"Where is my mother?"

He drew a breath, but paused. Finally, he looked Ruby in the eye. "She died in April."

Something flickered behind her eyes. Disbelief? Anger? "Now I know you're making all this up. You expect me to believe they're *both* dead?"

He shrugged as best he could with his hands

bound behind his back. The woman was darned good with a knot. "See for yourself. Your mother's things are all just the way they were when she was here."

Plain enough, that statement rang true. Some of the color drained from Ruby's cheeks.

He jerked his head to indicate an easterly direction, and winced when pain crept up his neck. "There are three graves up on the rise that overlooks Deer Hollow."

The rest of the color had drained from her face by now. "Three?"

He resented being the one to tell her all this. He resented talking about it at all. "Lost a baby four years ago."

She got up and left the room.

Ruby stood at the foot of the stairs, her hand on the worn banister, her heart in her throat. Crushing fear rose up and threatened to suck the air from her lungs. She squeezed her eyes shut, willing this nightmare to end...willing sanity and reason to return. Needing her world to settle back on its axis and stop careening out of control.

The dust everywhere, her mother's clothing, the vanity set and hairbrush... It all added up to confirm that man's claims.

But she didn't *know* him.

What reason would he have to make up a story like that?

She *didn't* know him.

Where else could her mother be if he wasn't telling the truth?

"Ruby!" The man's angry voice carried from the kitchen. "Come back here and untie me!"

Trembling, she lowered herself to the bottom step and rested her spinning head on her knees.

His story did explain everything, even the hay field she'd seen on her way here…her mother's forgotten vegetable garden. If all his claims were true and Pearl and her mother were dead, Ruby was too late. She covered her mouth with a trembling hand. She could never make up for the past.

"Come back here now, Ruby!"

She disregarded his ravings and sat like that until her backside and spine ached. Sat there while the impact of that man's information sank in. Ruby became lost in her thoughts and the grief that bore down on her. She sank to the floor and half sat, half laid with her head on a step.

She'd waited too long.

He stopped yelling and she lost track of time and place. Eventually, with stiff movements, she stood and crossed the foyer to open the front door. The first rays of morning sun were visible behind the horizon. From the porch, she watched them creep above the cottonwoods that lined the river in the distance, until eventually she made out the yard and barn.

Ignoring her complaining body, she set out across a pasture, dew making the grass slippery under the soles of her boots. A cool breeze lifted her hair from her face and neck. At the top of a rise, silhouetted against the pale orange sky, stood three crosses.

Heart aching, not daring to breathe, Ruby approached.

In the dim morning light she made out the names burned into the wood. Margaret May Sommerton. Pearl Dearing Sommerton. And the last—the newest—in the same neat lettering: Laura McWhirter Dearing.

Ruby dropped to her knees in the dewy grass.

All the way to Nebraska she'd planned what she would say to her family. A million times she'd imagined the scene and their conversation and reactions. She had so much to make up for, so much to explain. She'd made plenty of mistakes, staying away so long being the biggest, but she'd hoped for forgiveness. Now she would never get to say the things she needed to say.

She would never be able to tell her mother she was sorry. She'd missed her last opportunity. While she'd been singing in theaters, eating and sleeping in hotels across the eastern states, her mother and sister had needed her here.

All those years her mother had believed Ruby didn't love her or care enough to come home— to stay home. But she'd loved Mama. *Of course* she had loved her.

Tears came then; great racking sobs rose from her belly and her chest heaved.

She hadn't said goodbye.

Her grief combined with overwhelming guilt and regret until it hurt to breathe. It didn't seem right to be here with the breaking sun on her face or to hear the sound of birds chirping in the nearby trees when the rest of her family was gone.

Finally, through her tears, Ruby turned her gaze to her sister's grave. Now that the sky had brightened, the neatly mown grass in this spot and the beds of violets planted at the head of each plot caught her attention.

Never again would she see Pearl's bright smile. Gone was the person who'd shared her memories of growing up, the sister who shared her father and knew the same pain of loss. Now there was no one to remember him with. No one with the same curly hair or blue eyes. Ruby was alone.

She turned her bleary gaze to the grave marked Margaret May. Buried here was the baby Pearl's husband had mentioned. Ruby didn't know if Margaret had died as a newborn or if she'd lived a short while, but in either case, Ruby felt Pearl's loss now, and it became her own.

The wetness that had soaked through her skirt made her knees ache. Pushing herself to her feet, she studied the dip in the landscape and the trees that outlined what her father had named Deer Hollow, because of the deer that tiptoed from cover to feed in the early morning and late evening. A pair grazed in the valley below her now. The largest one lifted its head to look right at her, obviously finding her no threat, because it went right back to feeding.

A dim memory swirled into perfect clarity. Many years ago she and Pearl had lain here in the grass watching the deer, several of them with fawns. The sisters had looked at each other, marveling in silence. Ruby had admired her sister's ability to wait and watch, while she herself had itched to creep closer. Her heart ached for that moment. For the years since. That same impatience had led her away, and pride had delayed her return. The land and the house were familiar, but everything else was different. Everything that mattered was gone.

Eventually, Ruby turned and made her way back across the pasture to the house. Making mistakes was nothing new for her. At least this one with Nash Sommerton was fixable. If she hadn't addled his brains with that skillet.

She walked all the way around to the back door and opened it without pause.

Rather than seeing her sister's husband tied to a chair, she discovered a pile of splintered wood.

Chapter Three

Nash's hands had gone numb before he'd had the sense to hobble to his feet and bash the chair against the cast-iron stove.

Mad enough to spit fire, he'd stormed through the house, finding that Ruby was gone. Finally, belly rumbling, he made himself something to eat. He figured as soon as it was daylight, she'd want to prove his story true or false and make her way to the grave markers. He pumped water, lit the stove and put the coffeepot on to boil.

He'd downed two cups before she returned.

Her appearance was startling. The front of her suede skirt was blotched dark. Not only did she look disheveled and exhausted, but her nose and eyes were red and puffy. Her hair looked as though she'd crawled backward though a bramble bush.

"So you're Ruby."

At the sound of his voice, she started and turned to where he sat.

"You're not what I expected."

She looked toward the coffeepot, shuffled to the cupboard for a cup and poured it half-full. Easing onto a chair at the opposite end of the table, she took a sip and met his eyes. "How did my mother die?"

Her voice was even raspier now.

He drew a breath and released it. "About five years ago the doctor said her heart was weak and that she needed to take life easy. Everything made her tired. She was pretty feeble." He picked up his cup, but then set it back down. "A Cheyenne woman from nearby made her teas and poultices, and for a spell they seemed to help. At first she'd sit on the porch or in the rocker in the parlor, but eventually she couldn't go up or down the stairs. She stayed in her room, mostly."

Ruby kept her focus on the cup in her hand, obviously absorbing his words with great difficulty.

"Pearl took care of her," he added.

Ruby's gaze flickered to his momentarily. He could make this easier on her, but he wanted her to know how hard it had been on his wife—on the whole family. He needed Ruby to see how her irresponsibility had been a burden. He didn't want it to be easy for her.

She stared into her coffee for a long time before raising her eyes. "You said Pearl died before Mama."

He nodded.

"Who took care of my mother after that?"

"My mother came as often as she could. And Little Bird, the Cheyenne woman I told you about. Between the two of them and some of the ladies from church, we kept her as comfortable as we could."

Ruby didn't shed a tear now, but it was plain she'd done plenty of crying before coming back to the house. Her fingers trembled on the handle of the cup, and she quickly moved her hand to her lap.

Had she thought she would come back after all this time and everything would be as she'd left it? "Where were you in April?" he asked.

She appeared to think a moment. "Chicago."

"Doin' what?"

"Theater."

He raised his eyebrows. "Acting?"

She nodded. "Singing."

He couldn't imagine that unusual, sandpapery voice of hers lifted in song. "Singing on a stage… in front of people?"

"That's right."

"They paid?"

"That's how singers make a living." She flattened her hands on the table. "Look, I know I wasn't here for either of them. I should have come back a long time ago, but…but I didn't. I sent Mama money every month."

"You could have visited. Written at least."

"I sent a couple of letters. I'm not much for writing."

"Pearl needed help," he said. "She took care of everyone and the house all by herself till she died."

"I'm sorry." Ruby set her mouth in a straight line.

"Sorry doesn't fix eight years of neglect."

She stared at her cup. "No. It doesn't."

"Did you get letters from your mother?"

"A few, but I never stayed in one place long."

"Too busy to come visit, were you?"

"I had my reasons."

"I'll bet you did." Stage performers didn't have the best reputations. Not that he knew the sordid details, but he could imagine. He reached into his pocket and pulled out his watch. "I have to get out to the stock. Thanks to you, I didn't get any sleep last night."

"I'm sorry about that, too," she said. "And for…" She gestured to his head. "Hitting you with the skillet."

"You could've killed me." He got up and set his cup near the sink basin, noting for the first time that all the other dirty cups he'd left there were gone. He paused. "What's your plan?"

"What do you mean?"

"What are you going to do now?"

"I have to figure that out."

"You plannin' to stay here?"

"This is my home."

He said nothing. Didn't look at her again, just walked out the back door and closed it firmly behind him. He felt half-sick at the thought of her being here. He hoped she'd be gone when he came back. He had enough people to take care of, and sufficient worries on his mind already. He didn't need her adding to his problems.

In the back of his mind was concern for the ranch he'd worked so hard to build. He'd sacrificed time with his wife and family to make it a success. Ruby hadn't been in the picture then, but now…now she'd likely lay her claim.

She hadn't stuck around before. To protect his children's inheritance and his investment in the land, he could probably convince her to take off again. Or wait her out.

Ruby headed out to the coop and gathered eggs. She found a ham in the pantry, cut off a slice and fried it with the eggs. The whole time she used the skillet, she thought about what she'd done to her newfound brother-in-law. Her mother had always said she acted before she thought things through, and as much as Ruby had hated hearing it, that remained a fact. She gave herself the excuse of fearing a robber, and cast her blunder aside.

A hot meal in her stomach felt good. After washing the dishes, she heated more water and searched until she found a copper tub on the back porch. She dragged it into the kitchen, filled it and then slid the bolt on the back door before washing her hair and bathing.

The hot water soothed her aching muscles. But relaxing in such a way caused her to let her guard down, and she sat in the steaming tub and sobbed until the water cooled and her fingers and toes wrinkled.

She would never see Mama again. Never hear her laugh or see her smile. Ruby had missed her opportunity to hug her sister and tell her she loved her. She'd lost everything dear to her. *Lost everything she'd turned her back on*, her pitiless conscience taunted. Everything she'd run away to escape.

If her mother and sister had been so dear, why had she taken off and not returned for so long?

That's what Nash would ask her. That's what anyone would want to know. She'd asked herself a hundred times, but she still couldn't explain.

She'd been close to her father. They had been very alike, she guessed. He'd been the one person she could talk to, confide in. After he'd left without notice, she'd been bitter and angry. Her heartbreak had been disguised in rebellion and resentment. Her mother had relentlessly nagged and insisted Ruby attend church with her.

Ruby had hated sitting in church. Everyone there was looking at them and pitying them because of her father's desertion. And all her mother had to say about his absence was that God was taking care of them. God hadn't lifted a finger to keep Abe Dearing on that farm—and after he was gone, God hadn't put food on their table or shoes on their feet.

At sixteen, Ruby had been fed up with rules and restrictions, weary of her mother's constant admonitions. Ruby had packed a bag and caught a train.

She'd been proud. Self-reliant. Adventurous.

Impetuous. Foolish.

Lonely.

More tired than she'd ever been in her life, Ruby stood, dried herself and then dressed in a wrinkled skirt and shirtwaist from her bag. She couldn't deal with emptying the tub at the moment, so she left it and climbed the stairs.

She chose the room that used to be hers, though the only familiar furnishing was the bed. After setting the doll aside, she opened the window for fresh air and pulled down the spread, climbing between the sheets and closing her eyes.

The best thing that could happen would be to sleep for days, wake up and find this had all been a nightmare.

Nash's head ached so fiercely he left the hired men mending fence and rode northeast to a strip of land near the river that nestled between the Lazy S and the Sommerton property, where his father owned and operated a grain mill.

Little Bird's husband had left her the strip of land, and she had remained after his death. There was nothing conventional about the landscape or the cabin. Wooden slews carried water to thriving herb and vegetable gardens that stretched toward the river.

Cages had been built against a squat, barewood barn, and at any given time half of them contained birds or small animals in various stages of treatment and healing. Frames made of willows and small saplings held curing hides.

Peculiar scents of distilling syrups and natural cures permeated the air.

At his approach, a slender figure in a simple fawn-colored dress and moccasins moved forward from one of the gardens. She was a handsome woman, probably a good ten years older than himself, and she'd been a good friend to his family. Her hair was plaited into two long braids that didn't show a strand of gray.

"Nash Sommerton," she called, one hand raised in greeting.

He slid from his horse. "Little Bird."

She held the back of her hand to his horse's muzzle. Boone inhaled her scent and pressed his nose to her chest. "He says there is much confusion in your heart today."

"I don't know about that, but there's a mighty powerful pain in my head."

"Come," she said, and gestured. "Sit by the fire and I'll make you tea."

He'd been inside the cabin a time or two, but Little Bird preferred to greet and treat her patients out of doors.

He took a seat on one of the slabs of rock situated around a fire pit. She added a chunk of wood before coming to stand behind him. Her deft fingers found the knot on the back of his head. "Did you fall?"

Nash held back a groan. "Not until after the iron skillet struck me."

"I sense it was not an accident."

"No. Pearl's sister meant to put me out of commission."

"I haven't heard news of Pearl's sister. She is visiting?"

"I don't know what she's doing besides knocking me senseless. She just showed up last night."

Little Bird headed for the cabin. While he waited, a squirrel scampered close and leaped to perch on its hind legs on another slab of stone. The beady-eyed little creature stared at him curiously. It watched when the woman returned with a wooden tray and a small pouch.

She took a pan from a pile of utensils beside the fire, poured water from a gourd pitcher and added dried leaves. She measured out and added several drops of a tincture before setting the pan over the fire.

While that heated, she made a poultice. "Lean forward." She separated his hair and pressed the warm compress to his scalp. "The arrival of Pearl's sister was unexpected."

He didn't reply. It pained him to think how much Pearl had missed that undeserving woman, longed for her return.

"Laura Dearing often spoke of her."

"Pearl, too." He probably knew everything about the two of them as children, because his wife had shared it all. There were so many times she'd needed her sister. He couldn't understand Ruby's selfishness.

"You're angry she left her family behind to seek her way. I, too, left my family when I married William McLeod. I haven't seen them for many years."

"That's different. You left to marry. Ruby didn't marry or start her own family. She just ran off."

"Pearl's sister had no way of knowing her mother would become ill."

"She'd have known if she'd stuck around. Or come back once or twice. My head feels better already."

"Hold the compress in place while I pour your tea and cool it."

He did as instructed. His neighbor ladled greenish liquid into a gourd dipper, added cool water and handed it to him. "Drink it all at once. Don't stop to take a breath."

He found out right off why she'd told him not to stop. The bitter tea tasted awful. He finished it and shuddered.

"Saint Anthony's fire," she told him. "Tastes bad, but will stop the pain in your head."

He trusted her. Once when his mother had experienced some sort of female infirmity, Little Bird's remedy had fixed her good as new. The woman had cured one of his father's mill workers from palsy in his hands, and last winter she'd made Nash an ointment for his cracked and bleeding knuckles that had healed them right up. "Yes, ma'am."

He went to his horse and opened the saddlebag to take out a sack of sugar. Little Bird never accepted cash, but she always appreciated items she didn't grow or gather herself. He carried the sugar to the doorstep and set it down.

"Thank you, Nash Sommerton."

"It's I who am indebted." He took his hat from the pommel of his saddle and settled it on his head.

"We must travel our own paths," she said. "Some try to tell us which turns to take and how fast to walk. But in the end it's our journey, and we must make it alone."

"Are you trying to tell me something about my wife's sister?"

"I'm suggesting you don't draw conclusions without all the information."

He had plenty of information. All of it incriminating where Ruby was concerned.

Little Bird raised her hand in farewell. Nash tipped his hat and headed back to the ranch.

Approaching the stables, he glanced toward the house, and his heart skipped a beat. Sheets and pillowcases flapped on the clothesline in the sunlight, a sight he painfully associated with his wife. But of course it hadn't been Pearl's hands who'd hung the bedding. Dressed in a plain brown skirt splotched with water and with her sleeves rolled back, Ruby lugged a washtub to the side of the porch and dumped it out onto the parched lilac bush.

She wiped her forehead with her wrist and glanced in his direction.

Even from this distance, the differences between her and his wife were glaring. He'd never seen Pearl looking disheveled, not even on wash day.

Ruby set down the tub and wiped her hands on her skirt. Then she walked to the stairs and descended, heading toward him.

He didn't want to talk to her. He didn't want to see her. She stirred up too many feelings he didn't want to deal with.

She approached to within several feet and stopped. "How's your head?"

"I'll live."

"I said I was sorry."

He said nothing.

"I was wondering about something. I noticed a couple of men coming and going from the stable and the barn."

He narrowed his gaze warily. "Yeah?"

"Could they help me for a short time tomorrow, so I can move out the furniture to clean the rugs and wax the floors?"

"My hands aren't maids," he replied. What was she trying to prove by cleaning the house? It was a little late to show up and pitch in now.

She set her hands on her hips and fixed him with an exasperated glare. "I didn't ask for a maid. I asked for strong backs." She glanced toward the barn. "Never mind. I'll handle it on my own."

She turned and headed toward the house. The sun caught in her crazy hair and set the golden curls ablaze. For a moment he couldn't breathe. Everything about her made him ache. His heart, his head…

A sound caught his attention.

Ruby shaded her eyes and discovered a black buggy drawn by a single horse moving toward them. Behind it a trail of dust rose into the air. "Company?" she asked.

Nash had turned to view the approaching conveyance as well. He slid his hat back on his head, revealing a strong profile and lean jaw. Ruby glanced from him to the buggy. His expression didn't give away his thoughts.

"Do you know who it is?"

"I know." He moved toward the lane.

She followed at a distance, straining to see the driver, who turned out to be a woman in a blue dress and a wide-brimmed hat with matching silk flowers and ribbons. She guided the horse to a stop.

Nash took the reins, pulled the brake and wrapped the leather around the handle. The woman gracefully accepted his help and he lowered her to the ground.

She wasn't alone. Two children crowded forward to be lifted down, but instead of placing the little girl on her feet, Nash enveloped her in a hug. With a gleeful cry, she wrapped her arms around his neck and her stockinged legs around his waist.

The smaller child, a boy in a pressed shirt and suspenders, jumped up and down impatiently.

Finally, Nash placed the girl on the ground and the boy leaped into his arms. "Papa! Papa!"

His cheerful cries penetrated Ruby's confusion.

Papa?

The woman turned toward Ruby, her expression curious. She was lovely, with dark winged brows, high cheekbones and glowing olive skin. She took in Ruby's hair and clothing before settling her attention on her face. Recognition dawned in her warm brown eyes and she asked, "Are you going to introduce us, Nash?"

"This is Laura's other daughter." He glanced at Ruby. "My mother, Georgia Sommerton."

"I thought so." Georgia extended a slender hand. "I remember you, Ruby."

"You do?"

"Yes, of course. You were an adventurous child, as I recall."

"I suppose so," she said, still distracted by the boy's exclamation. Now the woman's resemblance to Nash jumped out at her: her black hair and dark eyes...her defined cheekbones. Ruby studied the sturdily built little boy in Nash's arms. He had the same dark hair and winged brows.

The girl, however, was fair and slender, with radiant skin and shining pale ringlets that hung to her shoulders. She lifted her curious gaze, and Ruby's heart stopped.

Studying the child was like looking at her sister years ago. Her eyes were the same bright cornflower blue, her expression solemn and wary. With a small hand, she reached to grasp her grandmother's fingers. Apparently the doll and the clothing in the drawers in Ruby's old room belonged to this child.

Captivated, Ruby stared. Unexpected tender feelings brought tears to her eyes, but she blinked them back and retained her composure. The oppressive ache that had been a weight on her heart since the day before eased, and an unfamiliar joy rose inside her.

She tore her gaze back to the smaller child, keen to recognize a similarity to her sister. Nash's hair...his eyes....

"Who is she, Papa?" he asked.

There it was. The shape of his lips...the tilt of his nose. Elation lifted Ruby's spirits. She shot her attention to the surly man holding the little boy and pierced him with a glare. "Why didn't you tell me?"

Chapter Four

Nash scowled at her over his son's shoulder. "Tell you what?"

"That my sister had children?"

"Didn't know that you'd care."

Was this what Ruby deserved? She took a deep breath and composed herself. Why would he think any differently? She hadn't shown concern until now. His mother hadn't made any cutting remarks yet, but there was still time. Ruby cast her a cautiously apologetic look, but her anger at Nash's callousness simmered.

"Ruby, this is Claire," Georgia said, and raised the hand that the girl held. "That's Joel. Children, this is your aunt Ruby. She's your mother's sister."

Ruby couldn't have been more surprised at the matter-of-fact introduction.

Nash turned and headed for the buggy, with Joel looking back at her over his shoulder.

Georgia didn't miss the tension between her son and her late friend's estranged daughter. Nash had set his jaw in that stubborn way he had.

"There's a bag with lemons under the seat, Nash," she called after him.

He waved a hand in acknowledgment, and set the boy on the horse's back while he unharnessed it and led it to a spot in the shade of a tree.

"I'll make us lemonade and we can chat," Georgia suggested.

"I'll help," Ruby replied. The three females headed into the house.

Georgia noted the wet porch floor and the basket of clothing that needed to be hung up, but Ruby walked straight past them and held open the screen door. She resembled her mother and sister, but her features were stronger, more vibrant. Any other woman would have tamed her hair into a braid or a tight bun to do laundry, but Ruby's was loosely gathered into a tail by a faded red kerchief, with long spirals framing her face and trailing to her shoulders.

"I'm a little out of practice in the kitchen." Ruby located a pitcher and a few glasses. "These might need washing. Everything's still dusty. I'm working on it."

She was a strong-looking young woman, competent, not frail or delicate as her sister had been. Her strength had nothing to do with size, though she was taller. Her appeal was in her complete lack of guile or airs.

Claire was obviously reluctant to release her grandmother's hand, but Georgia gave her an assuring smile and gestured for her to take a seat.

"Where's the other chair?" Claire asked, calling attention to the missing piece of furniture. Georgia glanced at the spot where it had been.

"It got broken," Ruby replied simply. "How old are you, Claire?"

The child looked first to Georgia, her hesitation obvious. Georgia gave her an encouraging nod.

"Six," Claire answered.

"And Joel?" Ruby asked. "How old is he?"

"He's three," Georgia replied.

"Still just a baby." Sadness tinged the young woman's voice.

Georgia had visited Laura and Pearl often, and they had been to her home many times. She knew they hadn't been able to reach Ruby, so had to assume the new arrival had only just learned of the deaths of her mother and sister. Georgia didn't understand her motives, but was sure coming back to this news had been shocking.

"The children have been staying with Nash's father and me, so Nash can run the ranch. I bring them to see him as often as I can, and he comes to dinner on Sundays." She paused, realizing she had no idea what this woman's plans were. "You're welcome to join us this Sunday."

Ruby appeared surprised at the invitation. "Thank you. I'd like that."

Georgia was curious to know what had brought Ruby here now, after all these years, and whether or not she planned to stay, but she didn't want to bring up a sensitive subject in front of Claire. She touched the little girl's shoulder. "Why don't you run up and get the doll you wanted from your room?"

"Oh, yes'm." Claire darted from the kitchen.

Ruby had heated water and was washing the pitcher and glasses. Georgia took a clean towel from a cupboard shelf to dry them.

Ruby gave her a cautious, but straightforward look. "You must be surprised to see me."

Georgia nodded. "More than a little."

"Your son doesn't want me here."

Georgia could only imagine how Ruby's sudden arrival had surprised Nash. They had all wondered about her, but he had been here with

Pearl and Laura all along, so undoubtedly he had more questions than anyone else. "The last few years have been difficult for him. He has strong feelings about all of it. About you."

Ruby paused with her wrists over the enamel basin, suds dripping from her fingers. "All I wanted to do was make things up to my mama and Pearl. I came back to ask Mama's forgiveness and to start over." She shook her head, sending curls swaying. "Nash hates me for making things harder for them—especially harder for Pearl."

Georgia was aware of her son's resentment. "Hate is a strong word."

"But it's the right word in this case."

Georgia had no idea what was going on inside Ruby's head, but she knew her son well enough to know he'd directed a lot of anger toward the woman who'd unknowingly left all the care of her mother to his wife, and later to the kindness of his neighbors. "He's going to need some time."

The back door opened and closed, and Nash set the bag of lemons on the table. "We're gonna wash up at the well."

Joel rode his father's hip as Nash headed out again.

Ruby took the lemons from the bag and found a cutting board. "He told me you called on my mother. Were you friends?"

Georgia nodded, not wanting to reveal more than Ruby was ready to hear. "We became good friends, yes."

"Do you hate me, too?"

"Of course not. I barely know you."

"You know what I did."

Her frankness was surprising. "You headed out on your own and you sent money home."

Ruby met her gaze with penetrating blue eyes, eyes like her mother's, but more full of life and expression. "Mama told you that?"

Georgia nodded. "We spent a lot of time together. She told me many things."

Claire returned clutching a rag doll. "The sheets aren't on my bed."

Ruby appeared flustered and brushed hair from her face with the back of a wet hand. "I didn't realize that was your room when I chose a bed last night. I used to sleep there when I was your age."

"You did?"

Ruby dried her hands on a length of toweling. "I washed all the sheets today, though, so I'll leave them clean for the next time you sleep in your bed again." She turned to Georgia. "I'd like to talk more when there's time."

Georgia gave her a long, considering look. "I'll look forward to it."

Ruby wasn't sure what to make of the older woman's lack of animosity, compared to her son's, but she was thankful. No doubt Ruby would run up against a lot of people with the same negative opinion of her, so she might be smart to develop an even thicker skin.

It took a few minutes, but Ruby found a glass juicer and washed that as well. She then set to squeezing the lemon halves. "I have no idea how much sugar to add. I don't even know if there is any."

Georgia carried a chipped cup to the pantry and returned with it full. "This should do it."

Nash came back and set a ragged square of ice near the sink. A few pieces of straw stuck to the surface. Georgia rinsed it off, found a mallet and chipped ice for their drinks.

When the lemonade was ready, they carried their glasses to the front porch. Ruby waited until the family was seated in what she assumed were their usual places before taking a seat on a nearby bench. An awkward silence followed.

"When did you get here?" Georgia finally asked.

"About dusk last night."

"She slept in my bed," Claire said to her father. Nash didn't look at any of them.

"How did you arrive?" Georgia asked.

"I rode in." Ruby gestured to the corral, one end of which was visible from where they sat. She'd let her mare out that morning. "The Duchess is in the corral."

"What about your belongings?"

"I had a couple of trunks shipped to the station in Crosby. I don't own much that's of use on a farm, though."

"Ranch," Nash corrected.

"I saw the mares ready to foal," she replied. When he didn't respond, she turned to Georgia. "Are your family all ranchers?"

"My husband owns a grain mill." She glanced at her son, and Ruby picked up on something between them that made her wonder about his own family relationships. "Our daughter's husband works there, too. Nash is the only horseman."

When Joel got up and headed for the porch stairs, Nash followed. "Want to go see the horses, buddy?" He turned to his daughter. "Come to the barn with us, sweet pea."

Claire glanced at her grandmother.

"Go with your father," she encouraged. "We'll be leaving shortly, and he wants to spend time with you."

Claire set her doll on the porch swing beside Georgia and joined her little brother.

"She reminds me of Pearl," Ruby said.

Georgia picked up the rag doll and absently smoothed its yarn hair. "She's definitely the spitting image of her mother."

"Not only her looks," Ruby said softly, "but the way she's so hesitant about everything."

Georgia studied her. "Pearl was a good wife and mother. We all loved her."

Ruby still heard no accusation in her tone or the appreciative statement. She glanced at the horse in the shade. "She was a good daughter, too, I guess."

"She was devoted to your mother."

Of course. Pearl had always done everything it took to please their mother. She hadn't torn her stockings or misplaced her school books. She'd been a good student and had dutifully helped pull weeds, cook and put up vegetables and preserves. Ruby could still see them together in the kitchen, putting the finishing touches on a cake.

Her sister must have been a comfort to their mother. "How long was Mama sick?"

"Several years. There were times when it seemed she got stronger, but then she'd get weak again."

Ruby had missed it all. The good days and the bad ones.

She'd been gone from home only a year when she'd realized her blunder. She had the freedom and independence she'd always craved, but there were no glamorous jobs for girls like her. She'd always been overly optimistic and impetuous, and more times than she cared to admit, those traits had landed her in tight situations. Leaving home with overblown dreams had been the most monumental of her rash mistakes, but she couldn't run back to the place she'd escaped. There had been nothing here for her.

She'd been convinced she wasn't cut out for a mundane life of cooking and cleaning and going to church. School had been torture enough—all those tedious days trapped inside and chained to someone else's schedule. The world was too big and exciting, and life too full of possibilities to miss out on by following all the rules.

Besides, Ruby Dearing was not a quitter.

So she'd taken unglamorous jobs in saloons and gaming halls, avoiding crude advances and barely getting by, until eventually she'd joined a theater troupe and traveled. Sometimes the pay was good, other times just adequate. But she'd persisted.

If, at some point along that path, she could have swallowed her pride sooner and come for a visit... But there it was. She had held on to her dream until it was nothing more than a dirty rag. And now it was too late. She had always fallen short.

"Your mother loved you very much," Georgia said.

Ruby had never doubted her mother's love. Laura Dearing just hadn't known what to do with her. "I was a disappointment. Even when I was here I wasn't a pleasing child. I missed my father too much. I didn't fit in with Mama's routine or her plans. Not like Pearl."

"Nobody's perfect, Ruby. And everyone is different."

She could wallow in self-recrimination or she could do something to make up for lost time. "Is it too late to plant a garden?"

"Probably not. Ours just went in a week or so ago."

Everything she'd once thought tedious and unbearable now seemed like a lifeline to the stable life she had thrown away. "I'm going to get the house clean. And then I'll plant a garden. I need to learn how to cook and put up things for winter."

She didn't miss the sympathetic look Georgia cast her way, but the woman replied, "I'll help any way I can."

"It appears you do enough already, what with the children in your care."

"I have help at the house. If you need me, all you have to do is ask. Don't be shy."

"Shy isn't one of my traits," Ruby said with a smile.

Half an hour later, she trailed behind as Nash and his mother led the children to the buggy. When they reached the conveyance, Claire hugged him around the knees. Gently, he loosened her hold and hunkered down to look into her eyes.

Georgia deliberately stood a distance away to give them privacy, as did Ruby, but their words were still audible.

"I miss you so much, Papa."

"I miss you, too, Claire."

"I love Grandma and Grandpa."

"I know you do. But it's still hard to be away from home for so long?"

Claire nodded.

Nash wiped a tear from her cheek with his thumb. "It's hard for me, too. Thank you for being brave and helping with Joel."

Claire nodded, and they hugged. Nash stood, picked up his little boy and kissed his forehead. "Thank you for being a good boy for your grandmother, Joel."

Joel hugged his neck, and Nash peeled him away to lift both children up to the buggy and then assist his mother. He bent forward for Georgia to kiss his cheek, and she waved a friendly goodbye to Ruby.

Georgia led the buggy away. Nash straightened his shoulders in a deliberate motion, as though fortifying himself and keeping a lock on his emotions.

Ruby stood a few feet away from him on the grass in front of the house. "They're beautiful."

He turned slowly, his dark gaze ruthlessly taking in her features, her rumpled shirtwaist, her hair. He had a couple days' worth of growth on his chin and upper lip, but his black hair barely touched the collar of his laced shirt. His eyes were so brown they were nearly black, his brows two angry slashes above. "I have work to do."

"I have questions I'd like to ask."

"Can they wait?"

His dismissal was even more abrupt than previously. The visit with Claire and Joel had clearly set him on edge. Ruby nodded and glanced toward the stables. "Who cooks for the hands?"

"We cook outdoors. In the bunkhouse if the weather's poor."

"I wouldn't mind cooking for all of you. Might make things easier if you didn't have to do it yourselves."

His expression was unreadable. "You can get our supper then. Most days there are three of us."

She might have said something else, but he'd already turned away and headed for the stables. After taking the glasses inside, she finished hanging her clothes on the line. The sheets were dry by then, so she made up the beds. She tried to put herself in Nash's place and imagine how difficult the past few years had been. When she looked at herself the way he'd seen her, she couldn't blame him for holding her absence against her.

Resigned to leaving her old room to Claire, Ruby opened the windows in her mother's room, mopped the plank wood floors and shook the rag rugs. An upholstered chair with long fringe covering the legs sat between the two corner windows. Beside it a basket held skeins of yarn and knitting needles. Underneath them she found squares of fabric.

Ruby picked up the unfinished piece on top and looked at the white rectangle looped on the needles. She didn't remember her mother knitting, but back then Laura had been busy with feeding and clothing two children and caring for a house. Perhaps this had filled her time after she'd become sick.

Next, Ruby cleaned and polished the furniture,

which consisted of an old armoire with calico curtains on the doors and two small drawers at the bottom, a wood chest at the foot of the bed, a dressing table and chair, and the bureau.

Before placing the ivory comb back on top, she ran her thumbnail across the teeth once more. She could never get the tiny teeth through her curly tresses, but she liked looking at the comb her mother had used for many years.

Ruby got a fresh pail of water and tackled the coal stove in the other corner. Her mother had always set a vase of wildflowers atop it in the summer. Maybe Ruby would look for some spring flowers later.

In the bottom of the armoire she found the quilt that had always been on Laura's bed, shook it out the window and spread it over the mattress. Grandma McWhirter had made it for Mama as a wedding gift. Daddy hadn't stuck around any longer than it took to sire two daughters, but the quilt had been here for as long as Ruby could remember.

A resounding slam echoed up the stairway.

"Ruby!"

She straightened and hurried out into the hallway.

Nash stood at the bottom of the stairs, glaring up. "What in blazes are you thinking, woman?"

"About what?"

"About flapping your drawers for all the world to see!"

She came down two steps. "What are you talking about?"

"I'm talking about the clothesline. A rancher from Hope Valley came out to look over one of my mares, and your nether wear is hanging in plain sight. It's indecent."

"What am I supposed to do with my underwear to get it dry?"

Obviously exasperated, he took a breath and expelled it. "Be discreet, of course. Tuck it in between the sheets and towels. That's what Pearl did."

Ruby set down the pail she held and flounced down the stairs. "Well, forgive me for doing my laundry. I had no idea my drawers would get you all in a dither."

His complexion reddened and it wasn't from embarrassment. "I'm not in a dither. I'm a businessman trying to conduct a sale with a respectable gentleman who doesn't care to see your *drawers*."

"Then do your business and leave me to mine." She moved past him and hurried along the hall toward the back door. The front door slammed again.

Chapter Five

After pausing to wash her hands in the kitchen, she carried a basket out of doors and unclipped her clothing from the line, quickly folding and stacking. From the corner of her eye she caught movement as a man climbed to his wagon seat and shook the reins over his horses' backs. He turned his head and adjusted his hat, but it was plain he'd been taking a gander.

She waved in a friendly fashion and went back to her task.

A minute later, when she glanced over again, the wagon was rolling up dust along the road and Nash had headed back toward the stables. She plucked a wooden clothespin from the bag and threw it as far as she could. It dropped in the grass with unsatisfactory silence.

Ruby carried her clothing into the house and to her mother's room, where she sorted it on the bed. Traveling with the troupe, the girls had hung their clean garments anywhere they could—most often in their hotel rooms. Ruby felt foolish for not having the foresight to realize it wasn't polite to hang her things where someone might see them, but the sheets had already been dry by the time she got around to hanging her chemises and drawers. She wouldn't have the beds made now if she'd waited.

It irked her that Nash had pointed out her mistake, and it irked her more that he'd told her what Pearl would have done. Of course her sister had known how to do everything properly. She'd probably never even said words like *drawers* or *underpinnings* in front of her husband.

Ruby didn't like feeling foolish, and she wasn't going to let her sister's cranky husband make her feel bad. There were nice ways to say things, and he hadn't been very nice about anything yet.

Yanking open drawers in the bureau, she took out all her mother's stockings and cotton clothing, and unfolded and refolded each piece. Ruby didn't own much everyday wear, so she'd be able to use most of the items herself. Mama would have liked her practical thinking.

At the bottom of a drawer she found a rectangle wrapped in a scarf and uncovered it, revealing her parents' wedding portrait. Her mother looked so young and lovely, with a sweet girlish expression. Ruby ran a finger over the image, noting Laura's simple clothing and the plain veil she'd worn over her hair. Around her neck was the gold locket she'd always worn. Seeing it stirred up more memories for Ruby.

Her father stood straight and tall in his three-piece suit. He was fair, with a thick mustache and curly hair Ruby remembered well. Seeing his likeness brought an ache to her chest.

One morning he simply hadn't been at the breakfast table.

"Where's Daddy?" Pearl had asked.

"I don't think we'll be seeing him again." It wasn't until years later that Ruby had considered how controlled her mother's voice and actions had been as she'd hidden her panic and fear from her daughters. "He took the big brown suitcase and his clothes."

"But he didn't say goodbye!" Ruby had cried. "He must be coming back."

"I don't think so," her mother had said, ineffectively dousing hope. "You girls had best set your minds to the fact that your daddy's gone for good."

Pearl had cried, and their mother had wiped her tears and hugged her.

"He'll come back," Ruby had stated emphatically, sure of it. Certain he wouldn't just leave them without a word of explanation.

When her mother had reached to comfort her, she'd angrily slid from her chair and run out the back door. People didn't just give up on the ones they loved. But with every day and week and month that had passed, her hope had faded.

She'd never stopped wishing. Wishing he'd return with hugs and gifts and assurance that he loved her. Wishing life wasn't so hard for her mother, for all of them. But Ruby had also grown determined. She would not spend her life here, lonely and fading like dry flowers in the heat— like her mother. She was going to see places, meet people, live life without boundaries.

Obviously, the sight of the portrait had been too painful for her mother, so she'd hidden it away. Ruby set it on the bureau beside pictures of herself and Pearl as May Day fairies, with flowers in their hair, winding streamers around the maypole. She tested how she felt with the wedding picture in plain view.

Her father hadn't married Laura with the intent of leaving. He'd obviously loved her and planned a life together. What had pulled him away?

Maybe his leaving hadn't reflected on her or her sister. Maybe it hadn't been her mother's fault. Maybe he'd simply had a wandering spirit, and nothing could have tied him to this land.

Ruby discovered she liked the happy memories of her and her sister as children and her parents young and in love. The portrait reminded her she had been a part of a family once. They were all gone now, and her only relations were Nash and Pearl's two children. She was going to have to learn to get along with him—and somehow prove herself to him. She would look at the faces of her parents and sister in the morning and at night to remember the good times and remind herself what was important.

A glance at the clock told her it was time to prepare supper, so she put away the clothing and cleaning supplies.

Her lack of foresight had left her with few choices for a meal. Tomorrow she would go into Crosby and buy supplies.

Out back of the house, she eyed the chickens in the pen. She had no idea what to do with a chicken, but she sure liked them fried, so she went in search of her brother-in-law.

"Hello?"

At the sound of her husky voice, Nash set down a bucket and straightened.

Startled that Ruby had sought him out, he met

her in the opening of the barn door, where the late afternoon sun sent shafts of light across the hard-packed dirt. She walked into one of them, and the sun lit her hair like fool's gold. "Can you spare a few minutes?"

"What do you want?"

"I wondered if you'd show me how to get a chicken ready to cook."

Having her here made things agonizingly complex. He didn't want to help her, but she did seem to be making an effort to do something useful. His belly was already grumbling.

She planted her hands on her hips. "I want to learn. And I really want to eat."

He grabbed his hat and settled it on his head as he strode out the door. Since she was bound and determined to get in the way of a day's work, he might as well get a meal out of her effort. "Got hot water ready?"

"No."

"Not boiling, just hot enough to scald. Sit a big pot on the back porch there."

She hurried to do his bidding, and returned minutes later.

"Don't eat the sitters," he explained. "If they're on nests in the henhouse, let 'em be. You have to pay attention to know which ones lay regularly."

She followed him into the pen.

"That one's a rooster." He pointed. "I didn't know till it crowed the other day. Grab it by the feet and hang it upside down, so it won't flap its wings." It took Nash a couple minutes to demonstrate a humane kill and preparation.

If he'd thought she'd be squeamish, he was wrong. She watched the process with interest, listening as he explained, watching as he scalded the bird and pulled off the loose feathers.

"What about all these little ones that are left?"

"Burn 'em off over the stove. Then cut it into pieces for frying."

She took the plucked bird from him. "Thank you, Nash."

Simple words, but in that throaty voice, they seemed to hold more meaning. She made things personal with that voice. She had the uncanny ability to make him feel something besides anger and grief, and he didn't like it.

He nodded and went back to his work. He had responsibilities, and tomorrow didn't take care of itself.

His wife's sister was persistent and would hound him until he answered her questions. He carried an uneasy feeling about what she wanted to talk about. He'd been working at the mill until he'd married Pearl. She and her mother had been hanging on to the Dearing farm and scraping by. He'd offered to take over farming if that was what they wanted, but Laura had been ready to let him do whatever he wanted with the land.

It had always been his dream to raise horses, and these acres held rolling hills of pasture and fields ripe for hay. It had been a sensible arrangement for them to share the big house with Pearl's mother, and Laura had welcomed Nash and later their children.

Laura Dearing hadn't deserved the hairpin turns life had dealt her. She'd been a kindhearted, devout woman who loved her family and should have had a husband at her side. She should have lived to a ripe old age and seen her grandchildren's children.

And Pearl. She'd worked hard and sacrificed to help him get the ranch going. Their marriage had been convenient for both of them. She got a husband to take over the land and provide for her and her mother. He got the ranch he'd always wanted. He'd been preoccupied with the business end of things and the work. He'd figured there would be plenty of time for them to grow closer once the ranch was thriving. At least that's what he'd thought until their life together had been cut short.

He'd already learned enough about Ruby to know there'd be no avoiding her if she was determined to ask questions and get answers. He steeled himself for the inevitable.

Ruby was smart enough to know the men worked till dusk before stopping to eat, so she waited until she was sure they'd be coming before she set food on the table.

The back door opened and the three men entered the kitchen. They had already removed their hats and were freshly washed. Their gazes shot directly to the table laden with steaming beans, biscuits and fried chicken.

Nash introduced the hands. "This here's Silas Dean."

The middle-aged man nodded politely. "Miss."

"And Dugger Wiley."

The tall young man gave her a friendly smile. "How do, Miss Dearing."

"Call me Ruby." She gestured to the table. "Sit wherever you like."

They seated themselves and Nash picked up the platter of chicken.

"I never cut up a chicken before," she apologized. "The pieces look pretty odd."

"Don't make much difference to how they taste," Silas assured her.

"I found some recipes in Mama's handwriting, but nothing about chicken. I guess most people just know how to cook them and don't write it down."

"My mama always says you can't learn till you try," Dugger noted, and gave her an appreciative nod.

The beans were still a little hard. She hadn't quite figured that out, either. But she could make golden, flaky biscuits with one arm tied behind her back. She'd found honey and poured some into a small jar, which she passed around.

The men didn't complain a whit about the food, eating as though they'd been served a feast. She got up and poured each of them coffee. "I found a jar of peaches for dessert."

She had sliced peaches portioned into four dishes when she looked up and noted Nash's expression. He was looking at the jar with a bleak expression. "Did I do something wrong?"

He shook his head.

"Were these special? Perhaps I should have asked."

He reached for his dish. "They're just peaches."

Dugger finished first. "Thank you for a fine meal, Miss Dearing."

The others followed his lead and trailed out the back door. The last one to the door, Nash turned back.

She paused in picking up plates and tentatively met his gaze.

"Thanks." He shut the door behind him.

"That must've pained you," she said to the closed door. She doggedly washed the dishes, wiped the table and hung the towels to dry, before pouring a pitcher of water and heading upstairs, exhausted.

The silent house yawned in the falling darkness. In her mother's old room, Ruby stripped off her clothing, washed her face and sponged her body before unfolding a cotton gown and dropping it over her head. She touched the fabric, brought it to her face and inhaled, hoping to find a trace of her mother in its clean folds. The scents of lavender and sunshine were pale reminders. She sat in the corner chair and surveyed the room she'd so carefully scrubbed and waxed.

"I'm sorry, Mama." The silent room absorbed her voice. "I wanted to make it up to you—all the years I was gone. I hoped you'd forgive me and let me try to start over with both you and Pearl." Ruby let her gaze touch the molding around the ceiling. "If you missed me half as much as I miss you now, I know how bad it was. I'm glad you had Pearl."

She didn't want to think about how hard it must have been on her ill mother when Pearl was killed. "Your room looks real pretty. I'm going to get the rest of the house just the way you like it, too."

When she could no longer keep her eyes open, Ruby stretched out on the bed and fell into an exhausted sleep.

In the glow of a lantern, Nash opened the stall door and studied the magnificent horse Ruby called the Duchess. It was his job to know horses, and he recognized this breed from a livestock exhibition he'd attended a few years ago. While they weren't as perfectly proportioned as Thoroughbreds, Barbs were agile and fast, second only to Arabians as one of the oldest breeds in existence. Nash had saved for a long time to buy a Thoroughbred to improve his stock. He knew an expensive horse when he saw one.

Contemplating how Pearl's sister had come by this one puzzled him to no end. He didn't know of anyone in the country who bred or sold them. He ran a palm down over the mare's bony forehead, and she twitched an ear.

Everything he thought he'd known about Ruby Dearing was being turned upside down. Pearl had never spoken ill of her, but Pearl never spoke ill of anyone. A few years after their father had deserted them, Ruby had hightailed it out of their lives as well. What drove a person to leave their family behind and disappear?

He'd been young once, frustrated by his father's expectations that he work at the mill in hopes of one day taking over. Nash had told his father that he wanted something else—that he wanted to raise horses—but his father had turned a deaf ear. Cosmo Sommerton's own dream of building a milling operation and leaving it as a legacy kept him from recognizing or appreciating his son's ambition.

The few times during his youth that Nash had approached his father about going out on his own, Cosmo had become so upset Nash had backed down. He'd still been working at the mill when he was in his twenties. Through church activities he and Pearl had struck up a friendship.

Nash stroked the Duchess's shiny neck and patted her solid withers. "You're a beauty, all right."

The horse nickered. It had been no secret that Pearl and her mother were looking for someone to take over the operation of their farm. They could no longer afford to pay hands to do all the work, and had come to the place where they were forced to sell or combine efforts with another owner.

Pearl had been one of the prettiest young

women in the community. She was a sweet thing, devoted to her mother and a volunteer at church. There were plenty of fellows willing to court and marry her, but she hadn't given anyone the time of day until she and Nash became better acquainted.

Nash had taken his share of girls to local dances, but the idea of marrying one had made his future at the mill less and less appealing. If he had a wife—and most likely a young family—he'd be stuck there forever.

One evening he had shared with Pearl his hopes for having a ranch. After talking to her mother, she'd approached him a few days later with the offer of turning the Dearing farm into a ranch. The land was there, the buildings, even fertile fields for hay and alfalfa. Everything he needed for a start. He'd set aside some savings, which he could use to buy horses.

Nash let himself out of the stall and checked on the mares as he made his way toward the front of the stable.

As he'd pondered it over, knowing without a shadow of a doubt that he wanted that land, he'd considered his father's reaction. Nash had thought about their future living arrangements—and how everything would be more suitable and proper if he and Pearl married. His father would likely be more tolerant of Nash's choice if love was involved.

And so he'd proposed, and Pearl had cheerfully accepted. They'd made the best choice for everyone concerned, and Nash had his ranch.

It had been easy to love Pearl. She was kind and loving and never complained, even when he worked long hours and spent nights in the barn with foaling mares. She had Laura for company, and later the children kept her busy.

In his heart, though, Nash sometimes feared he'd cheated her. He'd always planned that there would be time to make it up to her, time when they could take trips and he could lavish attention on her as she deserved.

But the horses always needed his attention. And then Laura had become ill, and Pearl had devoted more of her time to her mother. Nash recalled one evening in particular, when he'd entered the house after dark and Pearl had still been in the kitchen. The sweet smell of peaches hung heavy in the air. A dozen Mason jars sat cooling on the table, and his wife was washing an enormous kettle. She set it on the stove when she'd dried it, and turned to greet him with a weary smile.

"Are you hungry?"

"I ate with the hands."

"Maybe a dish of peaches then?" One slender

strand of hair had escaped the neat knot she always wore, and touched her neck. She tucked it back in place.

"You need your rest." He stepped close and reached behind her to untie her apron. He hung it over the back of a chair. "Go on upstairs. I'll bring water."

The image faded in Nash's mind. He had more and more trouble remembering their exchanges, especially with Ruby here. Ruby's vibrant presence overwhelmed his senses.

Was that why he had so much trouble accepting her? Because she made him feel as though he was losing another part of himself? Just by being here she pointed out things he didn't want to admit.

Ruby had been making a visible effort to ingratiate herself. She had taken some pretty harsh news and done her best with it, all things considered. He couldn't argue about her right to be here. He didn't have to approve of what she'd done in the past.

When he thought about the situation like that, he went back over his decisions. What would Pearl want him to do? What would Laura expect? He extinguished the last lantern and looked toward the darkened house.

He owed it to Pearl to give Ruby a chance.

Chapter Six

The following morning, she was awakened by Nash's voice shouting up the stairs. "Ruby!"

"What did I do now?" she grumbled, climbing out of bed and tugging on a wrapper. She padded to the head of the staircase and looked down. "Good morning."

He stood in the entryway, looking upward. "Dugger and I are ready to move furniture before we head out to check stock."

She darted back the way she'd come. "I'll be right down!"

She had no idea what had changed his mind, but she was thankful. A glance in the mirror made her laugh. Her hair had a life of its own, and mornings weren't her best. She could only imagine what Nash had thought.

She pulled on one of her mother's brown skirts and a lightweight shirtwaist, found her shoes and tugged her obstinate hair into a tail.

Dugger handed her a cup of coffee as she landed at the bottom of the staircase. "Nash made a pot. Didn't know if you like it sweet or not, so it's black."

She noted the front door had been propped open with a length of wood. "Black is perfect, thank you."

She blew on the steaming cup, took a sip and steadied the coffee as she followed him to the parlor.

"How many rooms do you want to do?" Nash asked. "We can carry out the dining room furniture, too, if you like."

"I would appreciate that. I'll go take dishes out of the china cabinet."

He nodded and set to work. Within forty-five minutes, two rooms of furniture had been moved to the porch and the front yard. Her mother's dishes sat in neat stacks along one wall of the hallway.

"Is there a wagon I can use to bring supplies from town?" Ruby asked Nash before he could leave. "I'll hitch up my own horse."

He gave her a hesitant nod. "I'll move the buckboard out where you can get to it. Might want to introduce your mare to the big bay in the corral. He's good as the other half of a team. Doesn't spook easily."

Because Pearl's death had occurred when a wagon turned over, Ruby's question probably stirred up those memories.

"What's his name?"

Nash gave her a surprised look. "Boone."

"Thanks."

He nodded, and he and Dugger headed out.

All morning, Ruby scrubbed and dusted and polished windows. While the wax dried on the floors, she washed up, changed into clean clothing and headed for town. She would much rather have saddled the Duchess and ridden her, but that left the problem of getting things back to the farm. *Ranch*, she corrected herself.

Fences were in good condition, and the horses in corrals were handsome and healthy. She could see the results of Nash's hard work everywhere.

Butterflies attacked her stomach as she reached the outskirts of town. She hadn't been this nervous about going home. There would be a lot of people who remembered her from years ago, and most folks had known her mother and Pearl. As far as Crosby was concerned, Ruby already had a reputation.

One other buckboard sat in front of the mercantile, so she stopped behind it. The bell over the door rang as she entered the store.

"Be right with you!" a man called.

A combination of smells assailed her senses, bringing back vivid memories. Coffee, kerosene, leather and brine combined to transport her to her childhood, when she'd stand beside her mother as Laura made her meager purchases.

Two women, one older, one younger, stood browsing through fabric bolts. Ruby gave the mature one a smile when she looked her way.

"Ruby? Ruby Dearing?" the woman asked.

Ruby nodded, trying to place the face.

The younger one turned at her mother's exclamation. Ruby did recognize her. "Audra Harper?"

"It's Reed now, but yes, it's me." She laid down the fabric she'd been holding and walked toward Ruby. Her gaze traveled over the skirt that had been Ruby's mother's and over her barely restrained hair. "You're the last person I ever expected to see shopping in the mercantile today."

Ruby still wasn't sure of Audra's reaction to her presence. "I got here evening before last."

"Do you remember my mother, Ettie?"

"Of course. Nice to see you, Mrs. Harper."

"Well, I am surprised to see you after all this time," Ettie said. "How long has it been? Seven years? Eight?"

"About that," Ruby replied with a nod.

Ettie gave her a sideways look. "Some of us

thought we'd see you at your sister's funeral. Or your mother's."

Ruby fished in the pocket of her skirt and pulled out her list. "I didn't know of their deaths until two nights ago."

"Shame to lose them both like that," Ettie said, but Ruby didn't hear much sympathy in her tone. "Your mother was a wonderful, God-fearing woman. She never missed a Sunday service until she was too weak to ride into town."

"She always did set store by going to church," Ruby said simply.

The white-haired man Ruby identified as Edwin Brubeker had finished with his last customer, and now stood listening with interest. She turned and acknowledged him. "Hello, Mr. Brubeker."

"Hello, Ruby. I would have recognized you anywhere. You haven't changed a bit, and you strongly resemble your sister."

"Pearl's hair didn't look like that," Ettie interjected.

"And you're taller, aren't you?" Audra asked curiously.

"I wouldn't know. I haven't seen her since she was thirteen or fourteen."

"You're definitely taller," Audra assured her, as though it was important that Ruby know.

Wanting to escape their scrutiny now, Ruby handed her list to Mr. Brubeker. "I'll look around a bit while you put my order together." She dismissed the women with a brief, "I'm sure we'll be seeing each other again soon," and headed for a wall of goods in the opposite direction. She stood looking at small kegs of nails and rows of tools as though they were of extreme interest. She'd wanted a hammer just that morning, so she selected one and carried it to the counter, avoiding meeting anyone's eyes.

After she'd picked out a few more items, the store owner had her order ready. "On the Lazy S's bill?" he asked.

Nash hadn't said anything about paying for supplies, and she hadn't thought about it. The least she could do was supply these things. "I'll pay now."

Mr. Brubeker's white eyebrows rose. He looked at the cash she placed on the counter. "My grandson will load the wagon."

"Thank you." Audra and Ettie were still hovering near the aisle when she turned to go. "Nice to see you both," she said.

"What are you doing back in Crosby?" Ettie asked.

"Mother," Audra chided.

Ruby paused only briefly. "I'm figuring that out. Now if you'll excuse me."

Mr. Brubeker's grandson was a lanky red-headed youth with a charming grin and freckles spattered across his nose and cheeks. He was still loading the buckboard, so she strolled along the street, gazing into the windows of the printer, the barber and a locksmith. A commotion at the end of the block caught her attention and she made sure the Brubeker boy was still loading her purchases before walking toward the gathering.

Next to the livery, a small crowd had formed around the corral, where four horses stood listlessly.

Ruby inched her way closer to the barricade to see the animals. They were all appallingly thin, with splotchy coats, and one in particular, a speckled gray gelding, had bare spots on his hide and ribs showing.

"What's going on?" she asked the men beside her.

"That fella's tryin' to sell those horses, but don't look like he's gettin' any takers."

She observed silently for a few painful minutes. It was obvious the poor animals were undernourished and neglected. Ruby felt sick at first, but then anger swept over her. "Who do they belong to?"

"See the short bald fella over there? Him."

She skirted the gathering until she reached the man he'd indicated. "Are those your horses?"

He turned and looked at her. She was an inch or two taller and he had to gaze up. His eyes widened. "Who are you?"

She ignored the question. "These horses haven't been cared for or fed properly."

He narrowed his gaze. "Who the hell are you and what would you know?"

"My name's Ruby Dearing, and it doesn't take a genius to look at their coats and ribs and see they've been neglected." She glanced around, noting the curious faces of the bystanders. "Isn't there a law to protect those animals?"

A couple men shrugged.

"Well, little lady. If'n you're so fixed on the critters, why don't you fork over the cash to buy 'em and take 'em home?"

Ruby's skin burned hot. She shot the gathering of men a challenging look. "I'll buy one if the rest of you will buy one." She turned back. "How much are you asking?"

"Fifty dollars apiece."

The man was both cruel and a crook. She looked him in the eye. "You'll get ten dollars a head and not a cent more. Take it and leave before I find the marshal." Reaching into the deep pocket of her skirt, she pulled out her coin purse and plucked out paper money. Casting a challenging stare at those around her, she urged, "Don't let him get away with this. Take a good look at these mistreated animals. Someone has to do something. Buy one of these horses or you won't be able to sleep tonight for the guilt of not doing what's right."

Grumbles arose, but three of the men produced money. One by one they begrudgingly selected their horses, until only one was left standing. Ruby shoved her ten dollars at the seller and marched forward. "What's his name?"

The man glared at her and stuffed the money into his pocket. "Call the hay-burnin' bag o' bones any damned thing you want."

He turned on his heel and stormed into the livery.

Ruby stroked the gelding's neck and looked him over. He rolled his eye at her and bobbed his head. Patches of his hide were raw and he had sores on his legs. Her eyes stung at his suffering. The animal's obvious misery turned her stomach.

Those who remained near the corral watched her. She took the horse's lead and walked him from the enclosure, hoping he had the gumption to make it back to the ranch.

The buckboard was loaded, so Ruby led the

gelding to the trough, let him drink a minute and then tied him to the tailgate. After climbing up to the seat and unhooking the reins, she spoke to the Duchess and Boone. "We're heading back real slow. This fellow needs a good home."

Once outside town, she stopped the team, got down to untie the gelding and let him graze in the shade of a tree for a few minutes. Back on the road, she turned and checked on him often as they made plodding progress.

Finally reaching the ranch, she drove the buck-board to the house.

Dugger had seen her approach, and joined her to unload the items. "Where'd the gray come from?"

"I bought him from a man in town."

"Looks mighty sickly, don't he? I'm surprised he made it all the way here."

"Me, too." She untied the gelding and led him toward the stables.

Nash appeared at the corner of the building and faced her with feet planted. "What are you doing?"

"I've brought home a horse."

"I can see it's a horse. What's it doing here?"

"I bought it."

"You *paid* for that animal?"

"He was in a bad situation, and I wasn't going

to leave him behind." She stroked the horse's withers and stepped nearer his head to rub his bony brow.

Nash's expression didn't reveal his thoughts. He looked at the horse for a long moment. "You've taken on a big job."

"He's had a hard life. I'm going to take care of him."

"And just how do you plan to do that?"

"Well, feed him, first off. I'll give him plenty of oats and water."

Nash shook his head. "Can't do that."

"Why not?"

"This horse is malnourished. He's not used to eating. Feeding him as you would any other horse would kill him."

A bolt of concern rocketed through Ruby's chest. "I let him eat grass on the way home!"

Nash's expression softened. He visibly relaxed his shoulders. "Grass is fine. Hay, too. But no hard grains. You'll have to start feeding him slowly, making mash like wet slop at first."

"Out of what?"

"Soybean meal, linseed meal. It'll have to be ground until his stomach and intestines get used to it."

"Ground. Could I use the coffee grinder?"

"Don't see why not." Nash watched her stroke

the animal's neck. "Bring him inside, then get the grinder. I'll show you."

Nash didn't know what to make of this woman bringing home a badly neglected horse. It seemed she'd made herself right at home—and she was; he couldn't deny it. The land was legally hers. The agreement between him and her mother had been a verbal one. At the time Laura had been weak, but they'd all assumed Pearl would be here to retain the property and house.

Watching Ruby with the horse, recognizing her instinctive need to help the animal, played havoc with Nash's knowledge of the woman. What was a footloose and fancy-free honky-tonk singer doing caring about the fate of an abused animal? He didn't like this chip in his already polished opinion.

She headed for the house and returned carrying a big wooden coffee grinder with a cast-iron crank.

"Take the drawer out and set it over a pan in the back there," he told her. "I'll take him to a stall."

Nash led the docile horse away, and Ruby did as he asked. When he returned he scooped soybean meal into a bucket and scooted it toward her. She cranked while he went for a pail of linseed meal.

When she changed hands, he realized her arm must be growing tired, but she was relentless. "Let me do the linseed," he offered.

"I can do it," she insisted.

"We still have the rugs and furniture to put back," he reasoned. "I can do this faster."

She relented, but knelt close to do all the scooping.

After several minutes of silence he looked at her. "I have to ask. How did this horse purchase come about?"

"I was waiting for Mr. Brubeker's grandson to load the things I bought, and I saw a gathering at the livery. I was curious, so I walked over. A man had four horses he was trying to sell. They were all skinny and their coats were in bad shape. This one was the worst."

"And so you bought him?"

She tucked her hair behind her ear, glanced away, but then looked back at him. "Yes. I couldn't watch that man any longer, and I couldn't let him get away with mistreating those animals."

"What about the other horses?"

"Some of the men there bought them."

Getting to his feet, Nash studied the ill-treated animal and tried to picture the scene, but couldn't. He certainly didn't fault Ruby for her compassion, but she'd taken on a big job. "This should be enough food to last a few days. We'll make a pailful at a time. Want to dip water?"

"Sure." She got to her feet and soon returned, lugging a full pail.

Nash got a long wooden stick from the tack room and together they poured water and stirred. "Real thin," he told her. "Then you have to let it stand and expand for a few minutes before you feed it to him. Otherwise it'll swell in his belly."

While they waited he went for a salt block and set it in the stall. At the front of the stable Dugger could be heard unharnessing the horses.

At last Nash carried the pail in for Ruby, and together they watched the animal lower his head to the slop and eat.

"And he can have grass, too?" she asked.

"Hay, grass, alfalfa," Nash said. "You can't let him out in the pasture for a couple of weeks. His intake has to be moderate until he's doing well with this."

She met Nash's eyes. "You sure know a lot about how to take care of him. I would have done it all wrong and caused him harm."

Her comment flustered Nash, but he didn't let on. "Tomorrow you can wash him down. Then treat those sores."

"Thank you, Nash."

He never knew what to say to her. He had trouble acknowledging her, accepting her presence… Looking at her square on, he found she was nothing like he'd imagined or expected. Ruby was unusual. Provoking at times. But she wasn't a monster, and he hadn't wanted to admit that. Still didn't. He stepped out into the corridor between stalls. "You did the right thing."

Her eyes widened.

He turned and went back to work.

Chapter Seven

Early the following morning a sound woke Ruby. She sat up in bed. She'd been so worn out the night before, she'd barely had the energy to put the last clean dish away and sweep the kitchen floor. Three rooms were spotless. The pantry and cellar were full, and she had rescued a horse. She rolled her shoulders and stretched her arms. This domestic life was more difficult work than singing and acting, but here she didn't have to avoid the hands of lecherous men or sleep on a hard seat on a rocking train as it crossed the country.

Her youthful dreams had turned into unglamorous reality a long time ago, but she'd been too stubborn to admit her impetuousness, and too proud to give up without giving the effort her all. Nobody could say Ruby Dearing didn't follow through.

Another sound from one of the rooms reached her. The unaccustomed noise drew her out of bed. She pulled on a lacy dressing gown over her nakedness and opened her door, stepping out into the hall. The sound came from down the hall, so she padded to the doorway of one of the bedrooms.

She peeked around the partially closed door to discover Nash standing before a bureau, adjusting a black tie at his collar. Seeing her movement, he turned. His hair was wet and neatly combed, and he wore a pressed white shirt and dark trousers. "Morning."

She felt foolish for coming to look. Obviously, he and Pearl had shared this room, and his clothing was still stored inside. "Sorry. I wasn't used to hearing anyone in the house in the morning."

She pulled the robe around her more securely. As usual, she hadn't thought ahead when she'd jumped out of bed and into the hall, with only this thin garment to cover her.

He took several steps toward the doorway. His gaze dropped to the V at her throat, traveled across her breasts and down to her feet before he drew his attention back to her face. "It's Sunday," he said simply. "Are you coming to church?"

"I'm not much for church." Her skin flushed

under his perusal. "Your mother did invite me for dinner, though."

"I can come back for you," he offered.

"I don't want to trouble you. If you give me directions, I'll saddle the Duchess."

Nash came out into the hall and explained how to reach his parents' home. His gaze kept rising to her hair, as if he was deliberately not looking at her improper state of undress.

Ruby returned to her room. She'd slept hard and once again her hair was a wild tangle of curls, and once again he'd seen it. She had planned to make something to take to dinner, and there was much to do, so she washed quickly in tepid water, dressed and headed downstairs.

Her first order of the day was to check on the horse in the stable and make him fresh mash. He seemed less listless today, and even raised his head and snuffled when she entered the stall. "How did you fare last night, my friend?" The stall needed to be cleaned, so she turned him out in the corridor, raked up the soiled straw and laid fresh.

The sounds of Nash saddling a horse reached her, and then there was only silence.

She talked to the gray while she mixed the mash, but he didn't move from where she'd left him. She allowed the mixture to expand and led the animal out of doors. After finding several buckets and pumping fresh water, she located the concoction Nash used for shampooing in the tack room.

She washed the horse's tail twice and held up a pail to swish it clean. Next she cleansed his mane, working out tangles with a comb, and finally washed the rest of him, sponging and rinsing thoroughly. She sang as she worked, songs from the vast catalog of music she carried in her memory. The horse stood submissively, and she used great care around his sores, washing and rinsing those spots last.

She hadn't given a lot of thought to the fact that Nash didn't come to the house at night. He was obviously sleeping in the bunkhouse, and had been since before she'd arrived. Perhaps it was too hard for him to be in the bed he had shared with Pearl. Ruby had been concerned about sleeping in her mother's room, but since she'd resigned herself to it, she felt closer to Laura than she would have otherwise. Ruby was thankful the arrangement had turned out this way. If her old room hadn't now been Claire's, she might have missed out on the comfort of being surrounded by her mother's things.

"I guess you need a name," she said, walking the horse around the corral in the sun to dry his coat. She rubbed his bony forehead. He nuzzled the front of her shirt. "Something musical, perhaps. You seem to like my singing. Allegro. Tempo. Too girlish, huh? Crescendo. Or Volante." She looked at him. "That means flying. Vivo means lively. Which one fits you?"

She led the horse back into the stable to his clean stall. He stuck his nose right into the pail of mash. "When I come back later today, I'll let you graze for a short time." She secured the stall gate. "If I call you Vivo, I expect you to live up to your name real soon. Think you can manage that?"

With much left to do, she made her way back to the house. Sorting through recipes in her mother's neat handwriting, Ruby considered making something she could easily carry while riding. A solid pie should fit the bill, she thought, deciphering a recipe for caramel pecan pie. She had all the ingredients, so she set to work.

The first thing on the list was butter the size of a hen egg, which amused her. She decided to go gather eggs so she could be certain of the size when she measured butter.

Might as well make two pie crusts, since she was doing this, she figured. She could leave one pie at home for Dugger and Silas to enjoy the following day.

The crust recipe wasn't included in the ingredients. Obviously, by her very gender, a woman was expected to just know these things, like a bird knew when and where to fly south.

Ruby had seen her mother make crust, but that was years ago, and she'd never done it herself. Making pastry was not instinctive. In fact, it was downright awkward. She threw out her first attempt and started over with determination. How hard could it be?

Her second attempt met with better success, though her crust wasn't as pretty as it should have been. She burned wood in the stove and baked the two shells until they were golden. Then she brushed her hands together with satisfaction.

"Daisy, Daisy, give me your answer do," she sang. "I'm half-crazy, all for the love of you. It won't be a stylish marriage. I can't afford a carriage, but you'll look sweet on the seat of a bicycle built for two."

She still had the filling to make. She checked the time. Flour, egg yolks, canned milk, vanilla and pecans went into the mixture, and she watched the pan diligently so her filling didn't scorch.

An hour later, Ruby carefully packed her pie into a larger pan, wrapped it and carried it to the stable, where she saddled the Duchess and stepped into the saddle with the pie nestled safely in her lap. She hummed as she headed for the Sommerton home.

Nash had given her good directions, so she had no problem finding the property. The impressive three-story house had dormers, bright green shutters and an immense porch that wrapped two sides of the structure. The grassy yard held half a dozen mature trees that shaded the whole area.

A slender, dark-haired man met her as she slid from the Duchess. "You must be Ruby Dearing. I'm Tucker Gilchrist, Nash's brother-in-law."

"Nice to meet you." His friendly welcome pleased Ruby.

"I'll take care of your horse. She's a beauty. The ladies are in the kitchen. They're expecting you. Just take those stairs and go right in."

She straightened her skirts with one hand and carried the pie to the porch.

Ruby didn't have to consider walking right in, because a young woman with sleek dark hair and pretty brown eyes spotted her and opened the screen door. "Come on in. Are you Ruby?"

Ruby entered the square kitchen with its mouth-watering smells. "That's me."

"I'm Nash's sister, Vivian. What have you brought?"

"I don't know how good it is. It's a pie."

Georgia left her place at the stove and hurried over to greet their guest. "I'm so glad you joined us. I've planned a special dinner to celebrate your homecoming."

Her statement rendered Ruby speechless. *Celebrate her homecoming?* The words gave her a hitch in her chest. Nash certainly hadn't been in a celebratory mood when she'd arrived. She was glad his mother didn't share his dim view of her return.

Vivian uncovered the pie and set it beside two others with golden, sugary crusts and perfectly fluted edges. Beside them, Ruby's pie looked as though a ten-year-old had made it.

"Say hello to Miss Dearing, Claire."

Ruby hadn't noticed the girl sitting on a chair at the small table. "Hello, Miss Dearing," she said obediently.

"It's so nice to see you, Claire," Ruby told her with a smile. The six-year-old was arranging pickle slices on a scalloped cut-glass plate. "I see you're helping." She turned to Georgia. "Is there something I can do?"

"Certainly, dear. Just wash up at the sink, and I'll turn the potato mashing over to you while I thicken the gravy."

Happy for the chore, Ruby did her best to mash the potatoes smooth and free of lumps.

Vivian showed her the dining room, and together they finished setting the table with a beautiful set of oriental-patterned china and shiny

silver flatware. Vivian folded the pristine mono-
grammed napkins into bird shapes and set one
on each plate.

"Everything is beautiful," Ruby told Georgia.

"The men don't care, but I like to set a pretty
dinner table," the older woman answered. "Claire,
run and call your papa and the other men to dinner, please."

The little girl skipped from the room, her
blond braids bouncing on her back. She seemed
more at ease and cheerful here in her grand-
parents' home than she had when Georgia had
brought her to the ranch. But then the children
had been living here for a long time now.

The men filed into the dining room, Nash carrying Joel. Nash cut a handsome figure in his
shirt and tie. Joel wore a similar white shirt.

"This is Ruby Dearing." Georgia gestured.
"Ruby, this is my husband, Cosmo."

"How do you do, Mr. Sommerton?"

"Cosmo," he instructed immediately. He
didn't look old enough for his thick white hair
and bushy white mustache, a contrast to his
tanned skin. He wore a shirt much like Nash's,
though it was cream-colored. He immediately
moved to pull out a chair for his wife. Tucker
did the same for Vivian.

Ruby thought Nash might feel obliged to do

as they had, so she quickly seated herself before he finished settling Joel on the chair beside his. Nash glanced at Ruby before he sat. Claire had taken the seat on his other side.

Cosmo picked up a serving fork and knife and sliced the roast in front of him. Plates were passed until each person had a serving, and then the steaming bowls went from person to person.

"Church was full this morning," Cosmo said.

"It was a nice service," Vivian said. "Mrs. Chamberlain's baby is sure getting big."

For the first time Ruby noted that Tucker and Vivian apparently had no children. Tucker gave his wife a sideways glance and buttered his roll. "He's a sturdy little fella."

"What did you do this morning?" Cosmo asked Ruby.

"I washed Vivo and made mash." She glanced at Nash and back at his father. "I've named the horse I bought Vivo."

"That's a funny name," Claire said.

"It means lively," she explained. "It's a musical term."

"Is the horse lively?" Tucker asked.

"Not yet. I'm hoping he lives up to his name soon, though."

"I heard there was an interesting horse sale in

town yesterday." One side of Cosmo's mustache lifted in amusement.

Nash sliced Joel's meat and placed his plate in front of him. He cut his gaze to Ruby. After church the men had congregated in the sun. Their conversation, normally focused on cattle and horses or the price of corn, had taken a different slant when Ben Dodge brought up the topic of a man attempting to sell overpriced horses at the livery and the pretty lady who had stepped in.

Nash had absorbed the men's story, picturing Ruby lighting into that unscrupulous man and shaming those fellow churchgoers into buying horses from him. He could see her doing it, too. Color rose in her cheeks from that attention his family now gave her.

"What was so interesting?" Georgia asked.

Cosmo chuckled. "The men talked about it this morning. Seems Ruby here was indignant about the seller's neglect of his horseflesh. Not only did she insist he sell the horses for ten dollars each, she also told the bystanders they were buying the horses. And they did."

"Ten dollars is awfully cheap for a horse," Tucker said.

"Even at that, the dreadful man was a bandit," Ruby claimed. "He shouldn't have received a cent, but I figured ten dollars apiece would satisfy him, and the horses would have good care once they had new owners."

"So this morning you washed this horse you bought," Vivian said.

Ruby nodded. "Treated his sores and fed him. He's a docile fellow. Very appreciative of the care. It's difficult to imagine how someone could mistreat any animal. Especially a work animal. Why, a person can't travel or run a farm without a horse."

Nash admired Ruby for speaking up in that situation. And he admired her for making sure those animals got a better life. "Ruby did something no one else did," he said. "Takes courage to do the right thing."

His comment was met with silence around the table. Ruby shot her gaze to him, her surprise evident.

"Nash is right," Georgia said finally. "You did a very courageous thing, finding homes for those animals."

Cosmo glanced at him, but Nash ate without meeting his eyes. "So, Miss Dearing, you are a horse lover like my son."

"I do like horses," she agreed.

"She rode here on a nice-looking mare," Tucker pointed out. "Looks like a Dutch Warmblood I once saw."

"It's a Barb," Nash corrected.

"A what?" Tucker asked.

Cosmo glanced at his son with interest. "Never heard of them."

"It's a breed that originated on the Barbary Coast in North Africa. I learned about them at a livestock exhibition," Nash explained. "Barbs have influenced a lot of the other breeds. I'm no expert, but Ruby's appears pure."

"Horse like that must be worth a lot," Cosmo observed, and quirked an eyebrow at Ruby.

Nash studied her with interest now. He'd been interested all along in that horse she called the Duchess, but wouldn't have asked her about it. He was still curious how she had come by such an animal.

Ruby stared at her barely touched plate of food. "The Duchess was a gift. I have papers, but I don't know what she's worth."

No one said anything for a moment. No doubt speculation was worse than the truth. His family was probably thinking she'd performed sordid favors in trade—as Nash himself was imagining right about now.

"A man from Turkey came to me after a performance in Sacramento one evening," she said. "He asked me to visit his ailing mother...to sing for her."

She had Nash's full attention now—and that of everyone else at the table.

Chapter Eight

"I went with him. The old woman was very frail and sick, but wearing a beautiful satin embroidered gown. I sang for her, and she closed her eyes and tears ran down her cheeks. The man cried, too. And when I went to leave he gave me the papers and the horse. The Duchess had been hers, the old woman's. He said she no longer had a use for it and she wanted me to have it. I thought he should have sold her, but as soon as I saw the Duchess I loved her."

Georgia stared at Ruby.

Vivian wiped her eyes with her napkin.

Truth must really be stranger than fiction, because Nash had never heard anything like Ruby's tale. But then, he was learning she was an unusual person with unique experiences. And it did make sense that a woman from Turkey would own a Barb such as the one Ruby had ridden in on. He'd been looking at it in the corral and the pasture all week, wondering.

"What a lovely story," his mother said with a smile.

"Where did you keep the Barb while you were traveling from place to place?" Nash wondered logically.

"I paid to have her cared for," Ruby replied. "I was only able to check on her occasionally, so it was a pleasure to finally take her away with me for good."

"I'm interested to see this horse of yours," Cosmo said. "Both of them, actually."

"Let Ruby eat now," Georgia admonished.

Ruby gave her a grateful smile and took a bite of her meal.

Cosmo turned to Nash. "Would you want a horse like that?"

His question surprised Nash. He didn't think his father was just being polite, but he rarely showed an interest in talk of horses. Apparently, Ruby's stories had impressed him.

"I've made arrangements to buy a Thoroughbred," Nash told his father. "I'm headed to Colorado midweek. This is the one."

"To build your herd."

Nash nodded. He'd saved for two years and sold six good horses to buy the stud. He had a lot riding on the one he'd picked out being the perfect one.

Joel knocked over his milk, and Nash gestured for his mother to stay seated while he went for a towel to mop it up. Returning, he cleaned up the spill. Claire poured her brother a fresh glass, less full this time.

Ruby asked Cosmo about the mill.

"We have the biggest grain elevator in several counties," he told her. "Nearly forty employees. Tucker here is a foreman."

Nash's choice to start his own ranch had been a sore subject for quite a few years, but maybe Cosmo was finally coming to accept his choice. Nash hadn't asked for any help getting his ranch started, and his father hadn't offered any. Nash figured his father had given any inheritance he may have received to his brother-in-law. That was fine. He was doing what he'd always wanted to do.

Joel would have a choice when the time came. He could raise horses with his father or mill grain with his grandfather—or choose another path. Nash would support him.

Vivian carried in two pies. "Did you drop that one on the way to the oven, Viv?" Nash teased with a grin.

His sister gave him a warning frown.

"Ruby made the caramel pecan pie," his mother said. "I'm sure it's delicious."

Nash glanced at Ruby, expecting anger or embarrassment, but she only smiled at his mother. "Thank you. I guess it's pretty obvious it was my first pie."

"I'll take seconds if there's enough," Cosmo declared.

"I didn't do as well the first time I made a pie," Vivian told her. She slapped Nash's shoulder and served him last. Nash accepted a slice of Ruby's pie and gave her a contrite glance.

It seemed his family all liked Ruby. He couldn't argue with them. She somehow managed to pull off everything she set out to do. She had worked hard at cleaning the house and doing the cooking. And now this. He took a hesitant bite, and the smooth flavor of the filling melted on his tongue. "It tastes good."

Complimenting her didn't feel as awkward as he'd anticipated.

She gave her head a soft shake. "It didn't turn out very pretty."

After the women cleared the table and did the dishes, they met the men and children outdoors. Cosmo had already seated himself on the porch, a big yellow dog lying at his feet. Tucker and Nash finished setting up a net across a flat portion of the side yard, and Claire passed out racquets. She extended a handle toward Ruby. "Do you want to play badminton?"

"I've never played before. I'd better watch."

Georgia took the racquet from her granddaughter. "Ruby can watch a couple of games to see how it's done, then she will play."

They drew colored marbles from a cup to select teams. Nash and Vivian were paired against Tucker and Georgia. Ruby seated herself on the grass to watch.

Nash picked up Joel and gave him an affectionate hug. Joel patted his cheek. Nash set him on his shoulders and then moved back to serve.

"That thing with the feathers is the shuttle-cock," Claire told Ruby. "You have to keep it from hitting the ground and you must keep it inside bounds."

Her serious expression painfully reminded Ruby of her sister. Ruby studied the pale hair at the little girl's temples and the delicate sweep of her golden brows. Her beauty created an ache in Ruby's chest. She longed to reach out and stroke those locks, glide the backs of her fingers across the child's smooth cheek. But as dear and familiar as Claire already was to her, Ruby was still a stranger. Her affection wouldn't be welcome, so she held it in check.

"Look! Look!" Claire cried in delight. Ruby gazed in the direction she pointed.

Nash set the shuttlecock in motion and Georgia immediately swung her racquet and sent it back over the net. Vivian hit it next, and it went back and forth a few times before Nash couldn't move backward fast enough with Joel on his shoulders, and it fell to the ground.

Georgia and Tucker cheered for themselves and Claire clapped.

Ruby leaned to whisper to Claire. "It doesn't seem quite fair with Joel on your father's shoulders like that, does it?"

"Next time they will trade, and Uncle Tuck will hold Joel."

"What if your father and uncle get on the same team?"

"One of them still holds him until he gets tired and goes off to play alone. Grandmother will lay him on a blanket in a little while, and he'll nap."

Sure enough, Joel tired of the game, and Georgia spread a blanket under one of the enormous trees. Joel plopped down and she removed his shoes.

Ruby found what was so obviously the family's routine comforting. But their relaxed familiarity showed her how much she'd missed out on—and how much of an outsider she was.

Maybe if she'd tried harder to please her mother, to conform to the rules and tedium, she would be part of a family now, too.

A touch on her arm caught her attention. Vivian handed Ruby the racquet her mother had been using. "Your turn."

Ruby stood and hesitantly took her place. Vivian demonstrated the different swings of the racquet, overhand and underhand. "If the other team is close to the net, hit the shuttlecock hard, so it goes beyond their reach. If they're standing back, tap it lightly, so it falls just on the other side of the net."

Ruby nodded. "I'll do my best."

She took to the game with agility and speed, although her skirts got in the way more than once, and twice her feet tangled and she fell.

"I'd have this if not for these skirts," she told Vivian. "Next time I'll wear my riding skirt."

As soon as she'd said it, she regretted the words. She was a guest, and there was no guarantee she would be invited again.

As though she'd seen Ruby's distress, Vivian agreed immediately. "Next Sunday we will both wear our split skirts. How about men against the women? Maybe we can get Daddy out here."

Her father waved from the porch.

Vivian looked at Ruby. "You will come next Sunday, won't you?"

"Well, I... Thank you, but I don't want to intrude."

"It's not an intrusion. I won't hear no."

Eventually Georgia served lemonade and coffee, and they sat in the shade of the porch. Cosmo sent the yellow dog out to lie beside Joel on the blanket. The animal knew what was expected of him, because he sniffed at the hem of Ruby's skirt and then loped out to the shade tree and plopped down.

Ruby finished her lemonade. "Thank you so much for having me today. I don't know when I've had a better time. I promised Vivo I'd let him graze, and I should head back before dusk so he has time in the pasture."

"Keep his grazing time to fifteen, twenty minutes tops," Nash said to her.

Tucker accompanied her to the stable and saddled the Duchess for her. "It was nice to meet you," he told her after she'd hoisted herself into the saddle. "Vivian was glad to have you here, too. I could tell. She's missed Pearl being here on Sundays."

"Were they close?"

"Family," he said with a nod.

"Thank you, Tucker." Ruby rode away from

the barn and toward the road. Had any of the Sommertons been reminded of Pearl, or compared her to her sister? It was likely Pearl went to church with them and shared in their Sunday afternoon activities. Mama might have, too.

Ruby hoped so. She hoped her mother had been friends with the Sommertons and enjoyed their company. Maybe Ruby would ask Nash. So far he hadn't been open to her questions, and he'd been close-lipped about most everything. When he'd told his father he'd be leaving to fetch a Thoroughbred, it had been the first she'd heard of it. But then why would he tell her? She'd shown up out of the blue and knocked him senseless.

She'd imagined she'd be making things up to her mother and sister, but fate had a different plan. Now she had to prove herself to this man.

On Wednesday morning Ruby headed to the barn early to care for Vivo, and Nash was already gone. After taking care of her horse, she found tools and cleared the overgrown garden. She left a volunteer tomato and what looked like a melon vine, and raked the rest of the dry stems and vines into a pit and burned them.

The ground needed plowing, so she set about figuring out how. In the barn she discovered a single plow and determined which harnesses hooked to it. Just getting the heavy tool to the garden plot was a trial. Surprised to find Nash hadn't ridden Boone, she used the big bay to drag it. Then she set it upright and got herself situated in the harness. The first two rows were trial and error. She stopped and reassessed her plan, determining it was plain hard work and she should get on with it. After the fourth row, she noted how crooked her lines were, and the wooden handles had already blistered her palms.

"Miss Ruby! Miss Ruby!"

She turned toward the agitated voice to discover Silas. She waved.

He slid from his horse and hurried toward her. "Plowin' ain't no job for a woman, Miss Ruby."

She rubbed her bleeding palms on her skirt. "I think I'm getting the hang of it."

"Move aside, an' I'll finish that plot for ya. Go git yerself a drink. Yer face is red as a tomato."

She unlooped the harness from her shoulder. "I should have worn a hat."

"You shoulda asked for help is what you shoulda done."

He checked the harnesses and picked up the reins. "H'ya, Boone."

"I was doing all right." The horse moved forward, and Silas guided the plow in a straight line. How in blazes did he do that?

Ruby walked to the pump in the yard and drew a pailful of water to splash on her face and to wash her hands and arms. The water she drank from the tin dipper tasted wonderful.

She turned at the sound of a horse approaching. The brown-and-white animal carried a female rider wearing a tunic. The woman reined in and slid to the ground. She'd ridden the horse without a saddle, and pulled a bundle from a pack.

She wore one long, jet-black braid down her back, and was slim and agile. When she approached, Ruby realized she wasn't as young as she appeared from a distance. Ruby walked to meet her.

"I am Little Bird," the woman said in a velvety low voice.

"Ruby Dearing. It's a pleasure to meet you."

"Nash Sommerton told me of your return. I brought you herbs."

"That's kind of you."

Little Bird reached for Ruby's hand and opened it to look at her palm. "I have something for this, too."

"Would you like a cup of tea?" Ruby asked.

"I brought tea." Little Bird patted the bundle.

"You certainly came prepared. Come in, please."

She held open the screen door and ushered in her guest. Then she pumped water, stoked the fire and set the kettle on the stove.

"There is a strong resemblance to Laura Dearing in your eyes and the movements of your body."

Nash had mentioned the Cheyenne woman who came to help care for her mother. "You brought her medicine and looked after her, didn't you?"

"I came often to see Laura Dearing." Little Bird pulled out several packets from her bundle and unwrapped one. "I brought anise hyssop for our tea. It is good for a dispirited heart."

Ruby held the packet of leaves to her nose and inhaled a blend of lemon, pine, sage and…perhaps licorice.

"You must burn a few leaves and inhale the flower essence," Little Bird told her. "It will bring back sweetness after having indulged in unwarranted guilt. It also encourages communication."

Ruby's gaze shot to the woman's face. Did Little Bird have the ability to see inside her heart?

"And the seeds…." Little Bird opened a small scrap of leaf, which had been folded like an envelope. "You must plant these around your back door for protection."

Ruby set the chipped teapot on the table. "How many leaves at one time for a potful?"

Little Bird picked up several. "These will do."

They let the tea steep on the table between them and looked at each other.

"Did my mother suffer a long time?" Ruby asked at last.

"If you mean suffer pain in her body, I brought her herbs to help with the pain. They worked well."

Ruby blinked back the sting of tears. "Thank you. And thank you for caring."

"She was a strong woman. Strong in her faith in God. Strong in her belief in people. She believed in both of her daughters."

Her visitor's words were meant to encourage Ruby, but the truth only pointed out how she'd fallen short. "I wasn't a good daughter."

"Her memories of you brought her pleasure."

"I should have come back a long time ago."

"Regret never added a day to a man's life. It does not change the past. Regret is a stone around your neck."

Ruby nodded thoughtfully. "I miss them both so much. If they missed me even a small measure of how I miss them, I am so sorry."

"Looking over your shoulder prevents you

from looking ahead and choosing the shortest and safest path."

"I know." Ruby poured their tea, and the fragrance of the anise hyssop filled her nostrils. "I'm looking ahead. And now I'm doing everything I can to make up for the past. Hopefully, I can make a difference for Claire and Joel."

Little Bird merely nodded and sipped her tea.

Before the Cheyenne woman left, she gave Ruby several herbs, with the roots attached for planting, and a few salves and tinctures, explaining the use for each.

"Your thoughtfulness means a lot," Ruby told her. "Thank you for coming to visit me. And thank you for being so kind to my mother."

Little Bird's horse hadn't been tethered, but had moved only as far as the shade where it stood cropping grass. The woman nickered and it came right to her. She raised one hand. "Ruby Dearing."

"Little Bird." Ruby watched her go with mixed emotions. It was an unexpected pleasure to meet a friendly neighbor and be treated kindly. It was also sad to meet someone who had been with her mother and had so generously cared for her when she'd been ill.

Silas had finished the plowing and was breaking up clods of dirt with a rake and a shovel.

Ruby wrapped her palms, found a pair of gloves and went back to work. She had a lot to do, not only with this physical labor, but also in building relationships. She'd never been much good at it. She'd been forced to change her initial plans, but now Pearl's children were going to take priority. She might never earn forgiveness, but she wanted to make a difference for them.

She'd seen how much they missed each other, how difficult their separation was. If she convinced Nash she could pull her share of the load around here, he might see fit to bring the children home sooner. She was determined to help make a home for Claire and Joel. They were her family.

Chapter Nine

Nash had been gone a few days, and with Silas's help the garden was tilled, raked and planted. Ruby's blistered palms ached, but the salve Little Bird had brought helped. Ruby remained vigilant in monitoring Vivo's time in the pasture and carefully measuring his mash. The sores that had recently been open and raw-looking were now pink with new flesh and hide.

Ruby sang while she curried the Duchess and braided her mane and tail in the wide entrance to the stable. Morning sun warmed her shoulders. Doves cooed in the rafters. She'd forgotten the tranquility and peace of mornings away from the city, with all its noise and busyness. She'd let herself become accustomed to sleeping on rocking trains and in uncomfortable hotel beds, had for a time, she supposed, imagined it was normal and preferable. It had been a long time since those circumstances had seemed exciting.

She gazed across the pasture and gave the horse an affectionate pat. "I think we'll go for a visit, Duchess."

After changing into a blue skirt and a white percale shirtwaist with narrow blue stripes, she saddled the mare, hoping she would be welcome at the Sommertons'.

She needn't have been concerned. At the front door Georgia greeted her as though she were an old friend and welcomed her inside and through the house to the big, sun-dappled kitchen.

"The children are on the back porch," she said. "Why don't you go out while I make us a pot of tea?"

Joel was the first to notice her. He'd been sitting cross-legged, stacking a pile of wooden blocks. He smiled bashfully.

Claire turned at the sound of Ruby's boots on the porch floor. She set down the kitten she held, and it scampered away. Her bright blue eyes traveled to the door and back to her aunt. She took in Ruby's attire and her hair. "I didn't know you were here."

"I just got here." Ruby stood hesitantly and laced her fingers together.

"Did you come to see Grandmother?"

"I came to see you, actually. The two of you."

"Oh."

"May I sit over here?"

Claire nodded.

Ruby took a seat on one of the cushioned rattan chairs.

"Is Papa still gone?"

"Yes, he's been gone a few days now. I'm sure this will be the first place he comes after he brings his new horse home."

Joel got up and joined them. He wore a white shirt, dun-colored shorts and sturdy, brown leather shoes. "The kitty's hiding."

"Did I scare it away?" Ruby asked.

"The kittens always hide," Claire assured her. "The mama cat keeps them hidden, but Joel and I look for them. Today we found two under that big bush by the coach house."

"The gray one scratch-ded me," Joel told her with a serious expression.

"Are you all right?" Ruby asked.

"That was a long time ago," Claire assured her.

"Yeah, a long time ago. He's a naughty kitty." Joel went back to stacking his blocks.

"They want to get away from him because he's not careful," Claire whispered.

"We always had litters of kittens when I was a

girl," Ruby told her. "Mama liked them because they kept the mice away."

"That's what Grandmother says." Claire backed up to the nearest chair and hiked one hip to hoist herself to the seat, showing a flash of petticoat beneath the hem of her brown silk dress. "Grandmother said you and my mama were little girls together. She remembers you from back then."

"Yes. I was the oldest, but we spent a lot of time together."

"What did Mama like to do when she was a little girl?"

"Well, when we weren't doing chores, we played with all the baby animals. Your mama loved the baby chicks. We had to be tricky to get past the hens to pick them up. The hens were very protective and pecked our hands if we didn't escape in time. Once we got a chick, though, we cuddled and cuddled it." She gestured by cupping one hand over the other. "If you completely cup your hands around a chick, it will go right to sleep."

"At the ranch Papa has hens out back. Are there baby chicks?"

"I'm sure there must be from time to time. Sometimes a hen gets loose and hides a nest."

"Like the mama cat."

"Yes."

"What other pets did you have?"

"Someone gave me a goat once. Silly me, I thought it would give us milk and Mama would be so happy. Turns out only mother goats have milk, though, and this one was a boy. He wasn't much fun after he grew horns."

"What did he do then?"

"He chased us and knocked us down." Ruby smiled about it now, but at the time they'd run crying to their mother. "My mama promptly gave that goat back to its owner."

"What else?" Claire asked. "What else did you and my mama do?"

Ruby thought back to times that had been more carefree, when life had seemed simple and safe. "We saw posters for a circus once when we traveled to visit my daddy's father in a big city. We begged to go to the circus, but it wasn't coming until after we'd be gone. We stared and stared at those pictures, though, and my grandfather told us all about the circus he'd seen. When we got home I found a long board and set it across a corner in the barn," she told her niece. "We pretended we were balancing on it, high above the ground. We were really only a few inches in the air, but pretending made it seem real."

"That sounds like fun," Claire said.

"It was great fun."

The screen door opened and Georgia carried a tray with a stack of cups, a teapot and a plate of cookies to a low table.

"Is there cookies for me?" Joel asked, scurrying to study the tray.

"Two cookies for you, Joel." His grandmother pulled a wooden stool close and helped him sit on it. "And tea with milk."

"Have you ever been to a circus?" Claire asked her grandmother.

Georgia served Ruby a cup of tea and gave one to Claire diluted with milk. Ruby made a point of keeping her fingers closed around her unsightly palms.

"Your grandfather and I once took your papa and Aunt Vivian when they were young."

"Were there acrobats?" the girl asked, wide-eyed.

"I believe there were."

"Have you been to a circus?" Claire asked Ruby.

"More than once," she answered. "When I traveled, my path often crossed those of other entertainers."

"You said you sang for a lady and she gave you her horse," Claire said.

Ruby sipped her tea. "That's right."

"Did you ever sing at the circus?"

"No. There's no singing at a circus. There are men and women who swing on trapezes high above the ground. And tigers that stand on platforms."

"I want to see tigers!" Joel piped up.

Ruby didn't have the right to promise these children anything, so she simply smiled and told him about the performers and animals.

Joel finished his cookies and tea and squirmed down from the stool. He wandered across the porch, came back to the stairs and ran to where a sawhorse had been outfitted with a straw broom to look like the head of a miniature horse. Joel climbed on the toy, picked up the rope reins and bounced up and down.

"I like hearing about my mama when she was little," Claire said softly to her grandmother.

Georgia gave her a gentle smile. "It's a treat to have someone here to share memories with you, isn't it?" She looked at Ruby with the same kind expression. "I'm glad you're here."

Ruby didn't know what to say. She sipped her tea self-consciously. Georgia had been friendly and welcoming from the start. Nash's reaction, Ettie and Audra Harper's reactions—those had been what she was expecting. Perhaps even what she thought she deserved.

Her throat constricted with emotion, Ruby
swallowed and glanced at her niece. Getting to
know these children was dependent on the gener-
osity of the Sommertons, so Georgia's kindness
touched her. She had already missed a lot. From
now on, she didn't want to miss anything. "I'm
glad I'm here, too," she managed to say. "I'm
thankful I didn't lose any more time. I only wish
it hadn't taken me so long to return."

"There is a season for everything," Georgia
replied. "We can't waste time on regrets. Perhaps this was simply your season to come home
and start over."

Ruby nodded. "Perhaps it was."

Claire handed her cup to her grandmother and
got down from the chair. "Do you like to make
clover chains?" she asked Ruby.

Ruby exchanged a glance with Georgia, hoping her hands weren't too stiff. "I do. I haven't
made one for a long time, but if you show me,
I'm sure I'll remember how. Is the clover easy
to find?"

Claire nodded. "There's a big patch behind
the coach house."

Georgia stacked their cups. "Watch for bees,
girls."

Ruby took the hand Claire extended and together they headed down the stairs. Joel hopped

off his makeshift horse and joined them. Ruby let Claire guide her across the lawn.

Thankfulness might have filled her heart, but her grief was still new and raw. Pearl should be here. Ruby had no hope or desire to be her substitute. But she owed it to her sister to do everything in her power to help make these children's lives full and happy. She still had a lot to make up for.

The Thoroughbred that Nash brought back to the Lazy S was a magnificent, spirited animal. The new stallion pranced along the side of the tall fence enclosure the men had built for him. It sniffed the air for the scent of the mares in the pasture. The stallion was a sleek warm brown, with white stockings on all four legs—a horse of near-perfect proportions.

"He's high-strung, but he's going to sire magnificent foals," Dugger said.

Silas and Dugger stood on one side of their boss, Ruby on the other, admiring the new animal.

"I want you all to hear this and hear it good," Nash said. "Flint is a dangerous animal, and he's to be treated that way. For his safety and ours we follow the rules. Nobody works with him alone, and nobody turns their back on him for a second." He glanced directly at Ruby while he added, "Stallions will snap off fingers, take nips right out of your flesh or even kill you with a bite to the neck. Until we learn his temperament and see how he reacts around the mares, we're taking no chances. Even if this boy appears mellow, his temperament can change in an instant."

She nodded in understanding.

Nash turned back to study Flint. "He was raised with other horses, so that should make a difference in his behavior around the others. But his sole job in life is to procreate, and nobody gets in his way. I intend to keep him happy by breeding him often and charging other ranchers for the privilege."

The men nodded in turn. Ruby listened with interest.

"How tall is he, boss?" Dugger asked.

"A little over sixteen hands."

"He has long hind legs," Silas remarked.

"That's the Arabian influence," Nash replied. "Good for speed."

"Are you going to raise horses for racing?" Ruby asked.

"Not necessarily. Flint's principal use will be to improve the other breeds we have now."

"That makes sense." She looked the stallion over appreciatively. "So, what happens next?"

"It's spring, so many of the mares are going

through their cycles," Nash told her. "We offer the mares and he does the rest. Under close supervision, of course, for their safety."

"And when will the foals be born?"

"If we're fortunate, early next spring. Some later in spring if they don't take right away."

"The mares carry them that long?"

He nodded. "Eleven months."

He sensed her attention and glanced at her. She was studying him with a thoughtful expression. The sun in her hair gave him an uncomfortable feeling in his chest.

"How about the Duchess?" she asked. "Is she ready?"

Her question caught him off guard. "What do you mean?"

"I mean…" she waved her hand toward the stallion "…in season to be bred."

"Matter of fact she is." *What was she thinking?*

"You're welcome to breed her."

He didn't know what to say. Or to think. "We'll talk about it."

She kept her gaze on his horse and didn't answer, even when she might've said Nash hadn't been willing to talk about anything else up to this point. She didn't have much hope he'd bring it up later.

That evening at supper, Ruby's movements

weren't quite as graceful as usual as she moved pans and carried bowls. Once, she paused in shifting a kettle from the stove, and straightened her back. Since Nash was strangely fascinated by everything she did, and couldn't seem to keep himself from staring when she was turned the other way, it was apparent something was off.

"Saw you got the garden tilled while I was gone," he said to Silas.

"Caught Miss Ruby doin' it and took over. She'd already made a hefty dent in the job."

He shot his gaze to her. "You *plowed*?"

She seated herself at her usual place at the opposite end of the table and picked up her fork. "More or less. I was getting the hang of it, anyway."

None of the women he'd ever known had the fortitude to harness a horse to a plow, let alone guide it to pierce the hard earth. Sometimes the plow jumped out of the furrow and had to be maneuvered back in. It took a lot of strength and was a hot, dirty job.

She hadn't asked for his help, and considering that fact made him think back to how he'd responded the last time she'd asked him for anything—help to move furniture.

She kept her fingers curled into her palms throughout the meal, and often rested her hands in her lap. After they'd cleaned up the stew and eaten slices of frosted apple spice cake, Silas and Dugger thanked her and excused themselves.

Nash stepped to where Ruby stood stacking dishes at the basin and reached for her hand. She resisted for a moment, but then let him open her fingers. Her skin was wet and warm, her fingers long and slender. He'd surprised himself by touching her, and belatedly had second thoughts. At the base of each finger were scabbed-over blisters. The other hand looked the same.

"I'm fine. Little Bird brought herbs and salves. As soon as the dishes are done, I'll use some and wrap my hands for the night."

"Next time just ask for help," he said.

She looked up. Her blue eyes held no accusation. Her stubborn determination held no anger. Why would she ask his help when all he did was rebuff her every effort?

"I know what you're thinking," he told her.

"I doubt that."

"I wasn't receptive when you asked for help with the furniture that day. But I rethought my actions."

She looked into his eyes as if trying to make sense of him. "I don't want to make more work for you. I'm trying to contribute."

"You've helped," he said.

He still held her hand, and she hadn't moved to pull it away. The slippery warmth sent a shaft of unexpected awareness through his belly. Unwelcome. Unsettling. The touch somehow seemed too intimate now, and he released her.

She had an expressive face, and she wasn't adept at hiding her reactions. He'd surprised her, and he found it sad that a simple compliment elicited her reaction. "Dry your hands now and use the salve. I'll finish this chore and we can discuss the horses."

After drying her hands, she wiped the table before getting a tin of ointment and clean cloths and sitting there. A minute later, he joined her. "That's not easy to do alone. Let me."

She didn't argue, just exposed both tender-looking palms. He held one wrist, gently dabbed ointment on the healing blisters, and then treated her other hand in the same manner.

He tore the fabric she'd set out into narrower strips, wound them around her hands and tied them securely. He had an inappropriate and almost irresistible urge to pull her hands to his face and touch her fingers to his cheeks. He closed his eyes briefly and imagined it. His skin tingled. His heart skipped several beats.

What had happened to the safe resentment and anger he'd stored up as a shield of protection? It had been easy to hold her at arm's length before he'd seen her rescue a pathetic horse, before he'd seen her look at his children with hope and longing.

It had been easy to resent Ruby Dearing before he realized he wanted her.

Chapter Ten

He looked up to discover her vivid blue eyes locked on him. He'd been angry when he'd told her she wasn't pretty. It had been a lie. Ruby took his breath away, and it had nothing to do with a resemblance to his late wife. She might share a few characteristics, but Pearl's sweet prettiness paled in comparison to her sister's seductive beauty and fire. It was difficult to look at Ruby without noting the feminine curves of her body, without admiring her alluring coloring and focusing on those full, mesmerizing lips.

Nash chastised himself, released her hands and put the lid on the tin. He had no business thinking carnal thoughts about Pearl's sister. He had a lot of regrets about his marriage, but he wasn't going to add more guilt to his list of issues.

"You said we'd talk," she reminded him.

He nodded. "You said you had papers for your Barb."

"The Duchess, yes. I thought you might want to breed her."

"The stallion is papered, too. Any colt he sires with the Barb would be valuable."

Ruby looked at her bandages. "I don't understand your hesitation."

"I don't need problems between us. Any dealings have to be legal and professional."

She flashed him a look of annoyance. "I'm not trying to cheat you out of anything."

"I didn't mean that."

"You can keep the foal. Sell it. Do anything you need to help the ranch."

She'd called the Lazy S a ranch this time. Her offer puzzled him. "You wouldn't want half?"

"There's nothing I need. You have children to raise. Expenses. If you sold a foal I'd feel like I'd contributed something."

He couldn't have been more surprised. They'd never discussed ownership of the property. He'd been too afraid of learning what she expected, of losing what he'd worked for. Nash had considered asking the lawyer in Crosby, but hadn't wanted to stir up gossip or give Ruby troublesome ideas if she didn't already have them. All along he'd been wary about her intentions, but she wanted to contribute—to the *ranch*.

Ruby's mother and sister had never had a bad word to say about this woman, and he'd always believed it was simply their character and deep love that didn't let them speak ill of her. Now that he thought about it, maybe all he knew about her were the opinions he'd formed without much to go on, except the fact that she'd left. "Ruby," he began.

She lifted her gaze from her bandages to his eyes. It was hard to put coherent thoughts together when she looked at him like that.

"What exactly does wanting to contribute mean? I need to know where we stand—where I stand with you and the property."

Her expression showed puzzlement. "The property?"

"What are your intentions? The house. The land."

"You think I've come to try to take the land from you? Why would I do that?"

"To sell it."

"But this is my home." It was unarguably the truth.

They stared at each other for a few silent moments.

Finally she nodded. "You don't know me."

"You're right about that."

"You don't know if maybe I want to sell it all and run off again."

He couldn't deny his misgivings. "Do you?"

She shook her head. "I want a home. I wanted a family." Her eyes got shiny, but she blinked hard. "I fully admit my rash decision to leave and not stay in contact. I regret not coming home sooner. But if this is our moment of honesty, I have to tell you I'm not sorry I left. I learned a lot about myself and about people. I made mistakes, but I did something I wanted to do. I *tried*. If I had stayed here I'd have still wanted to leave every day, because that's all I ever dreamed of back then. I would never have been content here. I'd have spent my whole life wondering what else was out there for me. I wanted more. I wanted to know. If I'd never gone I'd still be thinking what if I'd left? What if I'd taken a chance?"

Her reply caught Nash off guard. He felt a glimmer of admiration for her honesty and her courage. Not everyone could say they'd given something their best shot. She had. She hadn't been defensive or made excuses, but neither had she sounded repentant. She did, however, sound determined to stay now. He wasn't ready to admit the two of them might be similar in striving for what they wanted despite resistance from family. "You don't intend to leave again then."

"No. But I understand your hesitation about

trusting me. We can go to the attorney in town.
Take the deed with Daddy's name on it and see
what needs to be done to make it so we both have
equal share in this place."

Nash was doing a quick rearrangement of his
opinion. This woman confused and surprised
him at every turn.

"Unless you don't think we can make a partnership work," she added.

She was right about one thing. This was her
home, even though he could stubbornly argue
that she'd left and held no claim now. That would
have been wrong, and he couldn't do it. She'd
been born here, just as his wife had. He'd married
into his share. "I can make it work if you can."

"Everything straightforward," she told him.

Thinking, he drummed his fingers on the tabletop. He hadn't dared think this through before. Hadn't let himself imagine there was a
chance to bring his family back together. "After
that's done then, the legal parts, and you feel
you're settled…" *and I'm certain I can trust you*
"…there's one thing I want."

"What is it?"

His throat closed, so he cleared it to say, "I
want my children back here with me again."

Ruby heard the emotion in his voice, read the
pain in his eyes. She'd thought before how hard
it must be for him to be separated from his chil-

dren, even though they were nearby, even though they were with his parents. They weren't under his roof.

"My mother loves them and they adore her, but they belong here with me."

Ruby nodded in understanding. Emotion rose inside at the thought of having her niece and nephew close. Family. Real family. She would give anything to develop a true relationship with her sister's children—more than a couple hours together at the Sommertons on a Sunday afternoon. "I would be honored to help you take care of Claire and Joel," she managed to reply. "To help you raise them. I would do everything in my power to see them happy and well cared for, if…if you trust me."

"We'll have to work up to that," he said finally, and the hitch in her chest told her he still wasn't sure about her trustworthiness. That was all right. She would show him. "We'll go to town day after tomorrow. Take care of the legal part."

"And write something up about the horses, too," she insisted, gesturing with a bandaged hand. "That we will sell any colts from the Duchess and Flint and use the earnings for the ranch."

An owl hooted, the sound drifting through the open window. It had grown dark, and the lamps on the walls and one on the table illuminated the room. Ruby's fiery gold hair glowed. She wore it gathered at the nape of her neck, loose coils dangling to her shoulders.

They were discussing their future—a future that might eventually place both of them in this house with Nash's children. If anyone had suggested a year ago—a month ago—that there was a remote possibility he'd be having this conversation, even considering placing his children in her care, he'd have told them they'd lost their mind. "You're not what I expected."

She raised one corner of her lips. "I'm not what I expected, either."

He rose to his feet, and she wrapped her bandaged hand around his wrist to stop him. The warmth of her fingers burned his skin. It may have been his imagination that her hair smelled faintly of rain. "I already love your children, because they are Pearl's. But I want to be a family, and I want them to grow to love and trust me."

"They trust very easily," he told her. "When someone trusts you, it's a commitment. Honor that."

She didn't miss the warning in his tone. "I will."

She released his arm, and he grabbed his hat and headed outdoors.

* * *

A week later the local lawyer questioned them about their relationship more than once. "It's highly unusual for an unmarried couple to enter a partnership like this."

"We're not a couple," Ruby insisted. "Men have partnerships all the time."

"Yes, but that's different."

"How? Because I'm not a man? We want joint ownership of the Lazy S and all its holdings, plain and simple."

Mr. Buckley appeared to realize his opinion held little value regarding their plans. He picked up his pencil and made a few notes. "It is wisest to use wording to the effect that if one of you wants to leave, he—or she—must buy the other one out, or simply sign over your share of the property."

"That's perfect," Ruby told him.

He pursed his lips. "Come back in an hour and I'll have the papers ready to sign."

They stood on the boardwalk and Nash glanced along the street. "Doesn't look like there are any horse auctions today."

She attempted to gauge his expression, but his hat brim shaded his eyes. "Vivo is doing quite well. Have you seen how his coat is growing in and getting shiny?"

"I've seen."

"And I'm letting him graze for longer and longer at a time."

"He's friendly," Nash added. "Which seems unlikely after all he's been through. A lot of horses would be skittish and mistrusting of people."

"He just needed a friend."

Nash glanced at Ruby. She'd worn a blue dress with a small matching jacket, and the color set off her eyes and glowing skin. She'd swept up her hair and settled a jaunty hat with a feather at an angle on her head. Around the house, even dressed in her mother's plain clothing, she was a striking woman. Wearing something so feminine and fitted, she drew the attention of everyone who looked their way.

She didn't seem to notice people's reactions, however. Nash's ccuriosity about her life and the things she'd done and people she'd known had grown. Her past was a mystery, but he was probably better off not knowing the details.

"Let's get a piece of pie." He led her to the small hotel restaurant, where they each had a slice of apple pie. He was making the best of this situation. He had the ranch. She had a home. By sharing the land, they were making a commitment to each other.

Nash had coffee while Ruby enjoyed a cup of tea, and once they'd finished they picked up a few supplies and returned to sign the documents.

In his mind they'd made an agreement as serious as marriage. He was bound to her by the land and his love for it, but more importantly by his commitment to providing for and leaving an inheritance for his children. Some relationships had a lot less going for them.

With a start, Nash realized the direction his thoughts had veered. This was Ruby Dearing he was dealing with, not a fresh-faced girl with love and marriage on her mind. They were sharing their horses, the land. Eventually, he hoped to trust her with the children's care. She wasn't a replacement for his wife, and even if she had been, he didn't want one. He already had too much responsibility to take on another commitment.

Nash adjusted his hat and his thinking as he climbed on the wagon seat and headed the team toward home. But every so often his gaze inadvertently trailed to the woman sitting beside him. Whether he liked it or not, they had entered into a relationship. He was going to keep it on track.

The next time Georgia brought the children, Ruby introduced them to Vivo. The horse had grown surprisingly trusting of Ruby since she'd brought him to the ranch two weeks previous. He didn't shy away from Claire or Joel, so Ruby helped them to climb the corral fence and brought him close so they could reach out and touch his face and neck.

"We can wide him?" Joel asked.

She warmed to his wide-eyed excitement. The image of him on that sawhorse in the Sommertons' yard came to her. She didn't want to disappoint him, but she didn't have the right to make parental decisions.

"I couldn't let you do that without your father's permission," she told him. "If we see him before you leave, we will ask." She turned to Vivo. "I haven't had a saddle on him, but he does well with the harness. I will make sure it's safe first. Stand still, boy. Stand still, Vivo." Ruby climbed the fence and slid onto his back to see how he handled her weight. The animal stood placidly.

She took the reins and gently nudged him into a walk. The horse obediently moved forward, turned at her bidding and then came back to where the children waited. Georgia left the shade and joined them.

Later, they were drinking iced tea when Nash drove a wagon toward the barn, Silas on the seat beside him. Joel jumped down the porch stairs and darted toward his father.

Nash handed Silas the reins and climbed down to greet the little boy, swinging him up to his shoulder and sauntering toward the house.

"Can we ride Vivo, Papa?" Claire asked. Ruby had never seen the child's face so animated.

"Hello, Mother," Nash said, with a nod and a handsome smile. "It's nice to see you this morning." He turned his attention back to Claire. "Of all the horses in the pasture and stables, that's the one you want to ride?"

She nodded, sending her fair curls bobbing.

Nash riveted his gaze on Ruby. "You rode him?"

"A little while ago. To make sure he was calm with a rider. He's docile and obedient."

"I guessed that about him. He's easy to walk. Doesn't spook easily. He's also grown to like attention."

"And Miss Dearing's singing," Silas said from behind him.

Ruby laughed. "Help yourself to a cold drink, Silas."

"Come on then," Nash said. With Joel still on his shoulders, he reached for his daughter's hand.

"We can ride him!" Claire turned and motioned for Ruby to join them. As they reached the corral, she looked up at her father. "Joel can go first, Papa."

She possessed many of her mother's qualities, such as thoughtfulness and restraint. But her enthusiasm toward the horse showed Ruby a new side.

The two females climbed the fence and watched while Nash settled Joel on Vivo's back and walked the horse around the corral. The little guy's smile split his face. "I widing!" he called.

When it was Claire's turn, Nash lifted her to the animal's back and then gestured for Ruby to guide the horse. It was a small thing, and he stood close by, but she felt as though he had entrusted her with an important task.

Claire's smile touched her. Ruby turned her gaze from her niece to the man and boy at the rail, and an ache widened in her chest. She hoped Pearl somehow knew her children were well cared for and loved. This was all new to Ruby, but she intended to see they lacked for nothing.

She would do whatever it took to earn their trust—and their father's.

Early Saturday morning, Ruby took all the items from the pantry shelves so she could scrub the shelves clean and give them a coat of paint. Keeping busy took her mind off the quiet house for short stretches of time. The sun was high overhead when she washed the bucket and paintbrush at the pump. She set them out to dry and folded down the sleeves of her faded shirt.

A horse whinnied in the pasture, and she glanced up. A trail of dust indicated a rider coming fast. Apparently Nash had seen it, too, wherever he'd been, for he rode Boone right up into the dooryard and dismounted.

Ruby shaded her eyes with her hand. "Can you see who it is?"

It took Nash a minute to respond. "Looks like Tucker's horse."

Sure enough, Tucker Gilchrist galloped toward them. He slowed the horse and slid to the ground.

Nash exchanged a look with Ruby before walking toward his brother-in-law. "What is it?"

"You need to come to your folks' right away."

"What's happened?" Nash asked. "Is someone hurt?"

"Nothing like that," Tucker said, out of breath. "We all need to talk. The family is waiting." He turned to Ruby. "If you wouldn't mind, can you come look after the children?"

"I don't mind, but I have to change into clean clothing. It will only take a minute."

"I'll saddle the Duchess," Nash called to her retreating back.

Minutes later the three of them mounted and rode to the Sommerton place.

Nash's heart had a workout on the way. His brother-in-law's cryptic orders were disturbing, and his reassurances that no one had been harmed didn't satisfy him.

Vivian met them at the door, Claire and Joel with her. Nash gave them each a hug.

"Grandma had tears," Claire said softly.

"I'm going to take care of it," he promised her, although he had no idea what was going on.

"Thank you for coming, Ruby," Vivian said. "It might be best if you kept the children away from the house for a while. Mama said they haven't had any lunch, though, so you can bring them in the back to get them something when they're hungry."

Ruby looked puzzled, but she efficiently bustled the little girl and boy toward the side yard.

"What's going on?" Nash asked his sister.

"Mama sent one of the hands for us and I sent Tucker for you. Things are tense here, and that's all I know."

His parents were in the enormous sitting room. Cosmo sipped a brandy, though it was barely eleven o'clock. Georgia stood at a window, gazing out across the landscape. When she turned to look at her children, her ashen face shocked Nash.

"Mother, are you all right?"

She shook her head.

Nash realized for the first time that another person was seated in the room. A young man stood and looked their way as he, Vivian and Tucker approached. He was dark-haired and handsome, dressed in a white shirt and black tie.

"Be seated," Georgia said. "Your father has something to tell you."

The stranger remained standing. He extended a hand. "Miles Easton."

Nash shook it and introduced himself.

Miles studied him and Vivian intently and quickly resumed his seat.

"Miles is a doctor," Cosmo said.

"Is someone sick?" Vivian asked. Tucker reached for her hand and patted it.

Something was definitely wrong. The air in the room fairly crackled.

"No one's sick," Cosmo said. "Miles arrived yesterday. He had some things to get off his chest." Cosmo didn't look well himself. He got a handkerchief from his pocket and dabbed his upper lip.

"Will somebody please just get to the point?" Nash insisted.

"There's no easy way to say this…" his father began.

"Miles is your brother," Georgia interrupted.

Chapter Eleven

"Georgia!" Cosmo admonished.

"Did you have some way to sweeten the news? Diminish the blow?" she asked in a harsh tone Nash had never in his life heard his mother use before. But his mind was still back on the *he's-your-brother* part.

"Brother?" he questioned.

"May I speak?" Miles asked. When no one said anything, he continued. "I always knew of my illegitimacy. My mother didn't sugarcoat the facts. Once I was old enough to see how hard my mother worked and then how she scrimped and saved to send me to medical school, all I ever wanted to do was confront the father who never acknowledged me. She begged me not to. She died three months before my graduation, and all I wanted to do was find the man who'd made her life so hard, and give him a taste of his own medicine."

None of this sounded like the father Nash knew. "Papa, have you denied this?"

Cosmo shook his head. "I can't deny the boy's claim, Nash. I knew his mother years ago. Miles is nearly a year older than you. I met her when I went to Philadelphia to tie up my parents' legal holdings. She worked for the lawyer. It was a hard time for your mother and I. We'd lost a child, and she was grieving—we were both grieving. My parents had recently passed away." His father ran his hand across his chin. "I made a mistake. It was an inexcusable error. I was ashamed. I didn't want to hurt your mother, but I told her about it. I didn't want any secrets between us. I attempted to contact Miles's mother several times—not to continue a relationship, only to make sure she was all right, but she had quit the firm and was nowhere to be found."

Nash absorbed his father's words as though listening through a wall. Had he heard this right? This stranger was his own father's illegitimate son? A muted hum sounded in his ears.

"It was a grievous indiscretion on my part," Cosmo admitted. "I asked your mother's forgiveness, and I believe she forgave me."

Nash looked at his mother, and she gave a gentle nod.

"I worked hard to earn her trust again. Now I've asked Miles to forgive me. Had I known about him I would have provided for him." Cosmo looked to Miles. "I regret that your mother had a difficult life."

Miles nodded his understanding and then looked from Vivian to Nash. "I believed my mother had covered up for him, to protect his family, which she did. But after her death I found his name on an old letter. I wanted to hurt him— at first. I never thought about how many other people would be hurt. I'm sorry for that. I'm sorry, Mrs. Sommerton."

Georgia wouldn't look at him.

"It's not your fault, Miles," Cosmo assured him. "You have nothing to apologize for. I'm the one who caused the hurt."

Nash still hadn't absorbed the shocking information. He sat in stunned disbelief, listening to the conversation as though it was happening somewhere else and not right here in his parents' home.

In the chair beside his, Vivian wept quietly. He looked over at her slumped shoulders and the tears running down her face. Anger rose inside him. He slipped to his knees beside her and wrapped a comforting arm around her shoulders. Tucker met his eyes over her head.

His mother had been seated once, but had again bobbed up and stood at the window. She'd dealt with her husband's indiscretion years ago, and now she had to face it all over again. Miles was the living, breathing reminder of what had happened. How much was she hurting?

Georgia saw nothing as she stared across the lawn. Last night an angry young man had shown up to confront the father he believed had knowingly deserted him. Cosmo had apologized, and acknowledged his relationship with the boy's mother. He'd seemed almost relieved to know about Miles after all these years. She didn't know how to feel about that. About Miles.

She'd been so proud to raise her son and daughter. She loved being a mother and a wife. She'd believed Cosmo's mistake was behind them.

She hadn't slept a wink last night. Moments in time kept floating to the surface of her memory. Such as the Christmas morning Vivian sang in church and her sweet soprano voice had touched everyone. Tears had run down Cosmo's cheeks and Georgia had been so moved she'd barely been able to breathe. Or the time Nash and Pearl had planned a surprise anniversary party for them and invited all their friends and neighbors. She and Cosmo had spent the day holding hands, accepting congratulations and eating cake.

In the fragile young years of their marriage she had lost a baby, a tiny newborn who had died in her arms after only a few struggling days of life. Now Cosmo had another child.

This other woman's child had grown hale and hardy and become the stranger standing before her.

She thought of the young woman who had borne a son and raised him alone, while Georgia had been blissfully raising her own children.

It was painful for her, but she looked at her grown children's stunned expressions, felt their disappointment.

Nash got up from where he knelt beside his sister and came to her. His eyes held disbelief, but also compassion, and that compassion helped settle her nerves.

Her tall, strong son wrapped her in his arms and held her tightly. She had dreaded the moment when he and Vivian would learn of their father's unfaithfulness, hadn't wanted to see the shock and disappointment on their faces or the hurt in their eyes.

She wanted to hate that boy for stealing something precious from her children, but he was as much a victim in this ordeal as they were. More so, perhaps, because he'd been raised without a father, all along believing Cosmo hadn't wanted him. At least Nash and Vivian knew their father loved them.

She looked at her husband, recognizing his raw nerves and feelings. She took a fortifying breath. Easing away, she looked at Nash. "It's not Miles's fault," she said softly. "He's been hurt, too."

Nash couldn't say anything. A moment of weakness in his father's past had hurt his mother years ago, but was hurting her even more now. That selfish mistake had just turned their lives upside down. He studied his father. Could a person ever truly know another? A secret had come to light. Nash worked to tamper down his anger. He was no saint himself. He had made his own mistakes.

Nash took his mother's hand and led her to sit next to him on a divan. His curiosity got the best of him, and he looked at Miles. "Did you grow up in Philadelphia, then?"

"Upriver in Burlington. My mother had a sister there."

"You were able to go to medical school."

Miles nodded. "My uncle died and left us a

little money. We lived frugally, and both of us had jobs. My mother was insistent I would attend university."

"Did your mother ever marry?"

"Never."

Nearly an hour passed with an occasional question and long moments of silence.

"You'll stay here, Miles," Georgia said at last. "Have you any bags?"

Nash studied his mother with a combination of disbelief and admiration. Surely Miles had opened up a ragged old wound, a hurt she'd dealt with long ago, but she didn't show any of the anger he himself experienced.

"I have a few things at the hotel, but I don't expect you to—"

"I won't hear any argument. You will stay here and get to know Nash and Vivian." She couldn't bring herself to say "your father," so she left the invitation at that, implying he and Cosmo should have time to talk.

"Thank you, Mrs. Sommerton."

She placed her hand over Nash's, her lips pursed in a straight line. "I think it will be best for Claire and Joel if they go home with you today. I hope it's not inconvenient."

"No, Mother, of course not. Ruby is perfectly capable of caring for them."

She gave him a shaky smile. "Ruby has impeccable timing."

"You should talk to them before we go, though, so they see you're all right."

"I'll go freshen up a bit first." She stood and excused herself.

Nash composed himself and gave his father another assessing look. Cosmo met his eyes. "I'm sorry, son."

Nash fought down anger and went to stand near the window.

Cosmo got up and stood at the side of his desk. "I never meant for you or your mother to be hurt," he said. "You must believe me."

Nash stood stiffly near the window. "Selfishness always hurts others."

Vivian got to her feet and smoothed her skirts. "I'm sorry you had such a painful childhood, Mr. Easton. I never knew what it was like to wonder if my father cared for me." She looked directly at Cosmo for the first time. "Until today."

Cosmo's expression blanched. "This doesn't change anything between you and me." His tone had softened. "We do have another person in our family, but—"

"You're wrong," his daughter said, with her chin held high. "I don't care how long ago it was.

Knowing what you did changes everything." She turned and rushed from the room.

Tucker got up, gave Nash a confused look and followed.

Cosmo took a long swallow of his brandy.

When Georgia returned, she and Nash went in search of Claire and Joel. His mother took their hands and led them to a bench in her garden.

Nash motioned to Ruby. "Come with me to gather their things from their rooms."

She followed him up the stairs. "What's going on, Nash?"

Once inside the bedroom Joel used, Nash closed the door and leaned against it. His heart was a rock in his chest. He hadn't felt this way since the day Pearl had died.

"What's happened?"

It was difficult to form the words, but he explained about Miles's appearance and the family's reactions to the news of Cosmo's illegitimate son.

Nash's voice shook as he explained the details of what had taken place in his family. Ruby grasped his arm. "I'm so sorry. Is there anything I can do for your mother?"

He shook his head. "She was relieved to know you would be caring for Claire and Joel. Their lives have been on a pretty even keel here, and

I don't want to frighten them by taking them home, but this probably isn't the best place for them right now. Everyone needs some time."

Ruby let go of his arm. "Of course. We'll see to it their lives are kept as normal as possible," she assured him.

"Just gather a couple of toys and a few items of clothing," he told her. "They have plenty of clothes at home and we can get the rest later. One bag should do it." He reached into the armoire and brought out a satchel, which he set on the end of the bed and opened. He must have stood there awhile because he started when Ruby touched his wrist.

"I'm going to be right here with you," she promised him, her eyes wide and liquid blue with compassion. "With Claire and Joel. I'll protect them like they're my own. I promise you."

He nodded in appreciation and they finished quickly, hurrying to gather items from Claire's room. Nash glanced around and then met her eyes. "Thank you, Ruby."

"No thanks needed," she said. "I told you I wanted to be a family. This is what family does, right? Your children are precious to me, Nash. They're the only kin I have. I'm going to do everything in my power to see they don't lack for care or love."

He swallowed hard and glanced away. "We'd better go."

Georgia had explained to the children that they would be going with their father, so she hugged and kissed them, promising she'd see them very soon. Nash tied the bag to his saddle and lifted one child onto each horse's back.

Ruby took Georgia's hands and squeezed them. "If you need anything at all, you come see us, all right? Any time. If you want to talk, come by and we'll make tea."

"No doubt I'll be there sooner than you expect."

"Good." She gave the woman an impulsive hug.

She didn't like leaving Georgia behind, and Nash's struggle was obvious. Ruby pulled herself up behind Claire and did her best to tug her skirts down over her legs. "Do you think Vivian's all right?"

"She has Tucker. He's a good man." Nash gave his horse a nudge with his heels and led them away from the house.

Claire waved at her grandmother.

"Your grandma's fine," Ruby assured her. "You'll see her very soon."

"Did you put Nancy in that bag behind Papa?" she asked.

"Is Nancy your baby doll? She's in the bag."

It had been a long and stressful day, and by the time they reached the house it seemed as though it should be over. But the sun had just dipped toward the west, signaling it was time for Ruby to get a meal on the table.

"Ruby is going to take care of you here at the ranch," Nash explained, lifting Claire down and assisting Ruby.

"Is Grandma all right?" Claire's brow had furrowed with concern.

"Your grandmother is just fine," he assured her. "She's just very tired, sweet pea, and we're going to let her rest as long as she needs to. I'd like for you to help with Joel." Nash paused and hunkered down on one knee to look into his daughter's eyes. "There's nothing for you to be worried about. You can sleep in your own bed now, and you'll both have all your playthings. Don't be scared. Ruby is right here, and I will be here, too."

"I'll help, Papa," she told him with a solemn nod.

He enfolded Claire in a hug that brought tears to Ruby's eyes. She blinked and looked away. When she glanced back, Nash was ruffling Joel's hair. "You be a good boy."

"I be a good boy!" he answered with a nod.

Nash stood and left to care for the horses.

Ruby picked up the satchel. "Let's go put your things away."

In Claire's room, Ruby took the girl's few belongings out of the bag and set them on the bed.

"Your rooms are clean." She eyed the space, trying to see it through the little girl's eyes and hoping familiar surroundings were comforting. "Even the sheets and spreads are freshly laundered. I hope you're going to like being back in your own home." She stacked a few items of underclothing in a drawer. "If there's anything you need—anything at all—I want you to come to me and let me know. Will you do that?"

Claire nodded. "You used to sleep in here when you were a little girl?"

"I did." Ruby glanced at the small boy, considering his confusion about the change of circumstances. "How about you, Joel? Will you ask me if you want something, or tell me if you're scared? I'm going to take care of you and make sure you're safe."

The three-year-old lowered his gaze to the floor with sudden bashfulness.

"He'll tell me, Aunt Ruby, and I'll tell you."

Ruby's heart softened at Claire's address. Had Georgia referred to her as Aunt Ruby in front of them? She imagined so. And she liked the sound.

She offered them a warm smile. "Claire's a good big sister, isn't she?"

Ruby had a dozen things to do, but she looked from one child to the other, then moved to Claire's bed and settled herself on the edge. She patted the faded coverlet. "Come sit with me, darlings."

Both children joined her, though she had to reach down and help Joel up.

"We're going to be a family, the four of us. I can't tell you how happy that makes me, and I hope it makes you happy, too. I know how much you miss your mama. It's okay to be sad that she's not here anymore."

"Grandma Laura, too," Claire said.

"Grandma Laura, too." Ruby took a fortifying breath. "I miss them both very much. It makes me feel better to be here, though—in this house, in their rooms. Being here helps me feel closer to them."

"I think it makes Papa sad."

"Everybody misses people in their own way."

"Papa went to feed the howses." It was the first thing Joel had said to her, and it showed her plainly how a three-year-old lived in the moment. It was possible he didn't remember Pearl at all, but knew only what others had shared about her—and as much as a three-year-old could comprehend. It occurred to Ruby that coming home—coming here—might be more of an upheaval for him than for Claire. He'd been with Georgia since he was a baby.

"Yes, he did. You like horses, don't you?"

He nodded. "I like big ones, and baby ones, too."

"You can help me feed Vivo tomorrow. Would you like that?"

Joel nodded, his dark eyes wide and bright. "He's a big howse. I liked widing him."

"He's pretty skinny, though. We have to take good care of him so he gets better."

"I can help!"

"Yes, you can. I'm going to go make our supper now." Ruby looked around. "Why don't the two of you play with your toys or read a book while I fix the meal?"

"I can't read very well," Claire said.

Ruby got up and found a book on a shelf. She hadn't been around children, so she tried to remember what it was like to be one. "Why don't you just show the pictures to Joel, then? After supper I'll read it to you."

She fried bacon and made a batch of pancakes. When Nash and the hands came to the kitchen she was scrambling eggs.

Nash called the children, and within minutes

most of the chairs around the table were filled for the first time since she'd been there. Nash's gaze kept touching on his daughter and son. He poured milk, and tucked a napkin into Joel's collar.

Seeing him with his children touched Ruby. He was gruff and aloof with her, but he was like a different person with Claire and Joel.

After supper he said softly to Ruby, "I forgot to mention, you have to remind Joel to use the outhouse. Sometimes he forgets."

She nodded in understanding. "I'll remind him every so often."

"You have to keep an eye on him. He tends to get into things and sometimes takes off across the yard."

Nash's concern showed he still didn't completely trust her. "Okay. I'll watch him carefully. Maybe we need a latch high on the front door, in case I'm in the kitchen and don't hear him."

"I'll put one up tomorrow. There are other dangers to watch out for," he said. "The horses, of course, and the creek."

She nodded and offered him what she hoped was a comforting smile. "I grew up here, remember? I'll bet Mama had to watch out for me, too."

"I know," he said, and gave her an apologetic look. "It's just that…well…"

"I've never been around young'uns and I'm not known for being all that responsible."

"I didn't say that."

"You didn't have to. I understand, Nash. You're concerned about me looking after your children, and you wouldn't be a good father if you didn't point out these things to me and reassure yourself that your children will be safe."

It had been only a couple days since they'd signed the papers to share this house and land. At that time bringing Joel and Claire home had been in the distant future. The children weren't here because he'd had a change of heart or a sudden burst of confidence in Ruby. They were here because his mother needed the time.

"It's okay," Ruby said. "I can learn. I want to learn. Give me all the instructions you like."

His expression showed surprise, but he only nodded and thanked her. He took his children out to the porch while she washed and put away the dishes. Then she planned what she would prepare for meals the following day.

It wasn't completely dark when he brought them back inside. "Claire says you're going to read their bedtime story."

"Oh. Yes. Are we getting ready for bed? I'll dip warm water for them to wash."

"They need help washing."

"Yes, of course."

"You get Claire ready. I'll take Joel, and we'll meet in Claire's room for the book."

In the blink of an eye they were gathered there, with Claire in her bed, Nash and Joel on one side and Ruby on the other, with the book. The cover read *A Book of Nonsense*. "Nonsense?" she asked.

"It's silly poems," Claire told her.

Ruby opened it to find pen-and-ink drawings above limericks. "There was an old man with a beard," she read. "Who said, 'It is just as I feared! Two owls and a hen, four larks and a wren, have all built their nests in my beard!'"

Joel giggled and pointed to the drawing of a man with a huge black beard filled with creatures. "He has a biwd in his beawd."

"Read the lady with the bonnet," Claire urged.

"There was a young lady whose bonnet, came untied when the birds sat upon it. But she said, 'I don't care! All the birds in the air are welcome to sit on my bonnet!'"

"I don't want no biwds on my head," Joel declared with utmost seriousness, and patted his dark hair.

Nash's grin split his face and he chuckled, tucking Joel back against his chest in a hug and kissing the little boy's ear. Joel laughed and tucked in his chin to avoid the tickle.

The sight of Nash smiling and enjoying his children warmed Ruby's heart and brought a catch to her breathing. He'd been waiting a long time to get them back with him, but without Pearl or Laura to care for them, it must have looked impossible. Had he imagined he might have to wait until they were old enough to care for themselves while he worked the ranch?

When Ruby first arrived it had seemed as though she'd returned too late. Reconciliation was impossible and she had seemingly alienated this man who held all the cards regarding her sister's children. But maybe this was what fate had in store for Ruby all along. Perhaps, by being the key to helping her niece and nephew, she was exactly where she belonged.

She hoped so.

Nash kissed Claire and tucked her into bed with her doll. Ruby turned out the oil lamp on the wall, wished her niece a good night and then followed Nash to Joel's room.

The little boy looked awfully small in the bed, but Nash tucked a rolled quilt along each side of him, so he couldn't fall off. He ruffled Joel's hair and hugged him.

"Night, Aunt Wooby," Joel said shyly.

She gave him a warm smile. "Good night, darling. Sleep well."

In the hallway, Nash stood and waited until she joined him. "Figured I should let you know I'll be sleeping in the house now."

She hadn't thought that far ahead. Of course he wanted to be close. "Can I get you anything?"

He shook his head. "Thanks, no." He didn't make a move to leave. "I just want to tell you—to say, I mean..." He paused, obviously at a loss for words. With a nod, he finally stated, "I couldn't have brought them home without you being here."

"You don't have to say anything. I'm happy to be here for them." Even though he had his doubts about her, it was nice to be needed. It felt good to be important to someone. Because Claire and Joel needed her, she wasn't alone.

"Well. I'm exhausted. I'm turning in."

"Good night."

After she'd finished in the kitchen, Ruby turned out the lamps, prepared for bed and then lay awake with moonlight streaming through the window.

She thought of Nash's smile and the sound of his rusty laugh. His affection for his children, his mother and sister had given her unexpected glimpses into the person he was. She liked his voice, the sound of his laugh… He was Pearl's husband, and the way he made Ruby feel was probably inappropriate. He still didn't think much of her, but he needed her. She'd be pathetic to read anything more than that into what was going on here.

She had drifted into an uneasy sleep when a hard knock at the front door woke her. She shot out of bed and into the hall.

Chapter Twelve

"Hellfire, woman!" Nash gasped from the hall. "Don't you own a nightgown?"

She stood clutching her dressing gown to her breasts, and realized the rest of her was visible in the moonlight that streamed through the tall window at the end of the hall.

Dressed in only a pair of trousers, he padded past her and down the front stairs.

Ruby shrugged into the dressing gown and stood at the top banister. Dugger's voice carried up the stairwell. "The horse is gone, boss!"

"Which horse?"

"The Thoroughbred. He was in his stall and then I heard sounds. The other horses were restless. I checked and the stall gate was open and he was gone."

"I'm coming!" Nash turned and dashed up the steps past her. "Flint's gone!" he said on his way.

"Can I help?"

"You have to stay with the children."

She handled her disappointment well. "Of course."

A minute later, he dashed back out of his room, fully dressed, buckling a holster around his hips.

"You think someone *took* him?"

"He's valuable property, Ruby. I don't know, but most likely someone stole him."

Nash joined Dugger and lit lamps in the barn to investigate. Silas joined them, and they studied the floor and the footprints coming and going in the dirt. A jumble of tracks near the rail where a saddle was missing indicated someone had taken time to saddle Flint.

Distinctive hoofprints and a set from a pair of boots led out the side door and toward the gate. The boot prints disappeared, indicating the intruder had mounted the horse. A sick feeling settled in the pit of Nash's stomach. He'd saved years for this stud. The future of the Lazy S depended on breeding Flint.

The moon was bright enough to reveal the trail as it left the yard.

"Saddle up," Nash said to Silas. "We're riding after him."

Minutes later, mounted and carrying rifles, the two men headed away from the ranch.

"Only two choices," Silas said, when they reached the road.

Nash got down and studied the gravel, finally picking up the signs. "That way."

They rode at a quick pace, but not so fast that the horses might stumble in the dark or that they might miss their prey. It took over an hour before Boone pranced and lifted his head as though catching a scent on the wind.

"He recognizes something." Nash reined in.

"Might be a mountain lion."

"Nah. He's not scared. Might be Flint."

Sure enough, Boone whinnied and a horse replied with a nicker from off to their right.

Nash slid to the ground and placed his hand over his horse's muzzle to silence him. Silas did the same with his mount.

Nash glanced around and located a fallen log in the moonlight. "Tether 'em here and we'll move in on foot," he whispered.

Trees and high grass indicated they were near a creek or small stream. Nash led, picking his way as silently as possible. The scent of burning wood floated on the night air, guiding him. Maybe this wasn't their thief.

Through a stand of brush, the dim flicker

of firelight came into view. Whoever camped here was either not the person who'd taken his horse or not worried about being followed. Nash gripped his rifle.

The big Thoroughbred had been tethered in place and stood, his neck arched at their approach. Nash never forgot for a second that he was a dangerous animal and could injure or kill someone in the blink of an eye. There were no other horses nearby, however, and Boone was already familiar and not a threat, so Flint appeared calm.

The person in a bedroll wasn't as alert as the horse, however, and seemed to be sleeping—unless this was a trap. Could be an empty bedroll, and the thief hid in the nearby foliage, waiting for them to come out into the open.

Nash indicated he and Silas should split up and circle the camp to be sure. Minutes later, they met on the other side without incident.

Nash crept toward the form lying on the ground. With the barrel of his rifle, he nudged the fella's hat until it rolled away, exposing a shock of hair. He motioned for Silas to level his gun on the person.

With Silas in place, Nash reached for the blanket and jerked it away.

The horse thief lunged to a sitting position,

disoriented and…frightened. Their captive was no man.

A sleepy boy of about twelve stared at him in abject horror, eyes wide as saucers in the dwindling firelight.

Well, this day had been full of surprises, and not the good kind. Nash cursed under his breath, puzzled over this turn of events. "Get up."

The lad scrambled to slender bare feet and put his hands in the air. "You gonna shoot me, mister?"

His voice hadn't even begun to change. What was he doing, stealing horses at midnight? "That's my horse you've got there."

The lad said nothing, just looked at him, let his gaze sidle to Silas and back.

"He could've hurt you."

His chin came up. "He wouldn't hurt me."

"Oh? You sure about that?"

"Yep."

"Care to explain yourself?"

The boy only shrugged bony shoulders.

Nash stepped closer, and the boy flinched away. He had scratches and scrapes on his cheek and his hair was matted and filthy. "What's your name?"

No reply.

"Where are you from?"

Nothing.

"Skinny little thing like you saddled that horse and rode him all the way out here?"

"Yeah."

"Horse stealing is a pretty serious offense, you know."

"So's killin' kids."

"I'm not going to kill you. Get your boots on."

The kid stuffed bare feet into boots entirely too big for him, while Nash tossed dirt on the fire. There were no cooking utensils, no signs of food. The lad had been ill prepared for a trip.

Nash led Flint while Silas took the boy by the arm, and they headed back to where the other horses were tethered.

"What're you gonna do?" the boy asked.

"I have to figure that out."

Nash settled the kid in front of him and led Flint back to the ranch, the stallion's reins tied behind. The boy didn't smell any too clean. Whatever Nash decided, this kid couldn't sleep in one of their beds without a bath and a head washing.

Back in the stable, they took care of the horses. Nash thanked Silas and then led the boy to the house. "You gonna tell me your name?"

He remained silent.

Ruby met them in the kitchen. Her eyes widened.

"Here's our horse thief. If you'll heat water, I'll carry in the tub. He reeks to high heaven. He'll bunk with me tonight, and in the morning I'll take him into town. The sheriff will know what to do with him."

The boy looked at Nash with a plea of desperation on his dirty face. Nash had no doubt that if the kid thought he could have escaped, he would have run right then. His gaze even sidled to the door, but Nash stood between him and freedom, a lot bigger—and a whole lot madder.

Ruby pumped water, got the stove hot and then poured warm water into the tub. She gathered soap and toweling.

"Get out of those clothes," Nash ordered. "I'll find you something to wear."

The boy backed away, but Nash grabbed him by the arm and pulled him toward the tub.

Ruby didn't know what to make of the situation. What had the lad been doing all alone at night, and why had he stolen Nash's horse? It didn't make any sense. He looked so young and frightened that she felt sorry for him. Nash was right; he smelled and his dark hair was disgustingly filthy. Where had he been living and sleeping? Didn't he have parents or anyone to look out for him?

He didn't fight Nash, but turned away and re-moved two shirts and filthy pants. Averting her gaze, Ruby bent to pick up the offending gar-ments and toss them into the woodstove.

"Hey, them's my clothes!"

Nash picked up a pail and dumped water over the boy's head. A moment later, the pail hit the floor with a resounding clang and Nash jumped backward as though he'd been scorched.

"What's wrong?" Ruby glanced from the drip-ping boy to the man's shocked face. "Nash?"

He raised one arm and dropped it, and then he turned his whole body to face the other way. He pointed behind him. "That's not a boy!"

"What?" Ruby closed the door on the stove, where the clothing now burned, and hurried toward the tub. Sure enough, the skinny, un-dernourished child in their copper tub was not a boy, but definitely not a woman. If she'd been properly fed she may have had budding breasts, but this poor young girl was pathetically thin. "Oh," Ruby said with a heavy sigh. "Oh, my."

"Why didn't you say something?" At the anger in Nash's voice, the girl flinched. "You let me think you were a boy."

She didn't reply.

Over his shoulder, he said to Ruby, "You'll have to find her something to wear."

"I'll find something. She can stay in my room tonight. Go on to bed."

"I'll empty the tub in the morning." Not needing another word of encouragement, he disappeared.

"You sure enough surprised him." Ruby scraped some soap shavings into a cup with a splash of water and a little scented oil, and lathered it up. "Get on your knees and lean forward," she said. "We're going to wash your hair and rinse it."

The girl's hair had been cut above her shoulders, so it wasn't all that difficult to wash. Ruby lathered it three times and rinsed it. Then she had her stand to wash her body and rinse so she wasn't sitting in the dirty water. How could a girl get this filthy? This wasn't a few days' worth of dirt. Some of the grime was caked on her skin and took considerable scrubbing. Nor was it a few missed meals that had made her this skinny. Ruby couldn't help comparing Claire's and Joel's sturdy little bodies to this child's bony limbs and protruding hips.

The bottoms of her feet and her heels were blistered and infected, and she had cuts and scrapes on her legs and arms. One particularly nasty bruise marred a shoulder blade. Ruby resisted asking how she'd been injured. It was plain she didn't intend to open up.

"I'm Ruby. Ruby Dearing. I grew up here, and I've been gone for a while until recently." Ruby gently blotted the girl's hair with a towel. "Want to tell me your name?"

"Jane." One word. The first she'd said, and Ruby understood it was delivered with a slim measure of trust.

"That fellow who brought you here is my brother-in-law, Nash Sommerton."

"Not your husband?"

"No. He was married to my sister."

"Where is she?"

"She died." The words brought new pain. Ruby wrapped the girl in a blanket and sat her on a chair near the stove. After going for a wide-tooth comb and the salve Little Bird had brought, she treated all the visible scrapes and bruises and then applied the comb to the ends of Jane's hair. Ruby took a shaky breath and said, "My mama died, too."

She hoped the information would provoke the girl into sharing something about herself. "Do you have any family?" Ruby asked.

"Don't have nobody."

Ruby believed her. If Jane had a parent, she wouldn't have been as filthy or starved as she was. "Where are you from?"

The girl didn't reply.

Painstakingly, Ruby worked out all the tangles. They both stifled yawns during the process.

"Are you hungry?"

The girl raised one bony shoulder in a shrug.

Of course she was hungry. "My niece and nephew always have a bite to eat before bed. I'll make you some bread and jelly."

Jane waited silently and ate every last crumb of the offering. Ruby poured her a glass of milk and she drank it thirstily. "Thanks."

Jane's hair was partially dry by the time Ruby led her up the stairs.

"I ran across a trunk full of clothes when I was cleaning. There are some of my old things that might fit you. I saved them to use for scraps. They might be too big, but they'll do for now." She took out a flannel gown, offered Jane privacy to put it on and then laid out a dress and underclothing for the following day. "They're clean at least."

She ushered the girl into her bed and lay down on the opposite side in the dark. "How old are you, Jane?"

The girl didn't reply. Ruby guessed her at

about twelve or thirteen, and wondered where she'd been and how she'd survived. All the cuts and bruises made Ruby uneasy. Jane may have fallen or received those injuries many ways, but the girl's demeanor told her it wasn't that simple. She was untrusting, and rightly so.

The mattress trembled ever so slightly.

"You're safe here tonight," Ruby assured her. "No one means you any harm."

"Your brother was mighty angry."

"Brother-*in-law*. He would never hurt anyone. He's mostly bluster. You sleep and we'll figure things out tomorrow."

Ruby slept fitfully, waking often to check that Jane was still lying beside her, afraid she'd run off into the night. But Jane was obviously exhausted, because she was still asleep long after Ruby rose and dressed. Ruby had been on her own until recently, but now she had a lot of people depending on her. It was a good feeling to be needed, but these youngsters were a weighty responsibility.

Nash had already gone out to take care of stock, leaving a lamp on in the kitchen for Ruby, who lit kindling in the stove. She had three more mouths to feed today, so she set about preparing a pan of cooked meal.

Joel was up when she went to check on the

children. She took him to the outhouse and returned to help him wash and dress. Claire woke when Ruby opened her door. She blinked and glanced around. "I forgot I was home."

"Is it a good feeling to wake up in your own room?"

"I missed my papa."

"He missed you, too. Do you need help dressing?"

Claire scooted to the edge of the bed. "I can dress myself."

"I'll help you with your hair when you're ready. We have a guest this morning."

She rubbed her eyes. "Who's here?"

"A girl your papa brought home. She doesn't have any family, so she stayed here last night."

The simple explanation seemed to satisfy Claire.

Ruby found Jane awake, dressed in the clothing she'd left on a chair and sitting at the foot of the bed. "Good morning, Jane."

"Is Flint all right?"

Her question surprised Ruby. "As far as I know the horse is fine. Did Mr. Sommerton tell you Flint's name?"

"I already knew it."

"He's warned all of us what a dangerous animal Flint is. You could have been badly hurt. Killed, even."

"Flint's not dangerous," she argued. "Can I see him now?"

"We'll have to ask Mr. Sommerton about that. Maybe if you told him why you stole his horse, he'd be more likely to oblige."

Jane had an oval face and gray-blue eyes fringed with dark lashes. Her hair wasn't as dark as it had appeared the night before. Clean now, the shiny tresses varied from warm honey tones to a pale wheat color. Ruby got some pins and ribbon and set to work fashioning it the best she could away from Jane's face. She hadn't seen the healing bruise under her jaw until now. A faded scar marred one corner of her eye near her brow.

"He's going to find out where you came from eventually, so you might as well tell us."

Jane's gaze met Ruby's, as if she was gauging her words, and then lowered. "I stayed at the ranch where Mr. Sommerton bought Flint."

"Is it your home?"

Jane shrugged.

"Is Jane your real name?"

She nodded. "Least it's the name I got from the foundling home."

"So…you stayed at the ranch."

She nodded. "The Billingses got me from the

home. Mr. Billings said Mizz Billings didn't have
no girls to help with chores, but truth was Mizz
Billings was real sick, an' after I got there she
died. I had to cook for Mr. Billings and his other
kids. All of 'em's boys."

"Who hurt you, Jane?"

Chapter Thirteen

Jane looked at her hands in her lap. Ruby had scrubbed her nails clean, but she bore cuts and calluses. "James, mostly. Sometimes him and Sid. They're mean boys. Mr. Billings didn't care that they shoved me around, tripped me on purpose, and they ate my food, too. He made me sleep in the barn even when it was cold. I didn't mind none, 'cause I was better off there than around them mean boys."

Ruby agreed that the barn was probably safer, even though it was cold. Jane's tale was painful to hear. "And what about Flint?"

"He was the finest horse ever born on that ranch. Mr. Billings knew he'd get him a lot of money, so he got treated real special. I slept with 'im when he was a colt and sometimes even when he got bigger. Flint's the best friend I ever had."

"And Mr. Billings sold him."

She nodded. "Yes'm."

It didn't sound like a story a twelve-year-old would make up. Ruby's heart went out to the girl. A sense of panic rose in her chest. What would the sheriff do when he learned she'd run away? Take her back there?

No wonder Jane hadn't wanted to tell them who she was or where she'd come from. She was terrified of having to go back. If Jane had been treated so cruelly without cause, how much worse would punishment be?

Ruby put away her mother's brush and comb and showed Jane her reflection in the hand mirror.

"I look like a girl."

"You are a girl."

Jane touched her fingertips to the wispy hair near her ears. "Ain't never looked like a girl b'fore."

Ruby resisted reaching out to touch her, and waited to speak until Jane's gaze lifted to meet hers. "You're a lovely girl, Jane. You didn't deserve to be treated unkindly." She wanted to say more, but she had to talk to Nash. "My niece and nephew are ready to go down and eat breakfast. I want you to join them while I go speak with Mr. Sommerton."

"Yes'm."

Ruby led Jane into the kitchen, where Claire had already seated herself at the table and Joel was playing with a pair of wooden horses on the floor. Jane inspected the room in the light of day, her gaze landing on the stove. "Claire. Joel. This is Jane. She's staying with us today. I'm going to fill your bowls and give you the syrup and spoons, and I want you to eat while I go talk to your papa."

"Where did Jane come from?" Claire asked, curious.

"I stole your daddy's horse, an' he caught me an' brung me here," Jane said.

"Boone?"

"Flint."

Claire stared, wide-eyed. "But that horse is dangerous."

Jane looked at the bowl Ruby set in front of her and picked up her spoon, her gaze skidding from Claire to Joel as though one of them might snatch the food from her.

Ruby lifted Joel up to his chair. "Yes, Flint is dangerous and none of us should go around him without your papa there. Jane made a mistake. No one got hurt, and your papa's going to take care of it. No more questions for Jane now. She wants to eat her breakfast."

Jane had the bowl half-empty before the others ever picked up their spoons.

Ruby found Nash in the barn, making mash for Vivo.

"I could've done that," she said.

"Figured you had your hands full this morning."

"I'll bring Joel out and we'll give that mash to Vivo later. Right now you and I have to talk." Her tone belied her serious intent.

Nash straightened and wiped his sleeve across his forehead. "About what?"

"Jane is from the ranch where you got Flint. A foster child or something. She came after the horse because...it hurt her to lose him when Mr. Billings sold him. She's very attached to him."

Ruby told Nash everything Jane had said— about the cuts and bruises, about the rancher's two boys and about why the girl had finally been willing to talk. "She's afraid to go back. I think she'd run if someone tried to make her return."

Nash listened in dismay and then regret. Regret wedged its way into his conscience. He'd been pretty mad at the poor kid. "Hell."

"What are we going to do?"

He didn't want to say it, but he knew what was right. "We still have to go to the law, Ruby."

"You're not taking that girl to the sheriff."

Ruby took a step closer, giving him a full view of the fire in her eyes. "She's been abused and neglected, and she's only a child. I want to keep her here." Her disturbed voice betrayed her passion. He admired that about her. She was never afraid to say what she was feeling. And he admired her compassion. What she'd done for this horse would be nothing compared to what she'd do to save the girl. His gaze traveled her flushed face, the halo of hair she'd tried to tame, and settled on her lips. This woman tied him in knots.

"Well?" she asked, her stare never wavering from his face.

Adamant, Ruby was magnificent. Nash had no doubt she would take on the sheriff and anyone else who tried to do harm to the girl. He couldn't disagree with her. Perhaps most of his worries about her ability to protect his children had been for naught.

Ruby and Pearl may have had a few similarities, but where Pearl had been sweet and gentle, Ruby had a fire and zest that heated his blood. He wanted to take the remaining steps that separated them and kiss her senseless.

He entertained the appealing thought for a minute too long. Imagined she'd kiss him back. He shouldn't be thinking about kissing her. Now he would think of nothing else.

He brushed his hands together, took a steady-
ing breath…moved forward and caught her in an
embrace that surprised them both.

She flattened both palms on his chest.
"Wha—?"

The kiss cut off her question. Her body was
lush and curvaceous, her lips full and warm. He'd
given her appealing mouth too much attention
over the past weeks, and she didn't disappoint
him. She made a noise that definitely wasn't a
protest and pressed herself to him, bringing one
arm up around his neck and the other hand to
the side of his face.

She kissed him back as though she'd been
starving for his touch. She felt too good in his
arms, too right. He wasn't proud of how he'd
behaved when she first arrived. Self-dislike had
become a feeling he was accustomed to, and he
enjoyed kissing her as much as he'd thought he
would. From the first time he'd set eyes on her,
he'd known she had a mouth that would tie a man
in knots, and he'd been right.

This woman appealed to him on a sensory
level. Everything about her put him on alert. Her
body against his was strong and curvy, and he
splayed his hands against her back and pulled her
as close as he dared. Her heart pounded against
his chest. She was warm and alive, and she set

him on fire. His better judgment took over, so
he loosened his hold and brought his hands to
her upper arms.

Bracketing her face then with his palms, he
studied it, their breaths still mingling.

Ruby took a step back, forcing him to remove
his hands from her cheeks. She stared at him,
her chest rising and falling while she caught her
breath. He didn't see regret in her eyes, and was
relieved. "I can't handle anything else right now,"
she said finally. Frankly.

Nor was she angry. He nodded. "I know."

"We have so much on our plates, Nash. I can't
think about what just happened."

He didn't feel any regret, either, and while he
considered offering an apology, it wouldn't ring
true. He'd done what he'd been thinking about
doing nearly every day since she'd arrived.

He had regrets about his marriage. He'd married Pearl for convenience's sake, and he'd never
truly made an effort to make anything more out
of it. She'd been content, he believed. If not passionate or adoring, they'd been comfortable.
How he felt about Ruby was completely and
puzzlingly different. He thought about her constantly. Every time he saw her, a tingle of anticipation coursed through his veins. The feelings

she inspired were darned confusing, that was for certain, but they were pleasing too.

"Claire and Joel just got here. You have your family to see to, and now we have to figure out what's going to happen with Jane. There isn't time for this…this *other thing* with us right now."

She looked peeved, but her lips were pink and full, her already rough voice a little too breathy. This other thing. This other confusing and heated thing. This wild and certainly impetuous yearning that seemed mutual. Nash had poor timing, that was for darned sure.

He took a breath and attempted to think and speak normally. "I'll head into town and see the attorney after breakfast. I'll ask him to send a wire to the state." Nash glanced aside and then back. "I'm thinking I should ask the doc to come out and have a look at her, so we have someone to back us up about the neglect and cruel treatment."

Ruby extended a hand as though she wanted to touch him, but drew it back. What was she afraid of? A repeat of that kiss? "Thank you." The tears that formed in her eyes were uncharacteristic. "Thank you."

"Don't thank me. We're in this together."

For a minute he thought she'd move back into

his arms. He wanted her to. Her gaze searched his face, settled on his mouth.

Silas entered the barn, and Ruby stepped farther away from Nash, as though they'd been discovered doing something inappropriate. "I have breakfast ready."

"I'll join you this morning, but I normally eat biscuits and bacon with the men," he said. "It gives us time to talk over the plans for the day."

She nodded and hurried back to the house.

By the time Nash arrived at the kitchen, the children were nearly finished eating. He didn't recognize the girl he'd hauled out of a bedroll and brought home the night before—especially since he'd mistakenly assumed she was a boy the entire time. Now here she was, wearing a dress with a ribbon in her hair—hair that was unusually short for a girl her age, but shiny clean and a striking color.

In the daylight, her delicate features were pronounced. Pretty, even. Her sleeves had been rolled back over bony wrists that were scabbed and bruised, and she had bruises under her chin and a deep red scar near her eye. Immediately, Nash understood Ruby's protective instincts. His heart went out to the girl and her plight. Even though Claire was without a mother, his daughter was loved and protected. He didn't want to think of what could happen to Jane if no one looked after her. "Ruby told me where you came from," he said.

Her bowl was empty, and she set down a glass with milk residue on the sides. Her dark-lashed eyes lifted and she met his gaze. "Yessir."

"I'm not taking you back to the Billingses."

Relief swept over her delicate features.

"I'm going to speak with someone about you staying here with us."

Her eyes widened in surprise. "Why would you do that?"

"We don't want to break the law," he replied. "Any arrangement should be legal. Do you understand?"

"Yes, but… Why do you want me to stay? To work? I'm stronger than I look."

Her question pained him, a pathetic plea for the security and the food she'd already learned was available. No one had ever treated her kindly, offered her concern or affection. "Not to work. Though we do have chores." He glanced to Ruby for help, but no explanation was forthcoming. "Because it's the right thing to do. You need a place. We have a place."

"Jane is staying here, Papa?" Claire asked. "Is she going to be our sister?"

"I can't promise," he told them both. "I'll do my best to find the right people to help us."

"But I stole Flint," Jane said in a small voice. She stared at a spot on the table.

Nash studied her for a moment. "That was wrong, but I might have done the same thing in your shoes. I don't know. But from here on, you won't take anything that doesn't belong to you. Understood?"

Her gaze swept back to his. It pained him as well to think of the years she'd been without simple provision or family. His children had suffered a loss, but they were loved and well cared for. It was unthinkable to imagine Claire growing up in a similar situation. He cleared his throat.

"Yes, sir. I won't steal nothing."

"Your word is good enough for me." Nash's statement and his obvious empathy for the girl touched Ruby. She shouldn't have been surprised. She'd seen him with his children, with his family and the horses. He was a caring, kind man, though a bit gruff and opinionated. His initial animosity toward Ruby seemed to have lessened, or perhaps he simply needed her so much he'd chosen to set that aside for now. *We're in this together,* he'd said.

She didn't want to think about him kissing her or her kissing him back, or the rush of feelings his strong embrace elicited. If he thought so poorly of her, why would he have done that? He was still mourning her sister. Wasn't he?

He finished eating. "Thanks for breakfast. I'll most likely stop to talk to my mother on my way back from town. See if my father has gone to the mill today."

"Thank you," Ruby replied in a soft tone, and they both knew she meant for his acceptance of Jane. She'd expected him to be difficult, and before now he'd deserved that standing in her eyes. He needed to change her opinion of him.

He got up and settled his hat on his head before heading out.

Ruby thought about Georgia throughout the morning, wondered about the atmosphere at the Sommertons, thought about Vivian. Her concern continually wavered back to Nash, and how he was dealing with the appearance of an unknown brother—on top of seeing that his children were cared for, getting a new horse settled in and now Jane. Ruby had no place prying into his family's business, but she hoped he would tell her how his mother was doing once he'd seen her.

There hadn't been time to discuss anything with Georgia before Ruby had been given charge of her niece and nephew. She didn't think Claire was old enough for school yet, and no one had spoken of it.

"Do you go to school?" she asked her that afternoon while Joel napped.

"Papa said I can go after my birthday."

"Okay. Well, until then I suppose we should work on letters and numbers." She glanced at Jane. "How about you?"

The girl shrugged. "Can't read. Never been to school."

"We will have class in the afternoons, then, while Joel sleeps." Ruby would do the best she could now, but the girls needed slates and readers. Thankfully, Claire had several books on a shelf in her room.

As she was reading to the girls, the sound of an approaching horse caught her attention. Ruby went to the kitchen window and held back the curtain. A buggy pulled to a stop in the dooryard, and a slender man in a brown suit climbed down.

Opening the back door and crossing the porch, she greeted him in the yard. "Hello?"

He removed his hat. "Ruby Dearing? I haven't seen you in years." At her blank look, he said, "David Morris."

"David? Of course. I remember you."

They'd attended school at the same time. David had been a diligent pupil, while she'd spent all her time gazing out the window and watching the clock. He'd also been friendly, and one of the few students who had ever spoken of her father. He'd never been condemning, but openly concerned. While others sometimes whispered behind their hands, David had asked how her family was doing. She'd once spotted him buying all the jars of jam her mother had sold at the mercantile.

"Your father had the livery," she said.

"That was him."

"You have a little sister. Penny?"

"She's married and living in Washington County."

"What brings you here today?"

"Nash sent me. I'm the doctor."

"You?" She'd briefly considered that perhaps Nash would ask Miles, but of course that situation was too new and strained for favors.

"I know. Surprising, isn't it?" He grinned. "Doc Stevens passed on a couple of years ago. I had started a practice in Illinois, but the town council convinced me to come here for a while."

"So. Nash told you about Jane?"

His expression turned serious. "He thought my observations would help in a legal proceeding, and he's right. Once the state is aware of the situation, they will take action."

"Thank you for coming. I could have brought her into town, but she'll be more comfortable here. She's like a skittish colt."

Ruby led him into the kitchen.

"Hello, Claire," David Morris said.

Nash's daughter said a bashful hello from her seat at the table.

"Jane, this is Dr. Morris," Ruby told the girl. She considered removing Claire and Joel from the room while the doctor spoke to Jane, but then decided the conversation would be over Joel's head, and Claire would learn about her situation eventually. Hearing it in Jane's own words was probably best.

"I ain't sick," the girl declared.

"No, of course you're not. The doctor is going to take a look at your cuts to make sure they're not infected."

"Miss Ruby doctored 'em just fine." Jane gave the man a long, assessing look and then gauged Ruby's matter-of-fact expression. "I guess it's awright, though."

"Mr. Sommerton tells me you were living at the Billings ranch up north," he said conversationally.

She nodded.

"He said the rancher's boys were mean to you. What did they do?"

Again, Jane looked directly at Ruby, who kept her expression calm and nodded encouragement.

"They slapped me. Pushed me down a lot and kicked me. Took my food."

"Did you get three meals a day? Have plenty of milk?"

"I cooked for them—with whatever supplies Mr. Billings brung from town and whatever he killed and cleaned. Mostly rabbits and squirrels, sometimes fish or some beef. Din't never taste very good 'cause I don't know how to cook it. He kept a sack of beans, and I got the hang of that."

"Did Mr. Billings hit you?"

She shook her head and glanced at Ruby. "He just watched when them boys did it. Din't say nothing when they took away my food."

Ruby's chest ached, but she put a confident smile on her face for Jane's sake.

"Why don't you sit on the edge of the chair here for me, Jane?" David asked. Her story was a difficult one to hear, evident by his careful expression.

She complied and let him look her over, listen to her heart, look in her eyes and ears.

"I want Dr. Morris to see your shoulder," Ruby told her, and unbuttoned the back of her dress to expose the bruises.

"Is this tender?" he asked, gently pressing around the area.

Jane winced. "Don't poke it!"

"I'm sorry. How long ago did you get these bruises?"

"Dunno. Couple weeks maybe."

"I think you may have had a fractured rib. Does it hurt less now than when it first happened?"

She nodded.

Claire had watched the whole process with wide, assessing eyes. "My papa won't let anyone hurt you anymore."

"That's right," Ruby assured them both. "Dr. Morris and Mr. Sommerton are going to see that you're safe from now on."

David spoke with Jane for a few more minutes and then Ruby told the girls they could go play in Claire's room.

"It's a crime that people get away with treating other human beings that way," David said in a low voice that revealed burning anger.

"And the horse he sold Nash is a magnificent animal," she told him. "He obviously treated the horse better than the child."

"Some of those marks are older than others, some newer. It's plain she's been mistreated over a span of time. I believe her story."

"What will you do now?"

"I'll send a telegram to the authorities right away."

Ruby nodded. "We won't let her go back there."

"It's not that the agencies are unscrupulous or don't care," he told her. "It's just that they place so many children, they can't possibly check on all of them." He gave her a kind smile. "I can see she'll be well cared for here."

Ruby shrugged. "I've never taken care of children before, but I'll do the best I can."

"I'm confident you'll be a big help to Nash."

"I hope so." She was thankful for his concern and grateful for the tender, matter-of-fact way he'd treated and spoken to Jane. Perhaps Ruby could repay his kindness with an invitation to supper. He might have a wife waiting at home, though.

"Are you married?" Ruby couldn't resist asking. She had enjoyed meeting someone from her childhood who didn't seem to hold her past against her.

"Sorry to say I have not had that pleasure," he answered. "Medical school and a job took all of my energies, and then I worked at establishing a practice."

"And then you did it all over again here."

He nodded. "That's a fact."

She offered him a smile. "Why don't you stay for supper? We can catch up while I fix a meal. Nash should be here soon, and the hands will show up."

"I'm not half-bad in the kitchen," he told her. "I'll stay if you let me help."

"Do you know how to cut a chicken without mangling it?"

"I can probably figure it out. Chicken anatomy wasn't part of my training, but bones are bones."

She laughed.

Ruby fried plenty of chicken for their supper that evening. David told her about his years at medical school and seemed genuinely interested to hear about her time spent onstage and the people she'd met.

Until now no one had shown much interest in her life during those times. She told him about her favorite plays, shared the excitement of leading roles and solo parts.

"It all sounds quite exciting," he told her. "I can picture you onstage."

"Some of it was exciting," she agreed. "But traveling is a hard life, and I was never sure of work. Some years were exceptional and others very lean."

"I should like to hear you sing, Ruby Dearing," he told her.

"Something quite glamorous, no doubt."

"Of course."

Steam from the potatoes warmed her skin as she mashed them. "Oh, I went down south for to see my Sal, sing polly wolly doodle all the day. My Sal, she's a spunky gal, sing polly wolly doodle all the day."

David chuckled and picked up the lid of her pan to tap with a wooden spoon in time to the song. The children heard the commotion and came running.

"Fare thee well, fare thee well, fare thee well my fairy fay. For I'm going to Lou'siana for to see my Susyanna, sing polly wolly doodle all day."

David joined in on the next verse. Joel danced, and Claire jumped up and down. Jane didn't seem to know what to think. She blinked and watched them as though they were all crazy.

"Behind the barn, down on my knees, sing Polly wolly doodle all the day. I thought I heard a chicken sneeze—"

The back door opened and Nash entered the kitchen.

Chapter Fourteen

Nash looked from one person to the other, Ruby's face flushed and her hair in wild ringlets, his children dancing, and David Morris wearing a grin so wide it split his face. Was Ruby cooking or holding a house party?

"Papa!" Claire spotted Nash and shot forward for a hug. He accommodated her, and Joel was next. Nash picked up his son and felt his little heart beating like a trip-hammer with excitement.

At Nash's sudden appearance, Ruby appeared flustered, and scurried about setting the table.

"I invited David to stay for supper, since he was out," she said. "He cut the chicken for me."

David, was it? "Thanks for coming out, Dr. Morris."

"My pleasure."

Yes, he could see that. The doctor looked to be

having the time of his life. Boots hit the wooden stoop behind Nash as the hands made their way in.

Silas and Dugger were subdued around the children and their guest. After they'd finished eating, Silas offered to wash the dishes, for which Ruby appeared grateful.

Nash invited the doctor into the other room, where they drank their coffee. David Morris had taken over after Doc Stevens had passed on. David had come to Crosby after Laura's death, so Nash knew him, but they hadn't interacted much.

"It was wise of you to have me look at young Jane," the doctor said. "It's clear to me she's been mistreated. She's small for her size because she's undernourished. I'd say she's closer to thirteen."

Nash felt sick all over again at the thought of Jane's abuse and hunger. "Can we take care of that? Will good food help her now?"

"Of course it will help, and she'll gain strength and put on weight, but I don't know about growth. Poor nutrition in childhood affects a body for a lifetime. Depending on how long she's been in this condition, her bones and muscles, possibly even her organs, may not have developed the way they should have." He sipped his coffee. "Or it could be a combination of poor nutrition and genetics, and she's small by nature. Only time will tell. I would very much like to watch her progress."

"Yes, of course," Nash replied. "I'd feel better knowing she was being checked on." He absorbed the information and tapped his fingertips on the arm of the chair.

"I will recommend she eat a balanced diet. Liver would be exceptionally good for her if she likes it. I'll give Ruby a few suggestions."

Nash looked him over.

"It's fortunate Ruby came back when she did," David said. "I'm sure you're thankful to have a woman around the house again—especially one like her. She always did light up a room. And she's sure not hard on the eyes." He raised a hand. "No disrespect intended."

Nash gave his head a half shake. "She's a big help."

"Well." The doctor sat forward in his chair. "I want to thank her for the fine supper before I head out. Thanks for the hospitality."

Nash shook his hand and followed him to the kitchen, which was empty.

In the semidark dooryard Ruby and the children were playing tag under the moon. Ruby's deep-throated laugh rang out, countered by high-pitched squeals.

"She's something else, isn't she?" David said,

with admiration in his voice. "She'd different from how I remember her. She seems more content."

Nash looked at his expression and back out at his sister-in-law. He had to admit she was beautiful and spirited, and he'd never seen anything but kindness in her demeanor. The way this man spoke about her and looked at her didn't set well with him, but Nash had no right to feel protective and no reason to feel uneasy.

David took his hat from his buggy and settled it on his head. "Thank you for supper, Miss Ruby!" he called.

"You're welcome!" she replied with a wave. "Come back anytime."

Once the buggy had pulled away, Ruby led the youngsters to the house. "Time to get ready for bed."

Nash took Claire and Joel into Claire's bedroom to read to them. Ruby took Jane to her room and let her undress and put on her nightgown herself. "I'll prepare the room beside mine. Whenever you're ready, you can sleep there if you want."

"A room all to myself?"

Ruby stood at the mirror, worked a brush through the ends of her hair, and then used her wide-tooth comb on the rest. "There are plenty of rooms in this old house. Nothing fancy, but they're clean and comfortable."

Jane studied the room that had been Ruby's mother's, and her gaze lifted to Ruby's in the mirror. "Do you want me to sleep in there now?"

Ruby set down the comb and braided her hair in a thick plait. "You're welcome to stay in here with me as long as you want, but when you're ready for your own room, it will be there. I only want you to feel safe. That's all, just safe."

"I don't hardly know what to say, Mizz Dearing."

"You can call me Ruby. It feels more like family, doesn't it?"

Dressed in an oversize nightgown, Jane perched on the side of the bed and glanced toward the door. "What is Mr. Sommerton reading to them?"

"I'm not sure." Ruby folded Jane's clothing thoughtfully. "Did anyone ever read to you?"

"No."

Ruby opened one of her trunks. She moved aside clothing and trinket boxes until she uncovered several books. She found the one she wanted and pulled it out. "This was my favorite when I was a girl."

Jane peered to see the cover as Ruby approached. "What is it?"

Ruby perched on the edge of the bed. "It's

called *Hans Brinker, or The Silver Skates*. It's all about a boy and his family who live in the Netherlands."

"Are the Netherlands far away?"

"Indeed. The amazing thing is an American woman wrote this story without ever being there. I read about her. She did a lot of studying, and she had Dutch neighbors who helped her with the background and customs."

"What's customs?"

"Well, every country has its own way to celebrate holidays. We call them traditions or customs. Like for Christmas here we cut trees, bring them indoors and decorate them with popcorn and paper rings. We hang up stockings for Santa Claus to fill with nuts and fruit. People in other lands have their own traditions."

"Did you ever have a tree like that?"

"Every year when I was a girl. My sister and I used to go with my daddy to choose the tree, and we'd watch while he chopped it down. Then we'd drag it home on a sled."

"And you hung stockings? I know there isn't really a Santa Claus."

"Yes, we did." Ruby paused for a moment. "Did you ever hang a stocking or have a Christmas tree?"

"Nah. But I seen a tree before. There was one in the window of the bakery across from the home where I stayed." Jane focused her attention back on the book. "What's the story about?"

"Well, a young boy—I think he's fourteen or fifteen—enters an ice-skating race along the canal with his sister in hopes of winning a wonderful pair of silver skates."

"Does he win them?"

Ruby opened to the first page. "Why don't we read it, and you'll learn what happens?"

"All of it?"

"Not tonight. We'll read a little at a time. Would you like that?"

Jane raised uncertain eyes to examine Ruby's face. "What if I have to leave before we finish?"

Her doubt and fear touched Ruby. The girl kept up a good front, but she was scared and alone. A child adrift in a world that didn't offer many chances. Ruby held back tears to say, "Let's not think about that, all right? If it should happen, you could take the book with you."

"But I can't read by myself."

"We're going to work on that," Ruby assured her.

She didn't want to let on that she had any concern, but it troubled her that the authorities might not let Jane stay. In those moments it became imperative that Ruby read this story to Jane, that she teach her letters and numbers, that she give

her the things she'd missed out on. Ruby opened
the familiar book, remembering anew the magic
and hope within its pages.

After tucking in his son and daughter, Nash
waited nervously for Ruby. She hadn't wanted
to deal with what had happened between them,
and neither had he. But he figured they'd better
get that kiss out in the open so it wasn't hanging
between them, making their arrangement dou-
bly awkward.

Maybe she would go to bed without coming back downstairs. He stood looking out the
kitchen door into the darkness. He should turn in.

A step behind him alerted him to her presence.

"I thought you'd gone to bed," she said.

"Probably should have. I wanted to talk to
you."

"About Jane?"

"That, too. And about what happened between
us."

She turned as though she would leave the
room. "I told you I don't—"

"You don't want to talk about it, I know. It
won't go away."

"What is there to say? You're my sister's husband."

When she put it like that, it sounded wrong. It
hadn't felt wrong. Maybe that was the problem.

"You made it pretty clear I'm not like her," Ruby stated.

"No, you're not."

"But I'm available, is that it? Even though you don't really like me."

"I never said I didn't like you."

She stared at him in disbelief.

"I was angry at you, Ruby. I was angry at the whole situation. You were easy to take out my frustrations on."

"And now? Now you're not mad that I wasn't here for Pearl and my mother?"

He rubbed the back of his neck. "It still makes me angry, yes. But you're not who I thought you were."

She took a few steps until she was close enough for him to reach out and touch. She had braided her hair and it hung over her shoulder and across her breast. "And what about that kiss? A mistake?" She lowered her voice. "A mistake you might want to make again?"

Her words and sultry tone shot tremors of heat along his spine…through his abdomen. His fiery reaction caught him unaware. What was happening between them? Was it only him or did she have these feelings, too? When he'd come inside to see her enjoying herself with David, Nash's insides had seized up.

Now he looked at her through the doctor's eyes and saw a beautiful and appealing woman with a full, alluring mouth and a flush on her cheeks. She was dynamically alive and vital, and that scared him somehow. There wasn't a red-blooded man alive who could look at her and not have thoughts of kissing those lips.

Acknowledging his attraction definitely muddied the waters and complicated things. "It didn't feel like a mistake," he admitted.

Her eyes widened in the lamplight, and she studied him with a mixture of surprise and hesitancy. "It didn't?"

"No." He flattened his lips and thought for a minute. "I'm not sorry. But I don't want it to cloud our thinking or get in the way of the things we need to do."

"The children have to come first," she agreed. "They are our priority, and we're not going to let things get complicated."

He hadn't answered her question about wanting it to happen again. He couldn't lie. He would definitely be thinking about it. She overflowed with verve and passion. She was fearless, and undaunted by others' opinions or her own shortcomings.

David Morris had been impressed by those qualities, too. It wasn't only her sensuous beauty that made her appealing. It was her unflagging spirit and her vitality.

Nash held back a comment about how well she and Morris had gotten along. "The doctor said Jane's undernourished." He explained everything he'd learned.

"We can find out how long she was there, and that might give us a better idea about her growth," Ruby mused. "She mentioned living in a home across from a bakery. That might have been a foster home or a foundling home, but it wasn't a ranch situation, so the worst of the neglect may be more recent. She's never had a family or participated in things the rest of us have enjoyed. She feels like an outsider here, but deep down she's terrified to leave."

Ruby's genuine concern mirrored his. "I'll do everything I can to keep her here. You have my word."

She gave him a look filled with appreciation. "Thank you for putting aside your resentment and giving me a chance."

"Don't thank me yet." He took a step back. "Good night, Ruby."

She offered him a soft smile. "Good night."

He locked the kitchen door and went up to his room. Thanks to Ruby he had his children back under his roof, and he could rest easy about that.

Her presence here wasn't conducive to sleep, however.

He thought of her traveling the country with her theater friends and riding that horse all the way to Nebraska on her own. In a way it bothered him, but on the other hand she impressed him beyond measure. He couldn't think of another woman who would be so independent or daring. Pearl would certainly have never packed a bag, saddled a horse and ridden alone for weeks and weeks. Few females would have.

Ruby was not like other women.

And those differences kept him awake at night.

Georgia hadn't slept well since Miles had shown up. Cosmo's son—the son he hadn't known about—brought back to life something that had been over and buried. Her husband had disclosed his mistake all those years ago. They had dealt with it, put it behind them and gone on with building their lives. Now those experiences had come to life again, and her grown children were forced to deal with them, as well. She had mixed feelings about Miles, but even though his appearance made things uncomfortable, he was a young man who deserved to have his feelings recognized. She did feel compassion toward him.

Miles had accompanied Cosmo to the mill for a couple days, but last evening she'd asked him to stay at the house today. Cosmo finished his breakfast and gave her a customary kiss on the cheek before leaving.

Georgia got up and poured Miles a fresh cup of coffee before seating herself closer. "I'd like to hear about your life growing up in Burlington, Miles."

He studied her for a moment. "You've been very kind to me."

"I can only imagine what you must have thought about Cosmo. About his family. You are as innocent in what happened between him and your mother as my children are."

"And as you are."

She shrugged. "The point is we have to figure out how to go on from here. I think we can do that if we get to know each other better. I hope so, anyway."

He took a sip of his coffee. "For a long time I believed that my father had died. Of course, that's the story I got from my mother, the same story my aunt and uncle told to explain why Mother had no husband.

"I was curious, so I asked questions. I asked to see their certificate of marriage, something of my father's, asked why there were no photographs.

Eventually, my aunt convinced my mother to tell me the truth. She told me my father had been married when she met him. And she made me promise not to seek him out."

"How old were you then?"

"Twelve, I think. Old enough to understand the stigma of illegitimacy. But I respected my mother's wishes and would never have humiliated her."

"She must have been a very brave woman."

Miles met Georgia's gaze with a question in his eyes.

"Letting someone else raise you would have been the easy thing to do," she explained.

"Her life was never easy. She did office work for a steelyard during the day, and in the evenings she cooked and cleaned for a judge."

"You said you worked, too."

"After school I went to a cabinetmaker's, where I cleaned brushes and swept floors. I had no idea how much it took to live comfortably, but we stayed with my aunt and uncle. So thanks to them, apparently my mother was able to save a lot of what we earned. When my uncle died he left money to both my aunt and my mother, and I was able to go to college."

"She sounds like an amazing woman, Miles."

"I only wish she would have lived long enough

for me to do something for her in return. She died before my graduation."

"I'm so sorry."

"All along I had planned to start a practice and get her a house. I wanted her to take it easy and let someone else take care of her. After her death, I could think of nothing but retribution. My father became the target for a lot of anger. I believed he'd deliberately used and rejected her."

"Cosmo would never have done that. If he'd known about you and your mother, he would have done something. I don't know what, but he would have helped." Cosmo had always been a loving and attentive husband and father, had always provided for Georgia and their children. She had no doubt he would have taken care of Miles and his mother, too, at any cost to his reputation.

"I regret the pain I've brought your family," Miles said uneasily. "At first I didn't care who I hurt, but now that I see who you are and understand none of you had any ill intentions toward me or my mother, I'm sorry."

"I think you're lost, Miles. That's what I think. You lost the person who took care of you and saw to your future. That kind of grief can consume us. In your grief, you wanted to lash out at the man you believed made your mother's life so hard. Your need to settle the score kept you going. Then you learned Cosmo is not the monster you imagined. What do you do with those feelings now?"

He glanced away and his jaw worked.

Georgia placed her hand over his on the white tablecloth. He flinched, but moments later he turned his hand to clasp hers and met her gaze again. "How is it you're so forgiving?"

"You've done nothing you need to be forgiven for. As for my husband...well, I forgave him a long time ago. He's done nothing since to prove he didn't deserve that forgiveness."

"Nash and Vivian don't feel that way."

"They've only just learned of it. Discovering the unpleasant truth about one's father takes some time to come to terms with. Am I right?"

"You're right."

The sound of the front door opening and closing arrested their attention.

Footsteps sounded along the hallway and Nash entered the dining room. His gaze took in the two of them seated at the corner of the table and then shot to their clasped hands.

"Nash! I'm glad you stopped by." Georgia stood and got a cup and saucer from the sideboard.

"Am I interrupting something?" he asked.

"I should go," Miles said, and started to rise.

"Please don't," Georgia said, stilling him with an upraised hand. "Have a seat, Nash."

He seated himself on the chair Cosmo normally occupied and looked at his half brother.

"I asked Miles to stay this morning so we could talk. The more we know about each other, the more that's out in the open, the better we can deal with this situation. With each other." Georgia set a full cup in front of Nash and rested her hand on his shoulder. "Miles is welcome to stay with us for as long as he wishes, of course. Among other things, your father and I have talked about how we will introduce him to people, and I'd like to know what you think. Will you stay and talk with us?"

Nash nodded. "Yes. Of course."

Chapter Fifteen

On Sunday Ruby stayed behind while Nash took the children to church. She had learned where Little Bird lived, and so she visited her. Remembering the woman's intuitive concern, she hoped to find guidance for how to help Jane through this transition. Little Bird didn't let her down. She shared herbs and a tincture to improve the health of Jane's organs.

It comforted Ruby to know another person who remembered her mother and held no criticism toward Ruby's life and decisions.

Nash returned after church, mentioning nothing about going to see his family, so the rest of the day was spent like a weekday.

On Monday Dugger prepared the buckboard, and Ruby took the children into town, where she ordered books and slates, and several pieces of clothing for Jane. She had prepared Jane for a visit to the doctor, and David Morris was in his office, so he looked her over, declaring her injuries much improved and noting her overall health.

"I visited my Cheyenne friend yesterday," she told him. "I explained what you'd told us about Jane's health, and she gave me a tincture to help with healthy growth."

"Little Bird's reputation is a good one. I don't know much about Indian medicine," he told her. "I'm curious to know what it is and how it affects her. I want to keep a close eye on Jane.

Ruby nodded her agreement.

"I enjoyed myself at supper the other night."

"It was the least I could do."

"Perhaps you could join me for lunch at the café?" he said, while the children studied a drawing of human bone structure on the wall. "The children, too, of course."

Ruby was taken aback by his invitation. She had enjoyed his visit when he'd come to the ranch, and she liked talking to him, but she didn't want him to think they were more than friends. She didn't hold romantic feelings toward him. "Thank you, but I still have a lot to accomplish today. I need to get back to the Lazy S."

"Maybe another time, then."

She had gathered the children and ushered them out.

It was obvious that Nash had been watching for their return. He rode out to meet the wagon and looked relieved to see them. Her first thought was that he didn't trust her, but then she remembered how her sister had died and amended her thinking.

Even though they'd talked about the kiss and agreed they couldn't let anything interfere with the attention and focus the children needed, Ruby and Nash had tiptoed around each other since the previous week. She breathed easy when he headed out the following morning.

She browned meat and peeled potatoes, listening to the children's conversation on the porch. Midafternoon, she had settled them at the table with sliced apples when a buckboard pulled into the dooryard. "Stay here while I see who it is," Ruby told the children.

"Is it Grandmother?" Claire asked.

"No, it's not a buggy."

She walked toward the fellow who climbed down from the seat.

"Howdy, miss." He whipped his cap from his head. "You Ruby Dearing?"

"That's me."

"Willie Nestor," he said by way of introduction. "Got a couple of trunks in the back here." He gestured to the rear of the conveyance. "They been at the station for a few days, so I figured I'd just bring 'em on out for ya."

"I'd forgotten all about them. Thank you so much for your trouble."

"Weren't no trouble, ma'am. I'll haul 'em in iffin you tell me where you want 'em."

"Well, they actually go upstairs, but I don't want you to trouble yourself with that. If you leave them on the porch, my brother-in-law will take them up."

"Nash Sommerton your brother-in-law?" At her nod, he continued, "Won't be no trouble a'tall. Just show me where."

Belatedly, she realized the man had brought her trunks in hopes of payment for the job. Hauling them was likely his livelihood. "Thank you. I'll hold the door."

While he went back for the other one, she got coins from her room. After he'd deposited the second trunk, she paid him. He thanked her and went on his way.

"What's in those big trunks that man took up?" Claire asked, wide-eyed with interest.

"The rest of my dresses and a few costumes. Things I collected on my travels. You know, I've been getting along just fine without them. I'd forgotten there was so much. I don't suppose I need all that now."

Her niece wore an expectant expression. "Can we look?"

Jane gave Ruby an interested glance, but said nothing.

"There's nothing here that can't wait," Ruby answered. "Let's go upstairs."

Claire squealed and ran for the stairway. Joel picked up a wooden horse and followed. Jane trailed after them.

The trunks had been set end to end in the open space, taking up a good portion of the floor in her mother's old room. Ruby went to a drawer and took out the keys that unlocked them.

She opened the first one, and the children crowded around.

On top were half a dozen hats she'd carefully packed in tissue paper and nestled together.

"Ohhh," Claire said with awe. "They're so pretty. Did you wear all these?"

Ruby nodded. "People in the big cities dress up every day to shop and eat in restaurants, and just to stroll and be seen."

"Put one on," the little girl begged.

Ruby selected a green felt hat with a long feather plume and a silk bird, and adjusted it at a jaunty angle on her head.

"It's so beautiful!" Claire exclaimed.

Ruby removed tissue from another and settled it on Claire's head. It was too big, but the girl rolled her eyes upward to look at the brim and then ran to the cheval mirror and studied her reflection. Ruby set an elegant gray hat with pearl-studded netting on Jane and adjusted the smart veil across her eyes.

Jane blushed, but she moved to stand beside Claire and look at herself.

"My want a hat, too!" Joel said with a pout.

Ruby remembered a wool-and-silk knit cap she'd worn one Chicago winter, and dug to the bottom of the trunk to find it. "Here's one for you, Joel. It's very handsome for a boy."

He grinned and wore it while he galloped his miniature carved horse across the windowsill.

"I want to wear beautiful hats and dresses when I grow up. I hope I look just like you, Aunt Ruby," Claire said, with an admiring gaze.

"I imagine you will," Ruby told her. "Since you look just like your mama, and the two of us were very similar."

The little girl touched the brim of the hat she wore and turned sideways to look at herself from another angle. "Daddy told me you're not like Mama at all."

Ruby absorbed Claire's innocent disclosure

and focused her attention on her niece, uncertain how to feel about Nash saying that. "He did?"

Claire nodded with all seriousness. "He said looks don't mean anything, because two sisters couldn't be more different than you and Mama."

Being compared to Pearl was nothing Ruby hadn't heard before, but hearing it from Claire was different. "When did he tell you that?"

"After I saw you the first time and I said you looked almost like Mama." She studied Ruby in the mirror. "I look like Mama, but maybe I won't be like her at all. Is that so?"

It was true she was nothing like her sister, though they'd been similar in appearance, Ruby mused. She had always sensed her mother's disapproval, but to be honest, she hadn't tried all that hard to please her—not like Pearl had.

Of course their differences were plain to everyone, including Nash. He'd insinuated upon their first meeting that he'd expected her to be prettier. Ruby had known he didn't like her from the beginning, so she didn't take it personally. People said a lot of things when they were angry. But he hadn't been angry when he'd talked to Claire about her.

Facts were just facts. She was nothing like her sister. She'd never wanted to be like Pearl or her mother, yet here she was in the home they'd loved, with the children Pearl had given birth to, with the man her sister had loved.

Ruby still didn't want to be like Pearl…but what she *did* want had changed.

Ruby wasn't insulted or offended. Nash wasn't wrong. "I'm afraid he's right. Your mama got all the good qualities, like staying neat, always saying the right thing, being a good cook. Me, on the other hand, well, I never quite got the hang of being the perfect lady. My hair's always a sight, and I didn't know the top end of a chicken from the bottom until your papa showed me."

Claire turned away from the mirror to look up at her. "I like you just fine the way you are, Aunt Ruby."

Her acceptance touched Ruby's heart and sparked an unfamiliar vulnerability. *Just the way you are.* Ruby studied her niece and her heart filled with love and appreciation. "Thank you, Claire. You're the first person who ever said that to me." She touched the backs of her fingers to the child's smooth cheek. "You do look like her to me, because I remember her from when we were girls. And you're kind and tenderhearted like her, but I believe you are your own person. You won't be like anyone else, because you're special."

"I want to be like you, too, Aunt Ruby. I want to be brave and have adventures."

Claire's declaration touched and frightened Ruby at the same time. "You have plenty of growing up to do before you decide what you want."

She'd been caring for these children for only a short time. She hadn't given birth to them, but they prompted powerful, protective feelings. She could only imagine how her own mother must have felt when Ruby had run away and not kept in touch. Ruby would be crushed if Claire grew up and wanted desperately to get away.

The child had already moved back to the trunk. "What else is in here?"

Ruby showed them colorful dresses and costumes from a few of her plays. She selected one and lifted it, letting the skirt fall out. Most of the costumes cost several hundred dollars to have made, and she'd had to fund them on her own. The play in which she'd worn this particular dress held both good and bad memories. It had been one of her few starring roles, but the musical comedy itself had been panned by reviewers.

Jane reached to touch the bright blue dress and ran a single finger over the beaded edges and the sequined bodice. "It's the prettiest thing I ever saw."

"I'll never have cause to wear it again. I should've gotten rid of it instead of packing it."

"Put it on now!" Claire suggested with a hopeful lift of her eyebrows.

Why not? Ruby carried the dress to Claire's room and changed in privacy. She returned, and all three children stared.

Claire jumped up to perch on the edge of Ruby's bed. "Sing us something!"

Jane joined her, and Joel scrambled for his sister's assistance. They waited expectantly.

The children were indeed the most enthusiastic audience she could hope for. Ruby moistened her lips with her tongue and searched her memory for a song from this particular play. "I'm a lady not unknown to fame, critics call me by my Christian name…"

While singing, she pushed the trunks away to make room for the dance steps and continued on. It always surprised her how the lyrics and notes of so many songs came right back to her as though she'd performed them only yesterday.

The children laughed and smiled, though they couldn't have understood half the things alluded to in the words. They clapped at the appropriate times and Joel nearly pitched headfirst off the bed. Ruby shot forward to catch him and then resumed her impromptu show.

"And the little dancing girl may be married to an earl, for you never never never know your luck luck luck, no you never never never know your luck!" Finished, she took an elaborate bow, with flourishes and a sweep of her hat.

At the sound of additional clapping behind her, Ruby spun to find Georgia in the doorway, a smile on her face. "Indeed, you are a marvelous singer, Ruby!"

"That wasn't my best performance, but thank you."

Claire and Joel slid from the bed to give their grandmother hugs. Georgia knelt and gathered them close, kissing their cheeks and knocking off Claire's hat in the process. She placed it back on her granddaughter's head. "I've missed you, but I'm happy to see you're having a good time with your aunt Ruby." Her gaze trailed over the top of Joel's wool cap. "And you must be Jane." She glanced at Ruby and then back. "Nash stopped by the house. He told me about you."

Ruby extended her hand. "Jane, come meet Mrs. Sommerton. This is Nash's mother and Claire and Joel's grandmother."

Jane removed the hat she'd been wearing and came forward hesitantly. "Ma'am."

"It's a pleasure to meet you," Georgia said.

"I trust you are enjoying your stay here. I hope my grandchildren have welcomed you politely."

"Oh, yes'm."

"Good. I brought chicken salad sandwiches for lunch." She gave Ruby a questioning look. "Unless that doesn't fit into your plans. I don't want to intrude."

"You're not intruding at all. My plans were to teach letters and numbers, but you can see how well that went."

Georgia glanced at Ruby's vivid beaded dress. "You're a little overdressed for a country lunch."

"Oh!" Ruby laughed and backed out of the room. "My clothes are on Claire's bed. I'll be right back."

Georgia served them and they sat at the kitchen table and shared thick sandwiches on fresh bread with cold glasses of milk. She fussed over the children, including Jane in her questions and conversation, though Jane held herself in reserve.

Georgia's pleasure in seeing her grandchildren was evident. Having them gone from the house after all this time must be difficult for her. Ruby had a lot of questions about how their family was coping, but she wasn't comfortable intruding on Georgia's privacy.

Later, Georgia read the children a story. Joel

fell asleep and Ruby carried him, still wearing the oversize cap, up to his bed. She removed the hat and his shoes and then smoothed his hair, thinking how long he'd been without his mother, how Pearl must have loved these beautiful children.

Seeing to their well-being was a big responsibility, but one she was more than ready to accept. Ruby vowed she would keep Pearl's memory alive for her niece and nephew. It was the least she could do.

Georgia had brought along a bag with more of the children's things, so Ruby carried it in from the buggy.

The day before, she had opened a bureau in the attic and discovered dolls and doll clothes that had belonged to her and her sister. She'd cleaned up the dolls and washed and pressed the clothing, and so she got them out now for Claire and Jane.

"I thought you'd have fun dressing the dolls."

The girls settled on a worn quilt at the end of the porch, the clothing arranged between them. Jane appeared hesitant.

"Do you think she's too old to enjoy the dolls?" Ruby asked Georgia.

"I'm thinking she's following Claire's cues about everything," Georgia replied. "She's obviously interested, but I believe she feels awkward."

"Do you suppose she's never had a doll?" Ruby whispered.

"It's entirely possible."

Ruby studied the girls. It was painful to imagine Jane growing up in a foundling home, without love or attention, with no one to care about her well-being. "I don't want to treat her like a child, but maybe a bit of a childhood is what she needs."

Georgia nodded. "Looks to me you're doing just fine—with all of them. It's plain they adore you."

Warmed by the unaccustomed praise, Ruby looked at Nash's mother. "I loved Joel and Claire from the first moment I saw them. Jane, well, she's earned a place in my heart, too. I don't know if love is enough, but I want to take care of them like they deserve."

"I have always believed love is enough," Georgia answered, her deep brown eyes moving from the girls to Ruby. "Love has brought me through some difficult situations. Still is."

"Mrs. Sommerton—"

"Georgia."

"Georgia. I don't know what to say, but I want you to know I care about you and your family very much."

"Thank you. That means a lot." She smoothed

her skirt over her lap and raised her gaze to the blue sky. "What's done is done. There's no changing the past. I believe each of us wants to do the right thing with our future. Miles is as much Cosmo's son as Nash is. As shocking as that may be."

"I'm so sorry."

"This was a blow to Nash—to all of us. Cosmo never meant for anyone to get hurt. He's as shocked by Miles's appearance as anyone. He feels responsible for the turmoil."

Ruby took a deep breath and considered her words before she spoke. "I know what it's like to make mistakes and hurt people you love. Hurting someone you love is a burden. It's painful to live with." She was silent a moment, picking at a thread on her sleeve, before adding, "Regret brings its own punishment."

Georgia turned and studied her thoughtfully. Her expression held questions. "You're very straightforward."

Ruby raised a shoulder in a half shrug.

"I like that about you." She seemed to think a moment. "There has always been tension between Cosmo and Nash. From the time he was young, Nash talked about horses. He never had any desire to work at the mill with his father. He did it because it was expected of him. He put in his hours after school and Saturdays. Even though Cosmo encouraged him in business or accounting, he was eager only to study animal husbandry at university. Thankfully, my husband gave in without a big fight.

"When Nash returned and resumed his job at the mill, I was concerned about him. I knew he was only doing it to please his father, and I didn't want him to regret missing out on his own dream."

"And then he and Pearl and Mama made an arrangement," Ruby interjected.

Georgia nodded. "Cosmo had accepted it was inevitable by that point. He didn't speak a single word of objection when Nash quit the mill, married Pearl and transformed the farm to a ranch. But there was always something unspoken between them. Maybe that's why learning about Miles this way is so difficult for Nash."

"It would be difficult for anyone," Ruby reminded her.

"Yes. Of course."

"Your husband has spoken to Nash and Vivian?"

"Oh, yes. He's accepted the wrongdoing and apologized. This is a fresh hurt for them. Miles and Nash have spoken as well, and Cosmo is calling on Vivian this afternoon. I only pray they can find it in their hearts to forgive him. Like you said, hurting someone you love carries its own punishment."

"Your husband told you the truth and explained himself right away," Ruby murmured. "You had the opportunity to hear him out. There's a lot to be said for that."

"I feel selfish for thinking about what we're going to tell people about Miles. I can live with the humiliation if the truth is best, but the truth might embarrass him, might embarrass my children. But the truth is always best, don't you agree? Even if it's uncomfortable."

"Would you be more uncomfortable telling people Cosmo had been married before?"

"I don't think so. Even a small lie leads to trouble down the way. If people don't accept us for who they know we are now, they aren't really our friends."

"Did he attend church with the family last Sunday?"

Georgia shook her head. "He declined our invitation. Probably because the truth will be difficult and he doesn't want to feel responsible. It takes courage to own up to our pasts. Even when it's for the best. Forgiveness isn't always easy."

Ruby rubbed Georgia's hand in a comforting gesture. "I understand perfectly."

Georgia gave her an understanding smile. "I know you do."

"Your husband got the chance to make it right, though. I can't say I'm sorry, or make it up to the people I hurt. It's too late to say the things I needed to say to Mama and Pearl." Ruby stared out across the green countryside and swallowed hard. Finally, she brought her gaze back to Georgia. "I waited too long. At first I was proud, and then I was ashamed and embarrassed. If I'd put away that pride and shame and done the right thing sooner, I wouldn't have to live the rest of my life with regret. But I'm making it up the only way I can—to Claire and Joel. In some way to Jane, too. And hopefully to Nash. I understand why he blames me for not being here and for making everyone's life harder. I can't deny his resentment is justified."

"Don't be so hard on yourself, Ruby."

Ruby swallowed around the knot in her throat. "It's hard to live without forgiveness." Her whispered admission trembled from her lips.

Chapter Sixteen

Georgia's eyelashes fluttered momentarily as she closed her eyes and opened them again. "I know your mother would have welcomed you back with open arms."

"I want to believe that's so. Now I'll never know."

The older woman turned over her hand and grasped Ruby's.

A lingering question remained in Ruby's heart, and she needed to ask it. "Georgia, did my mother ever join your family on Sunday afternoons? Did you see her in church before she got sick?"

"Laura and I were friends for a long time," Georgia replied. "After Nash and Pearl were married, she often came to Sunday dinner with them."

Ruby smiled at the heartwarming news. "I am so glad to learn that."

"After she became ill I'd come see her, and we would sit right here and quilt together. We made quilts for missions and wedding gifts. I have many fond memories of our afternoons together."

"I'm so thankful she had you for a friend." Ruby pictured the two women on this porch, heads bent over their sewing. It was an image she liked a lot. "I found squares of fabric Mama must have saved for quilting in her sewing basket—and more in the bottom of her trunk. Much of her clothing I wear because it's practical, but there are more of her dresses I won't use," Ruby told her. "I'd love to use them to make a quilt or two—maybe one each for Claire and Joel—to remember her by, but I don't have the first clue how to do that. I can sew a little, but I've only worked on a couple of costumes."

"It's not all that much different," Georgia told her. "If you can stitch, you can put together a quilt. I'd love to show you how and help you work on them."

Ruby smiled with pleasure. "Oh, that would be wonderful! When can we start?"

"Why don't I come over a couple of afternoons a week? While Joel naps and the girls play, we will work on the quilts and talk."

"I can't think of anything I'd like better. I can still teach the girls on the other days."

"As much as I miss them, Nash needs to have Claire and Joel here," their grandmother told Ruby in a low tone. "It was time for them to come back, and you are the best person to take care of them. It's plain they've already taken to you."

Georgia had welcomed and accepted Ruby from the moment she'd first met her. Her confidence in Ruby's ability touched her. Ruby didn't know what she'd done to earn it, or to deserve her kindness, but she needed a friend as much as her mother had.

On Saturday afternoon Nash told his children and Jane to change into clothes they could get dirty. "We're going to go see if fish are biting in Whisper Creek."

The three of them scrambled up the stairs.

"I'll go help Joel," Ruby said, and put a foot on the bottom stair.

"I figured you could use a little time to yourself," Nash said from behind her.

She paused and turned back. She could get accustomed to this side of him. She noticed the width of his shoulders and the becoming wave of hair across his forehead. She could get accustomed to him. "That's thoughtful. Thank you."

He stood within touching distance, but only their gazes locked. "I didn't want you to think I hadn't invited you because I didn't want you along."

These past weeks had shown Ruby why her sister had fallen for this man. Yes, he was stubborn and sometimes quick-tempered, but he was also kindhearted and straightforward. He expected a lot from people, but he expected more from himself. At one time she would have looked at someone who so clearly lived in the present and thought him unimaginative, but she'd learned Nash was driven to make the best of the present for the sake of a better future. She admired his ambition.

She gave him a soft smile now. "All right."

Once Ruby had helped Joel change clothing, and Nash drove out of the dooryard, with Boone pulling the buckboard, Ruby seated herself on the porch steps and listened to the breeze rustle the leaves of the tall poplars that formed a windbreak to the east. Her gaze touched on familiar landmarks and eased to the pasture, where Vivo now grazed with the other horses.

She got up and strolled to the fence. The Duchess caught her scent and ran to where she stood. Ruby affectionately stroked her forehead and neck. After a few minutes Vivo joined them, and the Duchess touched her nose to the gelding's. He moved his attention from the mare to snuffle the front of Ruby's shirtwaist.

"I didn't bring you anything," she apologized. She gave him equal attention, but then left the horses and walked across the meadow and up the rise to the crosses that marked the three graves. She hadn't been to this spot since she'd arrived, weeks ago.

Tall blades of grass had grown in the beds of violets at the head of each plot. Nash had been a lot busier since the children and Flint had arrived. Ruby carefully pulled each stem out by the roots, made a pile and then carried the grass several feet away and discarded it.

This time she studied the location of the plots, wondering if Nash and Pearl had chosen the place for their baby together or if perhaps Laura had been with Nash. According to the dates on the crosses, the baby had been buried here first. Little Margaret May. Then a few years later the infant's mother had come to rest beside her, and lastly her grandmother, Laura.

Ruby had been shocked and confused the first time she'd come here. Her misery had been all about her personal loss, the trauma of what she could never do or would never have because her mother and sister were gone. The sentiment was still true, of course. She would never see them again. She would never be able to apologize or receive their forgiveness.

But this time Ruby mourned their losses, instead of her own. She grieved for her mother's suffering, and regretted how difficult it had been for Pearl to care for her alone. She mourned for how short her sister's life had been cut, how she'd missed out on holding her baby boy and how she wasn't here to see how beautiful Claire had become.

She cried heartfelt tears because Pearl had been robbed of life at such a young age and would not see her children grow up or marry.

Ruby thought of all the times her mother had said God was taking care of them, and knew these two women had trusted Him to the end.

Ruby's lack of belief had disappointed her mother. Their faith had given them comfort, and Ruby was glad for that. Obviously, the other women at church had been good to them. It was there that Mama and Pearl had become fast friends with the Sommertons. Ruby couldn't deny Nash and his family were good people.

She probably wasn't setting a good example for the children by avoiding church. She had vowed to do everything in her power to take care of them and raise them as Pearl would have wanted.

The sinking feeling in her belly told Ruby she'd lost an argument with herself. The Audra Harpers of Crosby, Nebraska, would just have to move aside their starched skirts. Ruby Dearing was going to ignore their snooty attitudes and do what her sister would want her to do. She was going to church tomorrow.

For two Sunday mornings Ruby had busied herself with Vivo. Last Sunday she had prepared breakfast, helped the children get ready and then disappeared. Something was different today, because she wore an apron over a two-piece green dress Nash had never seen, and her hair was uncharacteristically braided and wound around her head, with painstakingly neat corkscrew curls lying at her neck.

She set a platter of pancakes on the table and found him staring. The flush on her cheeks might have been from the heat of the stove, but he didn't think so.

"Doesn't Aunt Ruby look beautiful?" Claire asked without hesitation. "Her hair is so pretty. And look at mine, Papa. Aunt Ruby braided mine just like hers."

Ruby's complexion glowed with good health and the evidence of more sun than most women allowed their skin. The vivid blue of her eyes holding his made it difficult to breathe. Looking at her had always hurt, because she reminded him he was a man. A man with a beating heart and a lot of years remaining on this earth. A man who had missed a lot of opportunities to really love his wife the way a woman deserved to be loved. A man who hadn't stopped working long enough to consider the possibility of a heart-stopping passion in his life.

"Yes," he managed to answer. He'd dreamed of her last night, but thankfully, the memory had grown elusive in the light of day. Now she wore a proper dress, a matronly apron, and had tamed her hair, but in his dream she'd been wearing that deep red wrapper that looked like satin and showed every luscious curve of her body. Her wild hair had been soft to the touch. In his dream he'd been free to look, free to touch... and he had.

She moved away and returned to place a fork beside his place. He caught her scents, the crisp cotton of her apron, a hint of cinnamon, the fresh rainwater she used to wash her hair.

His awareness teased him mercilessly, while he kept a rigid lock on his body and his feelings.

He wasn't free. He had more than enough responsibilities…and qualms. She'd told him straight-
out she didn't have time for this thing between
them to grow.

She placed pancakes on each of the children's
plates. He buttered Joel's, poured maple syrup
and cut them into bite-size pieces. Ruby had
loosely tied a cotton towel around the little boy's
neck to protect his clothing.

Finally noticing Claire's quizzical expression, he cleared his throat and gave each of the
children a thorough once-over. "You all look especially nice this morning. Your hair is pretty,
Claire. Is that a new dress, Jane?"

Jane widened her gray eyes and gave him a
sheepish smile. "Ruby bought it for me."

"We have others ordered," Ruby told him.
"Jane looks especially nice in blue, I think." She
took a seat on the opposite side of the table and
avoided meeting his eyes. "I'll be going with you
this morning."

He had no idea what had brought about her
change of heart. "It will be nice to have you join
us. My mother mentioned we should join them
for dinner this afternoon."

"Will we play badminton, Papa?" Claire asked.

Jane set down her fork, though she had several bites remaining. She studied her plate with a solemn expression.

"You've met Nash's mother," Ruby said to her. "She makes newcomers feel very welcome. She will be pleased to see you."

Nash hadn't recognized Jane's concern about going. He appreciated Ruby's perceptiveness.

"We'll likely play badminton," he answered his daughter.

"Do you know how to play?" Claire asked Jane.

The girl shook her head.

"I helped Aunt Ruby learn. I can help you."

Claire's thoughtfulness brought a lump to his throat.

"All done. Can we go?" Joel had finished eating.

Nash grinned, removed the towel and wiped Joel's hands with it. "You can help me get the buckboard."

Nerves never got the best of Ruby. Opening nights in the theater had barely given her pause. She'd sung on stages in a dozen states without as much second-guessing as she was doing right now. Was she dressed appropriately? Maybe she shouldn't have come. She didn't want to embarrass the Sommertons. She had even remembered to dig a pair of white cotton gloves from her trunk.

As luck would have it, the first person she noticed when Nash halted the buckboard in front of the small whitewashed building was Audra Harper. *Reed*, she corrected herself, noting the fair-haired man escorting her to the door. She tried to place him, but couldn't.

Nash set the brake handle, jumped down and reached up for her gloved hand. She deliberately didn't look around to see if anyone was watching. She didn't want to know. When she'd taken the conveyance to town on her own, she'd jumped off the side to the ground, but she doubted Nash was going to let her do that. She took his hand and worked to keep her skirts modestly around her ankles as she stepped over the side and secured her footing on the wheel.

Nash reached for her, lowered her and then turned back for the children. "Wait here while I find a shady spot for the horses," he said.

Ruby looked up. Audra and her husband had already gone inside, thank goodness. Just then, David Morris separated himself from a small group of men and strode toward her. "Miss Dearing! How nice to see you this morning."

"Dr. Morris."

"You're looking well, Jane," he said.

Jane's expression showed a measure of discomfort, and she moved closer to Ruby.

David gave Ruby an apologetic glance. "I hope I didn't make things awkward between us."

"No. I'm sorry I got flustered that day when you invited me—us—to lunch. I've had a lot on my mind."

"Of course." He looked at something over her shoulder, his expression unreadable.

Ruby couldn't resist turning. Nash was making his way toward them.

"I'd like to be friends," David told her.

She found him studying her once again. "Certainly. I'd like that, too."

"David." Nash joined them and greeted the doctor.

He shook his hand. "Morning, Nash."

The Sommertons' black buggy rolled up just then, Georgia waving from the padded seat. Nash moved to help his mother down, kissed her cheek and offered to find a place for the buggy. His father got down, took his wife's arm and led her across the grass to where they greeted their grandchildren. Georgia glanced from Ruby to David, even as Claire and Joel hurried to hug her.

Several other churchgoers joined them, and Georgia introduced Ruby to those she didn't know, reacquainting her with others. Finally,

Nash returned, and the gathering moved inside the place of worship.

Ruby allowed herself to be led along the aisle, noting the familiar scents of wood and beeswax. The aged floor had been worn even when she was a girl, but it was still well maintained and smooth. The windows along each side had been opened several inches, so a morning breeze flowed along the plain wooden pews.

Nothing had changed except the faces in the crowd and the man who stood at the front in a black suit. Jane grabbed Ruby's hand, silently conveying that this was every bit as foreign and intimidating to her. Ruby gently squeezed her fingers and held on. The Sommerton family filed into a row, with Cosmo leading. Ruby sat between Nash and Jane, the girl's grip tightening on hers.

Ruby looked down to give her a reassuring smile.

Several minor chords sounded from the small organ, arresting attention. A man Ruby didn't recognize sat at the keyboard, dressed in a pinstripe suit.

"Let us turn to page seventy-eight in our hymnals," the minister called out.

Beside her, Nash opened a book with frayed corners on the cover and crimped pages inside.

Ruby had already made up her mind she wasn't going to sing. She didn't have a choir voice, and the last thing she wanted to do was draw attention. She was grateful it was a song she didn't know, even though she could read music perfectly well. Nash glanced over at her, so she mouthed the words.

Nash wasn't a great singer, but he held his own, and his voice melded with those around them. A couple of rows up to her right, David turned and glanced over his shoulder, his gaze taking in the family. He smiled at Ruby and she gave a barely discernible nod in return.

Nash looked at her, so she faced the front.

The songs were nice and the minister's preaching wasn't interminable. Jane relaxed her grip on Ruby's hand. Ruby enjoyed sitting in the midst of this family, and let herself warm to the soothing sound of the reverend's voice until the service ended.

A young woman with a baby in her arms greeted Ruby as the congregation moved toward the door. "I'm Penny Jacobs."

Ruby introduced herself.

"This is Henry," Penny told her. "Several of us ladies meet next door on Tuesday mornings. We'd love to have you join us. You don't have to bring anything, just come for tea."

"Thank you for the invitation," Ruby said sincerely. "The children keep me busy, so I don't come to town often. I will remember, though, if I should be in Crosby on a Tuesday."

"I knew your mother," Penny said. "She was a lovely woman."

Ruby found no malice in the other woman's expression. She swallowed. "Thank you. Thank you for saying so."

"You must be Ruby Dearing," the minister said.

Ruby diverted her attention to the man with his hand extended.

"I'm Reverend Colson. It's a pleasure to meet you. I was hoping we would see you on a Sunday morning."

She shook his hand. "Thank you. The service was—nice."

As she moved out into the sunlight, Audra waylaid her departure. "Hello, Ruby. This is my husband, Tom Reed. Tom, this is the woman you've been hearing so much about."

Chapter Seventeen

The fair-haired man blushed and greeted Ruby.

"This is the first Sunday you've come to church since you came to Crosby, isn't it?" Audra asked.

"There you are! I have a lovely dinner planned," Georgia interrupted. "Vivian is counting on you to help her set the table. And I want to find out how you make that caramel pie of yours. Mine just don't turn out the same." She glanced at Audra. "Good afternoon. Say hello to your mother for me."

Audra mumbled a greeting and took her husband's arm.

Nash joined Ruby and counted heads. "Walk with me to get the buckboard."

Georgia wasn't the only one to rescue her. And several people had been downright friendly. It was obvious that news of Ruby's return had gotten here ahead of her. Maybe she should have come right away, before they had time to speculate.

As they rode past young rows of corn, she thought how uncharacteristic it was of her to avoid people—or was it? Maybe she had shown a few cowardly tendencies, like not coming home to face her mother sooner. Ruby hadn't been ready to see the people of Crosby until now, though. She might have been defensive. She could have been hurt by their attitudes. The Sommertons' acceptance had made a big difference, and even David had helped influence her thinking. Perhaps the people of Crosby weren't as judgmental as she'd always believed—or at least not all of them. And those who did judge shouldn't have a hold over her.

Things at the Sommertons' had changed since the last time the family had gathered for Sunday dinner. Georgia had assigned Miles a place at the table. Seated at the head, Cosmo looked over each person, reached for his wife's hand and drew it close to kiss the backs of her fingers.

The touching gesture warmed Ruby's heart.

"There are a few things I want to say," Cosmo said. "I've spoken to my family members individually. Everyone had a chance to speak their mind."

"Daddy," Vivian said.

"I accept your disappointment as my due." He gestured to the others. "In all these years there was never a need for you to know about the past, and knowing would only have hurt you. Miles's arrival changed all that. I make no excuses. I respect your anger, and I have apologized for the hurt. With everything out in the open, I hope we can move on. A new start is what your mother wants, as well."

"Our family has two more people now," Georgia added. "Both deserve to be here as much as any other." She inclined her head to include Jane in her welcome.

Vivian reached for Tucker's hand. He gave her an encouraging smile. "If Mama can move on," Vivian said, "I can, too."

Georgia gave her daughter a warm smile and fixed her gaze on Nash.

"Are we gonna eat?" Joel asked from beside him. The little boy's puzzled frown moved from one person to the next.

Nash took a roll from the basket sitting in front of his son, halved it with his thumbs and placed it on Joel's plate. "Yes, we're going to eat in just a minute." He cast his father a stolid glance. "I don't have any hard feelings toward Miles. We've talked."

Ruby shared Cosmo's obvious relief. Nash hadn't spoken to her about his father or the situation with Miles, and she'd been concerned about how he was handling it. From things he and Georgia had mentioned, she knew he'd been here.

After getting things out in the open, the atmosphere changed from tense to friendly, and the conversation came easily. The family showed Miles and Jane the same courtesy they'd shown Ruby as a newcomer to their gathering.

"Will Mr. Easton play badminton with us?" Claire asked. The Sunday game was, of course, the most important thing on her mind.

"You can call him Uncle Miles," Georgia told her. "And you may need to convince him to join in."

"Two uncles," Joel commented, drawing attention to his milk mustache.

Tucker gave the child an affectionate smile.

"Can Jane call him Uncle Miles, too?" Claire asked.

Jane quickly ducked her chin against her chest, as though she wished to disappear.

"Jane, you may call me Uncle Miles if you like the sound of it," Miles graciously offered. "Or, should you need anything, you can just nudge me or call me that other fellow."

Several chuckles followed, and Miles grinned.

Ruby wrapped her arm around Jane's shoulders. "It takes some getting used to, being in a family, but this is a good one to belong to."

Ruby enjoyed time with the women as they cleared the table and stacked the dishes.

"Mrs. Gentry will stop by to do these and clean up the kitchen this afternoon," Georgia said. "We can join the others now."

"Mrs. Gentry?" Ruby asked.

Vivian uncovered a cake and tasted the frosting with a fingertip. "She helps Mother. Her husband worked for Daddy at the mill until his joints got too painful. Now Winter helps with the horses, brings in the wood, chores like that."

"And Mrs. Gentry helps around the house. There are a couple of gallon jars in the icehouse." Georgia removed her apron. "Perhaps a couple of you will fetch them later. The one with the checkered fabric under the lid is for the children."

Vivian studied her mother with a raised brow. "Mother, what did you put in the rest of the punch?"

"Only a little peach cordial and a splash of rum. I thought it would give our refreshment a festive flavor." She winked. "It did."

Vivian and Ruby exchanged a glance and laughed before heading outdoors.

* * *

Nash had difficulty keeping his attention away from Ruby that afternoon. She was striking in her vivid green dress. In the warmth of the afternoon sun, she removed the short jacket, revealing a white shirtwaist, wrinkled in all the fascinating and curvaceous places the fabric had been pressed against her body. After a few rounds of badminton, her carefully braided and moored hair came loose, and springy tendrils coiled down her back and beside her face. He liked it best all wild and curly like that. It suited her.

The teams changed, and he rested on the grass beside his mother. Her speculative smile warned him she'd caught him looking at Ruby.

"She's lovely, isn't she?"

Her observation and question disturbed him. He had confusing thoughts and emotions where Ruby was concerned. Everything about her looked good. She said the right things. She'd done the right things since she'd arrived. He should ease off his criticism about the way she'd left her mother and sister. She'd been—what—sixteen years old?

But her disappearance said a lot about her impetuousness, about how easily she could become distracted or bored or discouraged—whatever it took to make her pack up and leave again.

How long could she stick with this life of long workdays, caring for children, cooking and a rather ordinary circle of family and acquaintances? She and Dr. Morris had quickly developed a friendship, and it was plain that David had eyes for her.

Who wouldn't?

Ruby scored a point and win by whizzing the shuttlecock past Tucker's ear. She bent at the waist, a hand on her knee, and laughed.

Tucker set Joel down and the child ran over to his grandmother. "I'm thirsty, please."

Georgia smoothed his hair. She glanced at Nash. "Will you show Ruby the icehouse and help her carry back the jars of punch? There are two."

Nash got to his feet and lifted a hand to attract Ruby's attention. "Mother asked me to show you where the icehouse is."

Ruby glanced from him to where Georgia sat with Joel on her lap. She handed her racquet to Miles and joined Nash.

"Claire and Joel are happy to be here again," she said.

"Jane is hanging back," he replied.

"She's never done anything like this before," Ruby replied. "We don't know how many years she spent in an orphanage—and then going from one placement to another—before ending up with that horrible Billings fellow and his sons. Considering all she's been through, and her lack of trust, I think she's adjusting well."

"I hope you're right."

"She only needs a little time."

Nash led Ruby behind the house to a stone building only four feet tall. She blinked. "Is that the icehouse? Why is it so short?"

He grinned. "It's not short inside. It's built partially underground to hold in the cold. Have you never seen one?"

"Only big ice companies in the cities. Deliverymen take ice on wagons to hotels and probably to homes."

"My father buys the ice during the winter. There's a family north of Crosby who cuts it from the river to sell." Nash led her down several steps at the end of the building, turned a small block of wood that held the door shut and left the portal open so they could find their way inside in the dark. The interior was surprisingly cold.

"I would never have imagined," Ruby said.

"I want to build one of these at the ranch," he told her. "Haven't taken the time. I did start a pile of stones to use eventually."

"I wondered what those were for." She spotted two large jars side by side and bent to pick one up. "Here's the punch."

Unprepared for the weight and slick exterior of the glass container, she lost her grip.

Nash stepped forward and caught the jar before it hit the earth.

"That was clumsy of me," she said. The semidarkness and quiet of the icehouse created an awkward intimacy.

He'd moved so near, his shoulder brushed her cheek as he straightened. He turned to face her. "That was close."

"Too close," she agreed, looking up at him now. They both reached for the other jar at the same time, his hand covering hers. The warmth of his touch contrasted with the cold air surrounding them, and a delicious shiver traveled up her arm and along her spine. Ruby's fingers trembled.

"You're cold," he said, barely above a whisper.

"It feels good," she answered.

He lowered his head, and she rose on tiptoe to meet his kiss.

His lips were pleasantly warm and breathtakingly gentle. His breath mingled with hers, and she forgot the cold. She forgot everything except this moment and the way her heart responded by tripping in exultation. It wasn't decent, the way she liked kissing him. Without notice, she had intruded upon his life, and he didn't even much like her. She shouldn't be standing here wishing she had the freedom to reach up and touch his face, skim his jaw with her fingertips, fold herself into his embrace...

He was her sister's husband. Pearl had loved this man...kissed him and a whole lot more. She had given him children.

He'd most likely been without a woman since Pearl's death. Ruby shouldn't feel flattered. Or wanted. She should feel guilty.

She became aware of the jar pressing into her midriff. The cold and the reminder of their mission gave her the impetus to draw back.

She didn't feel shame. She felt regret. She regretted that she'd ever left Crosby, and that Pearl had found Nash first. She regretted that he loved her sister. Her sweet, perfect sister.

Ruby added jealousy to her admissions of regret.

She stepped back and picked up the other jar. "Everyone is thirsty. We'd better get back."

On Monday morning Willie Nestor delivered an envelope with Ruby's and Nash's names written in black ink. "It's from Mr. Buckley."

"The lawyer?"

"That's him."

Ruby paid Willie for his trouble, and he rode away. She considered going to find Nash in case this was something important, and she suspected it was. She hoped it was good news about Jane. But she couldn't leave the children alone, and Nash hadn't said where he'd be working that day, so she waited, glancing out the windows at every opportunity.

Midday, as she deliberately hid her laundered underclothing on the line between the rows of sheets, the sound of restless horses caught her attention. She told the children to stay put where they played near the back porch and found Nash in the barn.

He crouched outside the larger foaling stall, peering through the planks. Straightening, he motioned for her to accompany him back outside.

"Is one of the mares foaling?" she asked.

"Yes. So far she's doing fine on her own. Should be anytime now."

"Where are Silas and Dugger? Do you need any help?"

"No, they're working on a gate. Wait about half an hour and come back out. If all is going well, you can bring the children to watch. The last couple of births have been during the night, so they've missed them."

Following Nash's directions, Ruby returned later, after she put stew on the stove. This time Nash stood inside the foaling stall, but at the outer corner. He had removed his shirt. She tried not to study the firm planes of his abdomen and the solid-looking curve of his chest and shoulders, but abandoned the impossible attempt to appreciate the sight from her vantage point.

"It will be anytime now," he said in a low voice. "Bring them out. Tell them to be quiet so they don't startle the mare."

Ruby gave the children their instructions and led them to the barn, where they lined up along the gate and peered through the planks. Ruby watched over the top.

Nash was on his knees now, gently washing the mare's rump and hindquarters. The horse lay on a clean bed of straw, her head in the air, and gave Nash a preoccupied glance. Her side heaved up and down with labored breaths.

Nash set the bucket away silently and rested on his haunches.

After a few minutes Joel pointed. "What is that?"

"It's the foal's legs," Nash said softly. He moved aside the membrane, took gentle hold of the legs and leaned back, waiting for another contraction to push the baby out.

The mare rested her head on the straw.

Ruby held her breath.

Nash knew when to assist and when to pause, leaning back as more and more of the foal was exposed until the newborn horse lay on the stall floor.

"It's a baby," Claire breathed in awe.

Jane watched in fascination.

Nash released the squirming foal's forelegs and quickly removed the film from its head. With knowledgeable swipes, he cleared the animal's mouth. He gave its neck several affectionate strokes and checked its mouth again.

He glanced over to gauge their reactions and smiled. "She's a beauty," he said softly.

"Can we come touch her?" Claire asked.

"Not just yet," he answered. "These are her first minutes with her mama."

Once he made sure the foal was safely delivered and the mare was all right, Nash straightened and came to stand near the gate. "Be patient and in a little while she'll stand up and test her legs."

The mare lifted her head and looked at her new offspring. Within a few minutes she stood and touched her nose to the baby's.

The foal took its time. Joel grew impatient and sat, using a piece of straw to draw imaginary circles on a wood post. Eventually, the foal made several feeble attempts before struggling to its feet.

Jane released a relieved sigh. "She's up."

"She's up," Ruby agreed.

Nash opened the gate and joined them. "I'll give them a few minutes before I change the straw."

"Can I do anything?" Ruby asked, now faced with Nash standing before her, shirtless. She kept her focus on his face and waited for a reply.

"If you wouldn't mind getting me a clean shirt, I'm going to wash up."

"I don't mind." She hurried out of the barn and across the dooryard to the house. The rich aroma of stewing beef met her nostrils, and she hurried up the stairs.

Ruby opened a drawer and took out a neatly folded shirt. She ran her fingertips over the fabric, remembering the kiss they'd shared in the icehouse the day before. She had always considered herself strong, but she was weak when it came to Nash. She had become a different person since meeting him, and the difference frightened her. Closing her eyes, she recalled the handsome edge of his jaw, the strength of his brow, the length of his fingers. Her heart betrayed her and fluttered like a schoolgirl's. She raised her fingers to the base of her throat, humiliated by her racing pulse.

Opening her eyes, she looked into the small, framed mirror. What was she thinking? Her gaze fell to the photograph on top of the bureau.

Pearl.

Chapter Eighteen

Previously, Ruby had mopped the floor, dusted and changed the bedding in this room, and each time she'd glanced at her sister's likeness and been saddened. This time she picked up the frame and studied Pearl's sweet face, her orderly hair, the delicate lace of the blouse she wore and the heart-shaped locket around her neck—the same locket their mother had worn in her wedding portrait.

Had Mama given it to Pearl then? Vaguely, Ruby wondered what had happened to it after Pearl's death. One day it should belong to Claire.

Ruby set the frame back in its place and closed the drawer. She had an obligation to Pearl's children. Nash was counting on her to help raise them. She couldn't be awash with guilt every time she thought about her sister. She was doing all she could to fill the void.

The room suddenly darkened, drawing her attention to the window. Ruby glanced out and discovered a few puffy gray clouds creating shadows on the countryside. If a storm arose, Nash would need help keeping the mares calm.

As she neared the stable a few minutes later, Dugger pulled a wagon beside the barn. Silas got down and went around to retrieve a toolbox from the back. Apparently, the men shared her idea of helping Nash with the horses.

Jane led Joel out of the barn, holding his hand. Claire followed, and Nash approached Ruby. "Thanks."

She handed him the shirt, and he shrugged into it.

"Flint is in the south pasture," he said to Dugger. "Keep an eye on the sky, and if it looks like a thunderstorm, put him in the rear stall of the stable."

"Where's Vivo?" Ruby asked.

"He's in the east pasture with the mares that have foals. He's tame around them. Even seems to keep Peg, the skittish bay, calm. We'll keep an eye on 'im."

Ruby turned to Jane. "Will you and Claire take Joel into the house? I'll be right there."

The girls obediently led him across the yard.

Ruby turned back. "What about the letter?"

"The letter? Oh!" Nash reached into his rear pocket, pulled out the folded envelope and tore it open. After glancing at the paper, he handed it to Ruby. "The adoption agency sent all the paperwork to the lawyer."

She took the sheet and read a brief letter from Mr. Buckley, explaining the process for an adoption through the county. "He set up an appointment to sign the papers in front of a judge at the courthouse. But..." She frowned.

"But the papers are made out in my name only," Nash stated.

He was a respected citizen, a rancher, a father. She'd been living in the county only for several weeks. Of course the authorities considered Nash an acceptable father for an orphan. Ruby on the other hand—why, Mr. Buckley probably hadn't even bothered to include her name.

"It makes sense," she said. "You already have children. You're trustworthy and a member of the community. They don't know me. If they did..." She would only have to live down her reputation.

Ruby glanced at the sky and finally met his eyes. "What's important is that Jane will be safe. She doesn't have to go back to the Billingses, and she has a home."

"We'll tell her together," he said.

Ruby nodded. "I'll see you at supper."

She would keep her focus on exactly what she'd said to Nash. Jane would be safe. It was selfish of Ruby to feel hurt because she hadn't been included in the adoption paperwork.

She peeled potatoes for the stew and added wood to the stove. A person had to earn trust and respect. She still had a long way to go before anyone thought she was responsible.

Deliberately setting aside her feelings of not measuring up, she gathered books and slates.

Off and on for the next few days, a light rain settled the dust, sustained the hay fields and filled the stock tanks. On Thursday morning when Nash left the house, he noted Ruby had already scraped dried mud from the porch floor. Today the sun valiantly rose above the tree line along the eastern horizon, and he hoped for clear weather so the children could play out of doors.

Ruby hadn't mentioned the confinement. She'd showed saintly patience, but he couldn't help wondering if her dedication was boundless. Nebraska winters were harsh, and depending upon the snowfall, sometimes travel to Crosby for church or shopping was limited. Would she survive a winter of isolation?

This was one of the days that doubt assailed him. He didn't question Ruby's love for them, but he wasn't completely convinced of her commitment. Her compassion for Jane should have been enough evidence of her good intentions. She had been taken with Claire and Joel from the first moment.

But Ruby had loved her mother, too, and that hadn't stopped her from seeking an adventure. Life on this ranch couldn't compare to the pull of the big wide world. David Morris had shown more than a friendly interest, and if he pursued Ruby, the prospect of living in town and being married to a doctor might seem more exciting than life here.

Nash didn't like the doubts that only added to his disturbing preoccupation with this woman. He couldn't waffle back and forth about his confidence in her. Until she gave him a good reason to doubt her, he had to put these thoughts to rest.

They hadn't told Jane about the adoption yet, and it was cruel not to set her mind at ease. He didn't know what to say to Ruby, though. She'd been determined that Jane would not have to return to the Billingses, and had been adamant they do something permanent. She was the one getting to know the girl, looking after her day after day, but it appeared that Ruby wouldn't be included in the legal paperwork. If he was uncertain about her stability, maybe it was for the best.

He disliked himself for thinking that way. It seemed everyone at church had accepted her once his mother made it plain Ruby was part of the Sommerton family. His family had accepted her wholeheartedly, and the children adored her. He didn't know why he was having such difficulty trusting her.

Maybe he was afraid to care too much.

That night for supper she dished up noodles with chunks of beef and vegetables that were surprisingly good. No one made biscuits as well as she did. She was doing her best, even though he hadn't given her much credit.

"This is a fine meal," Nash told her.

She glanced up and met his gaze with a smile of surprise. "Thank you."

If she looked surprised when he complimented her, he didn't say nice things often enough. Had he expressed his appreciation to Pearl, or had he taken her for granted in his preoccupation? He supposed it was the latter.

"You're a good cook, Miss Ruby," Dugger told her. "You make noodles as good as my mama's."

"I shall consider that high praise," she answered. "Does your mother live nearby?"

"Yes'm. After my daddy died a few years back, she and my sister moved into town. My mama works for the tailor and I visit them on Sundays."

"She raised a hardworking son," Ruby told him.

"That she did," Silas said. "Mrs. Wiley is a hardworking woman herself."

"Grandmother was here again today," Claire told Nash. "She and Aunt Ruby sewed."

"I enjoy your mother's visits," Ruby said. "She's taught me how to make quilt squares from the fabric my mother had cut. We're using the material from several of Mama's dresses, too. Eventually we'll sew them all together."

While she learned more about her mother's last years, it had been reassuring to know her mother always spoke kindly of her. She should know because of her mother's nature that Laura didn't harbor resentment toward her, but Ruby would always regret she hadn't returned in time to make amends. She had to find a way to let go of those misgivings.

"Papa, may I have a blue dress?" Claire asked.

Nash turned his attention to his daughter. "A blue dress?"

"Aunt Ruby has a beautiful blue dress with beads and sequins. She wore it when she used to sing."

Ruby turned to Nash. "My trunks arrived last

week. I had kept a few costumes." She appeared to think for a few minutes. "I could take that dress apart and use the fabric to make skirts for Claire and Jane."

Jane set down her fork. She'd been sitting in relative silence, as usual, but she was eating more at a time and seeming more at ease with their family. At first she'd looked as though she'd dart under the table at a sideways glance, but now she listened with interest and occasionally even smiled.

Joel got down from his chair, went for a slate and chalk, and came to sit on Nash's lap.

Dugger stacked the dishes and Silas brought in firewood. "Gonna get another rain storm," Silas announced.

"Your knee's never wrong," Nash replied. "The hay can use another good soaking."

Both hired men thanked Ruby for the meal, excused themselves and headed out.

"You can help me wash these dishes," Ruby said to Jane.

It was a warm evening, and the breeze that came in the door felt good. Joel drew a lopsided circle with a couple of eyes Nash assumed were Ruby's. Then he handed his father the chalk.

Nash drew a horse that looked more like a dog, but his gaze kept traveling to Ruby. She was showing Jane how to shave soap and get suds for the dishwater. Again, she had uncharacteristically braided her hair today, and the thick plait hung over her shoulder and across her breast, drawing his attention as she moved.

She looked over and caught him watching. Ruby gave him a smile, wiped her hands on her apron, set the kettle on to heat and tossed a handful of sticks into the stove.

Once the water had boiled, she took a few leaves from a small bag, poured water over them in a cup and set it before him. She pushed the sugar bowl toward him. "Have a cup of tea."

He picked up a spoon and adjusted Joel on his lap so he could look into the cup. A pungent aroma met his nostrils. "Pine and…sage. What is it?"

She settled herself on a chair beside him. "Anise hyssop tea. Little Bird gave it to me for a dispirited heart. I shared some with your mother, too."

"Does she seem all right to you?" he asked.

"I believe she is doing well. She's strong…and practical. Since you and Vivian have been talking to your father and to Miles, I think Georgia is moving forward. Your parents seem to love each other very much. What they have together is…well, it's rare."

"Yes." He touched his nose to Joel's temple. "It is."

"I thought maybe you could use some of the tea, too."

He raised a brow. "You think I have a dispirited heart?"

"I wouldn't presume to know about the condition of your heart. The tea is soothing. That's all."

He didn't know about his heart, either, but his thoughts were chaotic. Ruby seemed to sense as much, because she simply watched him stir sugar into the brew. He trusted Little Bird's medicinal abilities, but he wasn't convinced a cup of herb tea would fix what was ailing him. He did enjoy sitting here like this, all of them gathered in the kitchen, the lanterns creating a warm glow. Ruby talking about her day and Claire asking about a new dress made everything seem normal, and normal was comforting. He sipped his tea.

Ruby left for a few minutes and returned with a book.

"What are you reading?" he asked.

"Ruby finished reading to me about a boy named Hans Brinker," Jane said. "He lives in a faraway place called the Netherlands."

Nash had never seen the girl so animated. "I've heard her reading to you a couple of times."

"She reads to us a lot. I can read some of

the words myself now," Jane said with a satis-fied nod.

"I'm proud of you," he replied. "You must be a good student."

"I need to know how to read by myself. In case I don't have anyone else to read for me."

"You must know how to read," Ruby agreed. "Even if you do have someone to read to you." She showed them the cover. "This is a brand-new version of an old English tale. Mr. Brubeker had two copies for sale in his store."

"The Merry Adventures of Robin Hood," Nash read aloud. "I remember Robin Hood from the penny dreadfuls."

"This author has written the tales more for children," Ruby said. "And there are color il-lustrations."

"Pictures?" Claire asked.

"Me see, too!" Joel leaned away from Nash, craning to get a better look at the book.

Ruby found the pages with the artist's rendi-tions and showed them. "Now sit tight," she in-structed. "And listen to the story."

Joel settled back comfortably on Nash's lap. He picked up the wooden horse that had been sitting on the table and held it.

Ruby turned to the front page and read aloud. Jane listened transfixed, and Claire warmed to the story, as well. Even as unusual as Ruby's voice was, her tone was soothing, and her expressive reading created a calm atmosphere that had been lacking in this home for too long. Maybe it was the tea, but Nash suspected the relaxed mood was due to Ruby's presence. He had grown accustomed to the tone she used, and enjoyed hearing her speak to the children. Whenever she talked to him softly her voice sent a shiver down his spine. He'd discovered a lot of things about her that affected him like that. The way she cast him a secret smile when one of the children said something amusing, the way she tilted her chin in interest when he spoke.

He shouldn't be having fanciful thoughts when there were serious concerns at stake. Jane was still uncertain about her future, and he couldn't let her continue to worry.

It was time they told her about the adoption.

A clap of thunder shook the old house, and the pans in the cupboard rattled.

Jane yipped and sidled off her chair as though prepared to run. Her eyes were wide with fright.

Immediately, Ruby got up and rested her arm around the girl's bony shoulders. She bent at the waist and leaned right down to speak near her ear. "That surprised me, too," she said matter-of-factly. "Silas's knee predicted a little rain, didn't it?" She glanced at Nash. "Don't we need more rain?"

"Rain is good for the hay," he replied, following her cue for reassuring the youngsters. His children were used to thunder and wind, but Jane was obviously uneasy.

The sound of hard rain filtered through the screen door.

Ruby stayed right beside Jane, her arm around her. "Are you enjoying the story?"

A burning scent wafted through the open door, alerting Nash to something amiss. He stood and set Joel on the chair seat. "I have to check on something."

"Stay right here," Ruby told the girls. "Keep an eye on Joel."

She followed Nash out the door and stood on the back porch, while he donned his wide-brimmed hat to keep the rain from his eyes and headed toward the barn. He scanned the yard as he went, and his gaze rested on a smoldering tree that had been split down the center by lightning. Its leafy branches lay on the ground. The pungent smell of ozone lingered.

Footsteps sounded in the puddles as Ruby darted across the yard and stopped before the stricken tree.

"Thank God it wasn't the house or the barn," he said.

Standing in the deluge, she brought both hands up to cover her face and then let them hang at her sides. The starch had gone out of her spine, and she stood staring while cold rain plastered her hair and clothing to her head and body.

"It's okay, Ruby," he told her. "The tree's not burning, and the rain will douse any remaining embers. You're getting soaked out here."

She said nothing, still staring through the downpour at the fallen tree.

He took a few steps closer. "Ruby? Are you all right?"

Without reply, she turned and headed back to the house.

Chapter Nineteen

Ruby's reaction confused him. Nash checked the animals in the old barn and the stable. Flint was restless, so Nash took a few minutes to stand beside him in the stall, stroke his mane and speak softly.

Dugger approached with soft steps. "We'll keep an eye on that tree tonight. Fire's already out, and it's still raining."

"Keep an eye on the mares for me, too. Another one of them is ready to foal."

Nash returned to the kitchen. "Where's Aunt Ruby?"

"Getting on dry clothes, probably," Claire answered.

"Let's get ready for bed," he said.

Ruby met them in the upstairs hall, dressed in her deep red wrapper over an ankle-length nightgown, feet bare, her loose hair towel-dried and hanging over one shoulder.

Jane moved to her side and asked in a hushed voice, "Can I sleep in your room tonight?" She had been staying in her own room for a week.

Ruby cradled the girl's cheek. "Yes, of course. You are always welcome."

Jane found comfort with Ruby, and for that Nash was thankful. He didn't like to think what it had been like for the girl, growing up with no one to care for her or show her love. A broad stroke of fate—or providence—had led him to the Billings ranch to buy Flint, thereby leading Jane to this place, where she'd found safety— and Ruby.

Ruby's heart seemed big enough to encompass Jane as well as his children. If he supposed destiny had arranged someone to care for Jane, how could he think differently about the provision for his own children? Maybe he didn't have a dispirited heart, but he sure had an indecisive one. He didn't want to consider that this hesitation might be because of his own fear of feeling too much.

Once he'd tucked in Claire and Joel, he noted Ruby's door was closed and no light shone from beneath. He attempted lying down, but after half an hour, he tugged his trousers back on and headed outside, intending to sit on the porch for a while.

The kitchen door stood open. The screen barely squeaked as he exited the house. Leave it to Ruby to have waxed the hinges.

She stood at the edge of the porch, staring across the darkness that stretched away from the house. She didn't move as he approached. She wore a loose-knit shawl over her sleeveless night-dress, but the shawl hung at her elbows, leaving her pale upper arms bare. The sight made his breath catch.

"Ruby?"

She didn't move. "The thunder let up. Jane is asleep."

"Are you all right?"

She didn't reply.

"Ruby?"

"I helped my daddy plant that tree," she said at last. "It's one of my best memories."

Nash took another step until he stood right beside her. He, too, studied the night. The steady rain sluicing from the roof formed a curtain across each end of the porch and played a steady rhythm on the water-soaked ground, creating a pleasurable intimacy.

"We planted it only a few months before he left," she continued. "I never understood why he started a tree when he wasn't planning on sticking around to see it grow. I still don't know."

"It was growing into a good shade tree," Nash answered inadequately.

"But then he didn't stick around to see his daughters grow, either." She shrugged. "I guess if Pearl and I weren't important to him, that tree sure wasn't."

The clouds parted, and in the sliver of moonlight that arrowed across her face, he could see tears glistening on her cheek. She looked away and made a quick swipe with the corner of the shawl in an attempt to hide her display of emotion.

A million things fell into place. Ruby had idolized her father, so of course her world changed when he'd left them. She put up a good appearance of being tough and resilient, but some things affected a person deeply, so deeply they couldn't explain their reactions to the pain. Nash had asked if she was all right. Now, knowing she wasn't, he had no idea what to say. "Pearl didn't talk about him much, but she said you and your father were close."

"I was a daddy's girl," Ruby agreed. "Pearl, she always stuck close to Mama's side. Even when she got older, and by then Daddy was gone."

"Had to have been hard when he left."

Ruby pursed her lips before speaking. "Mama

acted like nothing had happened. She believed God was taking care of us."

"She had a strong faith, your mother."

"God didn't pull weeds from the garden or gather us hand-me-down clothes from the church storeroom. That was Mama. And God didn't send money home to Mama all those years. That was me."

Nash studied the landscape, but wisely didn't reply.

The silence yawned between them. Finally, Ruby flapped a hand at him. "Go ahead. You want to say something. We've been honest with each other up until now."

He was uncomfortable under her scrutiny, and he didn't want to say anything to upset her.

"Go on. I might not agree, but I won't get mad."

He'd heard about her anger over the mistreated horses, and he'd seen her indignant about Jane's abuse, but he'd never seen her take offense. "I'm just a simple man, Ruby. I don't claim to have all the answers. But it seems to me that God does work in those ways. Through people."

The rain let up, and she tipped her head back to gaze at stars appearing from the darkness. "I thought she didn't care." Her tone was matter-of-fact.

He couldn't explain something like that. No one could. She was vulnerable where her father was concerned, and Nash respected her feelings. "Maybe your mother was being strong for you." A jagged streak of lightning in the distance caught his attention. A muted rumbled followed. The worst of the storm had moved on. "I wonder if Claire and Joel think I'm going on as though nothing has happened since their mom died. I'm just trying to keep things as normal as I can for them."

Ruby turned to look at him then. "Could be she was simply being strong for Pearl and me. I didn't make it any easier for Mama, that's for sure."

The added insight into Ruby's susceptibilities gave Nash more to think about.

"I dealt her fits and I was hard to get along with. Maybe I blamed her for him leaving. I don't know."

"You were just a kid."

"If I blamed her, then I didn't feel like it was my fault."

"It wasn't anyone's fault, you know."

"I know."

"He made the choice on his own."

She nodded absently. "He chose to go, and that means we weren't enough to hold him here—

none of us." She rubbed her upper arms. "And then I did the same thing to Mama. I ran off and didn't look back."

That statement surprised him more than anything else. He hadn't expected her to state the fact so plainly—almost like an admission. "You said you didn't regret leaving."

"I'm not sorry I had the experiences and did what I believed I needed to do at the time. I am sorry I hurt her."

He let her confession settle in his mind. "She never spoke unkindly of you, Ruby. Neither she or Pearl ever had a bad thing to say about you."

"She openeth her mouth with wisdom, and in her tongue is the law of kindness."

Nash couldn't have been more surprised. "Did you just quote Scripture?"

"I said I didn't set much store by it, but they did." Ruby took a deep breath, pulled up her shawl and hugged it around her shoulders. "It was just a tree."

Nash felt inadequate. After all his mental squawking about her selfishness and lack of commitment, he'd come to the astonishing conclusion that she was sincere. She'd been understanding and supportive of his family situation, while he'd done nothing but give her a bad time about hers. He had the urge to drape his arm over her shoulder and comfort her, but he stuffed his hands in his pockets instead. "I'm not one to give advice about fathers. I'm dealing with my own situation."

She laid her hand on his forearm, catching him by surprise.

"I wish I had something I could say to help," she said.

Her gesture of concern and caring took him aback. He shouldn't have been so surprised. Contrary to what he'd always believed about her—maybe what he'd *wanted* to believe about her—she'd shown nothing but kindness and empathy since she'd arrived. He gathered his thoughts. "I appreciate everything you've done. Being willing to take the children on short notice, being here for my mother."

"It's more like she's been here for me," Ruby told him. "It's been comforting to talk to someone who knew Mama so well."

He'd known Laura, too. But he hadn't been open to talking about her. He'd held Ruby at arm's length since she'd arrived.

He took his right hand out of his pocket and covered her hand on his arm. Her fingers were warm and slender. The innocent touch reminded him of how isolated he'd been. A deep sense of loneliness washed over him, chased by fleeting hope. The unexpected emotions were so powerful, he clung steadfast to his dignity.

"Georgia has helped me begin to deal with losing Mama. It's good to be able to talk about her and find out things I had wondered."

Nash hadn't been very helpful in the talking department. Ruby showing up had scared him from the get-go, and he hadn't been willing to listen to her or offer information or condolences. He'd resented her, and in the process had been downright unkind.

"Claire talks with me about her mother," Ruby told him. "Does she talk about her to you?"

"Sometimes, yes."

"You're not going on like nothing ever happened. You're just moving forward, like you have to. You're making their lives as full and normal as you can."

He swallowed hard. "With your help, now."

"At first I thought you were going to keep them away from me."

He hoped she would understand, but he didn't know how to explain. "I made a mistake."

With his hand still covering hers on his arm, she turned to face him. In the shadowy darkness, her surprise was evident. "A mistake about what?"

"I jumped to a lot of conclusions...about you."

"You had never met me."

"Right. So I shouldn't have formed opinions."

"You thought what anyone would think. And what everyone does think. You should have seen Ettie Harper's face the first time I went into town. She took one look at me and you'd think she'd eaten a sour pickle."

"That's what her face looks like all the time. Don't take offense."

Ruby laughed, and he chuckled, the tension dissipating between them. "Your mother came to my rescue when Audra addressed me at church. I didn't want to talk to her, because I didn't want to be in a position to explain myself."

"That's understandable," he answered. "I'm glad my mother knew what to do."

"As long as we're getting everything out in the open," Ruby went on, "I'm sorry I hit you with the skillet and tied you to the chair."

"I accept your apology, but you should probably avoid reminding me of that."

She accepted his teasing advice with a nod.

"I'm sorry I said you're not pretty."

She shrugged. "It doesn't matter."

"Yes, it does. I was being bitter and I wasn't kind. You're very pretty."

Her smile disappeared.

Nash freed his other hand and rested both

palms on her cheeks. Hesitantly, she gazed up into his eyes, and then her focus slid unerringly to his lips. This close, the scent of her hair was as fresh as the rain, while her shawl and nightgown smelled like sunshine. She'd had this same crazy, heart-tugging effect on him from the first time he'd laid eyes on her—and that's what had scared him. Like the bright yellow primrose that flourished in the rocks and sand across the plains, she was a surprising combination of feminine beauty and unwavering grit. Her irresistible appeal constantly set off warnings, but his caution had consistently and effectively been eroded by her closeness and his emotional hunger.

Nash did the unthinkable and slid his fingers into the soft, cool ringlets at her nape. Immediately sensitized, his fingertips sent awakening signals to the rest of his body. He had no choice now but to lean down and seal his lips against hers, draw in her heady scent and untangle his hands to gently fold her against his chest. She sighed against his mouth, trembling as she returned the kiss and grasped his shirtfront possessively in both fists.

Ruby didn't want these kisses to complicate their relationship. She wanted to relive the same heady feeling she'd known that day in the icehouse, but she didn't want to regret it. She didn't want him to regret her.

A lot of men had tried to kiss her. A few had succeeded. None had made her feel this all-consuming desire to return their affection, to possess everything available and fulfill a longing. Her reactions confused her. While it was exhilarating to feel something so intense and natural, the cautious part of her knew he was the wrong person to have feelings for. But his arms were strong and reassuring. He was grounded here on this land, knew what he wanted, had deep feelings for his children, his family, held dreams for the ranch. His solid dependability was as alluring as his kiss.

When had she become so unsure of herself, so hesitant to take what she wanted? When had she ever let sentimentality or opinions sway her? She didn't want to miss out on this small measure of happiness, even if she did regret it later.

She kissed him back without hesitation, wholly absorbed by the fire that ran through her limbs and brought a song to her heart. It was true his initial insults and rejection hadn't fazed her—because he'd meant nothing to her those first days. Now a warning undermined her joy. Allowing him to mean something to her made her vulnerable, and Ruby didn't allow herself to be vulnerable.

She'd been on her own for a long time. She didn't depend on anyone else for her livelihood or her happiness, but she had the same basic needs as everyone—the need for tenderness, the need to be appreciated, the desire to share a human connection.

Nash inched his face away from hers to whisper, "Ruby—"

"Don't," she hurried to say, and covered his lips with her fingers. "Don't spoil this moment with regret or guilt or anything else."

Nash wished he could see her eyes more clearly, read her expression. Surprisingly, he didn't sense any hesitation on her part. She clung to him, her firm, lush body and warm, responsive lips enticements beyond resistance. He'd known the first time he'd seen her, had taken one look at her mouth and known it would tie him in knots. And it had. She had. She didn't need to tie him to a chair to hold him prisoner. He was already captive to this woman, to her inner strength and her vitality, a combination of qualities that enhanced her beauty and appeal.

Daring to move aside her shawl, he ran his palms over her flimsy cotton nightgown, down the curve of her back to the swell of her hips, and held her against him, where she could plainly learn the extent of his desire.

The fingers she'd placed against his lips changed from a restraint to a caress. A heady, sensual caress. She ran the tip of one finger across his bottom lip to the corner of his mouth and back again. Lowering her hand to grasp his biceps and raise herself on tiptoe, she duplicated the caress with her tongue.

His every nerve ending stood at attention. She was a seductive temptress in a sweet maiden's body. The scents and textures of her hair and skin set him on fire, reminded him he was alive, reminded him he was a man.

"Do you want to go inside?" he asked.

Chapter Twenty

"Yes," she answered immediately.

"Upstairs?"

"Jane is in my bed."

"Will you come to mine?"

"If you want me."

He touched his forehead to hers. "I want you, Ruby."

She released his arms and gathered her shawl close.

He followed her inside, through the kitchen, and joined her on the stairs. She walked barefoot, and behind her he took caution not to make a sound with his boots. He led her to the open doorway and stood aside for her to enter his room.

"I'll make sure Jane is sleeping first," she whispered.

With a nod he pointed to the other rooms and moved in that direction. After assuring himself his son and daughter slept soundly in their beds, he returned to find Ruby waiting for him. He closed the door and twisted the key in the lock.

She met him as he turned back, flattening herself against him, pulling him close with her palms on his spine and pressing her cheek against his shirtfront. Nash tried with all his might not to draw a comparison, but he was human and the differences between this woman and her sister were glaring. The last person he wanted to think about right now was Pearl, but whether he wanted it to or not, his mind linked his experiences. Pearl had been shy and self-conscious, definitely passive and not particularly enthusiastic in the bedroom. Ruby had already shown more enthusiasm in the enflaming kisses they'd shared than her sister had in their entire marriage.

Nash drew those thoughts up short and banished them from his mind. He refused to do either woman a disservice by continuing to draw contrasts.

Intuitively, she asked, "Do you want me to go?"

"No." He loosened her shawl and backed her up so he could drop the drape on the foot of the bed. He took off his shirt and hung it on the bedpost. "I want you to stay."

Ruby untied the ribbon at the neck of her

nightdress and pulled the garment off over her head. Her mane of hair snagged and she untangled it, letting it fall over one shoulder. The warm glow suffusing the room created shadows and highlights on her curvy limbs and shapely breasts. Nash caught his breath in surprise and wonder at the exquisite gift she offered. The sight gave him sensual pleasure, but her openness spoke of profound trust. He drank in this woman like an intoxicating brew.

"Well?" she asked finally, gesturing toward him.

"You're beautiful," he managed to reply.

"I wasn't fishing for compliments," she said with a low laugh. "I was pointing out that you're still dressed."

Nash perched on the bed's edge to yank off his boots and socks, and next left his trousers on the pile. She studied him openly, apparently not uncomfortable or embarrassed. He walked to stand before her, and she placed her hands on his chest. His skin jumped at her touch.

"I don't expect anything from you, Nash. This isn't a commitment of any kind," she said in her low, ragged voice. "This is just you and I. No promises or expectations beyond tonight."

Should he be insulted at her lack of commitment? Or perhaps she simply didn't want him to feel obligated. His meager ounce of concern didn't outweigh the promise of this night with her. "No promises," he replied, as his lips touched hers and passion overcame reason.

She was every bit as supple and silky as he'd imagined. Her skin intoxicated him; the satiny feel of her hair on his chest and arms was an aphrodisiac. Ruby held nothing back. She gave herself to this act as completely as she did in every other aspect of life, a willing, unreserved partner. He lost himself to the sensations, to the sounds and textures and tension. She spoke her encouragement in a raspy, full-throated whisper that was his undoing. He couldn't get enough of her. The press and tug, the brush and pull. Minutes passed that painfully stole his breath, but made him yearn to have the night last forever.

How had he ever said she was not beautiful? How had he resisted falling at her feet in adulation when he'd first laid eyes on her? How would he ever keep his word about making no promises to each other? Her incoherent murmurs fueled his ardor, but his only desire now was to please her. To *reach* her. To hear his name from her lips. Nash gave himself to this woman wholeheartedly. There was never a guarantee for tomorrow, so he let himself live for tonight, for the pleasure and comfort he found in Ruby's embrace. Tomorrow would take care of itself.

He woke before dawn to find she'd gone. He could smell her on the sheets, on his skin, closed his eyes and tasted her on his lips. His heart beat in a different cadence now. He was more aware of the weight of his body against the mattress, the feel of his skin against the sheets. He had changed. And the transformation scared him. He couldn't afford to take chances.

Their encounter had created no expectations, she'd said. Similar to how her previous life had lacked commitments. He'd ignored her words at the time—or pretended they meant nothing—but the reality stung now.

He'd fought his feelings so hard because he'd instinctively known that falling for Ruby would be a big mistake.

Had been a big mistake.

His biggest concern should be his children and Jane. While Ruby had taken charge and seemed to genuinely care for all three, she'd known only a life without obligation. She'd done exactly what she wanted, without regret, and last night she'd wanted the companionship and comfort he offered. Maybe she'd needed the reassurance that she was desirable.

He'd walked into this with his eyes wide open to her nature.

Nash stood, and the first thing he noticed was the portrait of his fair-haired wife on the bureau. Pearl gazed back at him as trustingly as she always had. She'd been committed to him, to the ranch, to their children and to her mother—no matter how hard things got.

He was making comparisons again, but how could he not? He was a man who faced reality. He couldn't kid himself. Ruby didn't want to make promises.

The smell of coffee diverted his attention, and he dressed quickly. When he reached the kitchen, Ruby didn't avoid his eyes. She met his gaze in her straightforward manner, and unexpected warmth rose from under his collar. He should have been the one to use better judgment.

She held out a steaming cup of coffee, a familiar challenge in her eyes. This was steadier ground.

He took the cup from her, and their fingers brushed. His jerked just enough to spill a few drops of the hot liquid on his thumb.

They were alone in the kitchen, the kindling in the stove crackling. The children hadn't awakened yet, so the atmosphere was uncomfortably intimate.

"No promises," he said, but his tone was nothing like the one he'd used the previous night. The words held a bitter taste on his tongue. Looking at her made him feel as though the floor was shaking under his boots. He wanted to promise her a lifetime. He wanted her to ask him for more. Demand more.

"No promises," she confirmed, without even a heartbeat's delay.

He turned and rested the cup on the edge of the table while he grabbed his hat and opened the door. "I will tell Jane tonight. At supper. It's not fair to leave her wondering what will happen to her."

"Yes, of course," Ruby answered.

He closed the door behind him.

Ruby had been holding her body stiff, so she deliberately relaxed her shoulders. She'd made a lot of impetuous mistakes in her life. She took a deep breath now, hoping last night hadn't been another of them. The lightning bolt hitting the tree had opened up old wounds before she'd had a chance to disguise them. The vulnerability she'd shown unnerved her.

She thought over every minute of what had happened between them. Nash was a widower. A man who'd been without his wife for two years. They'd talked about their fathers. That had probably been a mistake. He'd told her she was beautiful, but that meant nothing. Did she think just because she'd taken over the care of his children that she had any right to move into her sister's place in his affections? Or into his bed?

Ruby felt sick to her stomach at her presumptuousness. She stirred the mush she'd made for the children's breakfast and removed it from the heat. She regretted her rash actions. She lamented making things tense between Nash and herself.

What would Pearl think of this development? What would her mother think? Ruby took a brave look into her heart of hearts to admit what it was she wanted and what she thought. That's all she'd ever cared about, but this time she didn't want to hurt anyone in the process.

Even if she set her mind to it, Ruby didn't know if she could muster up any remorse over how Nash had made her feel the night before.

She put a lid on the pan. She had time to take care of Vivo before she woke the youngsters.

Nash spotted Ruby letting Vivo into the pasture. For a moment he considered heading the other way, but instead he watched. The horse thrived under her care.

Much like the children.

He was conflicted over his feelings. Sure one minute, uncertain the next. How long did he suppose it would take for her to prove herself to him? Six months? A year? Who was he to decide when she had done penance and could be trusted? He felt ashamed that he'd been so narrow-minded in the first place.

If he'd learned anything about her last night, it was that she'd been hurt by her father's abandonment. And then she'd lost the rest of her family. Learning about Claire and Joel had given her great joy. And she'd been eager to make a home for Jane.

How could Nash know the right thing to do next?

That morning he checked the mares with new foals and rode the fence line, making certain it was secure. A team of gray horses pulled a canvas-covered wagon along the road, and he trotted out to meet it. A weary-looking couple sat on the seat, and two youngsters poked their heads out from the interior.

"We're the Parkers," the man called to Nash. "Traveling to Sutton from Illinois."

"You still have a long way to go." Nash removed his hat and nodded to the man's wife. "Ma'am."

"I'm going to work at the lumberyard in Sutton, and my wife is a schoolteacher."

"Name's Nash Sommerton. You're welcome to stay on my land for a spell if you need to rest. There's a pretty stream just over the rise, with elders and cottonwoods for shade. And if you come by the house around suppertime—" he pointed in the direction of his home "—my sister-in-law is a good cook. She'd like the company."

"That's kind of you, Mr. Sommerton."

They waved, and Mr. Parker led the team off the road toward the refuge Nash had mentioned. Nash watched them go, thinking about the courage and determination it took to uproot a family and move them to a new location. He'd seen plenty of people traveling through Nebraska in his lifetime.

He'd been fortunate to start his ranch where he'd been raised. The land had been established, the house built, and he was near his family. People took opportunities wherever they found them, hoping for the best. Planning for the future.

He'd been confident in his plan, focused on buying horses, growing feed, breeding stock—and then everything had changed.

Laura's death had been a tragedy, but Pearl's death had shaken him to the core. He'd never imagined raising Claire and Joel without her.

He'd always thought there would be more time. He was a short-sighted man.

Stubborn. Demanding.

He didn't want to make the same mistakes all over again. The thought of asking Ruby to marry him had flitted through his mind, but she was adventurous and independent. She didn't need him, not like Pearl had needed him. Ruby had gotten along just fine on her own until now.

He slid from Boone's back, took the reins and walked the horse along the fence to release the tension his thoughts created in his limbs.

So she didn't need him for her livelihood or security. She'd told him she didn't want to make any promises, but maybe she wanted someone to make *her* promises. She'd been crestfallen that her name wouldn't be on Jane's adoption papers. If they were married, the legal complications wouldn't be a question. They would be a couple adopting a child together. Maybe she needed him so she could be a parent to Jane. So they could share in the role of parents.

Maybe she needed a reason to stay.

He shouldn't be so nervous. If she said no, things couldn't get more awkward than they already were.

He climbed into the saddle and galloped back to the stable, where he took off his shirt, pumped water and washed up beside the old barn. He got a clean shirt from his stash in the deserted bunkhouse and headed for the house.

Ruby looked up as Nash approached the porch where she sat with Jane and Claire. Joel was napping upstairs.

"Papa!" Claire set down her slate and came to wrap her arms around his waist.

"Hi, sweet pea. Miss Jane. Am I interrupting your studies? I need to talk to Aunt Ruby."

"They can use a break," Ruby answered. She laid down the book she held.

"Maybe over in the shade?" he asked.

She fell into step beside him. "Is anything wrong? Does this have something to do with Jane?"

"In a manner."

Ruby let Nash lead the way across the grassy lawn to the windbreak, hoping he wasn't going to bring up the previous night—or apologize. Her heartbeat got erratic at the thought of both what had happened and the idea of talking about it. She wasn't embarrassed or ashamed, but she certainly didn't want to hear him say he was sorry.

"Before you tell me you're sorry—" she started.

"I'm not sorry."

"Oh." She hung her hands at her sides and

glanced away, then back. His black hair was damp and his tanned skin glowed pink from a recent scrubbing. The strip of paler skin on his forehead revealed where the brim of his hat usually shaded his face. He smelled like soap and horse and sunshine. "Well, all right."

She waited.

"Not for last night, anyway," he said.

She thought of his hot kisses, his defined torso in the lamplight, the sounds and sensations of their intimacy, and a quiver started in her belly. *He wasn't sorry.*

"I am sorry I didn't give you the benefit of the doubt from the beginning."

"We talked about that. You didn't know me."

"And I'm sorry it took me so long to see you. I mean, *really* see you."

That admission must have cost him, but his expression was sincere.

"And I'm sorry you lost your mother and your sister. I added to your grief by not acknowledging how much you were hurting."

Ruby's throat felt tight and her eyes stung. She blinked, but held his dark gaze. She'd been so painfully alone, grasping at Georgia's friendship, hanging on the woman's stories of her mother, wanting desperately to belong and to have the love of her niece and nephew. Clinging to the idea that Jane would somehow be her own family...

Ruby wasn't comfortable with the susceptibility his recognition of her feelings created. He'd taken her by surprise, so it took her a few moments to pull her thoughts together. "You came in the middle of the day to say this?"

He pursed his lips and spread one hand on his thigh. He was obviously biting his tongue.

"I'm surprised, is all," she added quickly. "I don't know what to say." She thought about their history. "No, that's wrong. I do know what to say." She gave a little nod to affirm her decision. "I don't blame you for any of those things. You had your own hurt to deal with, and I'm responsible for what I did. But I forgive you."

He relaxed his shoulders.

A pair of barn swallows swooped in the direction of the poplars, disappearing into the branches, and a yellow-and-white-striped cat stared after them, swishing its tail in the grass.

"I've done a lot of thinking," Nash said.

"You certainly have."

"I don't want you to make me any promises. But I want to make a few to you."

She raised a hand to object.

"Hear me out," he insisted. "We signed a legal agreement for the horses. That's business. But the children are not business."

"Of course not."

"Adopting Jane will be legal, but it shouldn't be business, either."

"What do you mean?"

"I mean we should be family. All of us. Your name needs to be on the adoption papers with mine."

"But—"

"If you and I get married, we can be a family. We will both be Jane's parents. As well as Claire and Joel's."

"Married?"

"Don't tell me it never entered your mind."

"You *are* feeling guilty."

"No! No, I said I wasn't sorry."

"Sorry isn't the same as guilty."

He ran his fingers through his hair and grasped the back of his neck. "You are a frustrating woman."

"One you want to be married to?"

He dropped his hand to his side. "Yes. I promise to make a good husband. Faithful. Hardworking. I promise to always be here for you and the children. I can't say I'll never make mistakes or be stubborn about things, but I promise I will work on my faults."

Faithful...always be here. An acute ache arrowed through Ruby's chest. "You can't promise not to die."

Chapter Twenty-One

A knot formed between Nash's eyebrows. "You're right. I can't promise not to die. No one can do that. But I can promise that as long as I draw breath, I will stay on this ranch and be your husband."

She swallowed past the lump in her throat.

His expression softened.

The last thing she had anticipated today was a proposal of marriage. "Is this the most impulsive thing you've ever done?"

"I thought about it before I said anything."

"I know about being impulsive, and thinking about getting married to me is impulsive."

"It's logical," he added.

She put her hands on her hips and ducked her head for a moment, thinking. Thinking his suggestion was not the least bit romantic. Did she care? Was a fanciful proposal what she wanted or expected?

Could she simply step into Pearl's shoes and take on the responsibility of rearing the children, much as she was already doing? What would be different?

Warmth spread through her body, and her skin tingled in all the places it had touched his last night. Joy and pain warred in her chest until a pressure built. She placed a hand against her breast and straightened, concentrating on breathing in and out.

She looked into his mahogany eyes, searching for sincerity, craving an answer there.

Everything would be different if she agreed. They would share more nights like the previous. She would lie beside him each night until morning. She would be...*his wife.*

It terrified Ruby to acknowledge how much she wanted all that. Even if she became merely the fill-in wife, belonging was better than being an outsider.

She didn't doubt his promises. He wasn't like her father. Maybe Pearl would want this for her—for them. Pearl would want them both to be happy. And she could be happy married to him.

"You can have some time to think it over," Nash said. "We don't have to say more to Jane than to assure her she'll be staying here for good."

"All right. I'll think about it."

His gaze flickered over her hair and back to her face. "Is there anything you want to ask me?"

"I don't think so. Is there something else you want to tell me?"

He raised his eyebrows as though he'd just had a thought. "I invited a family for supper. The Parkers. Two youngsters, I think. They're passing through on their way to Sutton."

The change of subject derailed her train of thought. "Oh. All right. I'll make enough."

"I didn't think you'd mind the company."

"I won't."

He glanced toward the house.

Aside from the night she'd hit him over the head with a skillet, this had been the most peculiar encounter they'd ever had. They stood three feet apart, discussing marriage and the rest of their lives as though the prospect was unemotional.

"Is there anything you'd like to ask *me*?" she wondered aloud.

He studied her, and it was plain he was thinking how to phrase something. "About last night," he began.

"Were you disappointed?"

He blinked and widened his eyes. "No! Ruby, I was far from disappointed."

"What then?"

"I was not the first."

Her gaze didn't waver. "Does it matter?"

"No. It doesn't."

"I loved someone once."

Those simple words said everything without saying anything. Maybe someday she could tell him about the man she'd once foolishly believed loved her, and whom she'd hoped to marry.

"Did he hurt you?"

"Not as much as I hurt myself."

Nash tilted his head...raised his hand and skimmed her cheek with the backs of his fingers.

His gentle caress sent an enchanting tingle across her neck and shoulders.

"I shouldn't have asked."

"It's not a secret. I just don't think about him anymore."

He slid his palm down her arm to take hold of her hand. "What do you say we tell Jane now? Together?"

Ruby clasped his strong hand. "Yes."

Jane accepted the news with her usual restraint. "I don't have to go back to the Billingses? Or to an orphanage ever again?"

"Never," Nash assured her. "You will stay right here on the ranch and go to school with Claire. Your name will be Sommerton."

Jane gave him a solemn stare. "Like yours."

"Just like mine. We'll be family."

She looked at Claire. "Is it all right with you? I ain't your real family."

Claire looked to her father as though gauging his expression before answering. "I don't want you to leave. We're going to be real sisters."

Jane beamed at Claire's unquestioning acceptance. Her face was already fuller and held more color than it had only a few weeks ago. She looked up at Nash. "What will I call you?"

"You can call me whatever feels right," Nash said. "Claire and Joel call me Papa. You can call me Father or Daddy, or stick with Nash for a while."

"Okay."

Jane shot forward, pressed herself against Ruby's skirts and buried her face there, wrapping trembling arms around her legs.

Ruby disentangled them and knelt so she could hug the girl, whose whole body shook.

"I ain't never had no one to read to me or sleep close by when I'm scared. I din't know there was people what cared if I had clothes without holes or shoes that din't hurt my feet. I saw other young'uns with mamas and daddies, but I din't never think somebody would want to be mine."

Ruby's throat closed and tears stung her eyes.

She felt terribly selfish for feeling alone after she'd grown up with people who loved her. And guilty for leaving the mother who had always been there for her, even though Ruby hadn't appreciated her beliefs.

Jane straightened, loosening her hold on Ruby, and directed her next words at Nash. "Ain't nobody ever forgave me just because it was the right thing to do, neither. 'Ceptin' you."

Nash gave her a crooked smile, and he didn't try to speak.

"You know that question you asked me earlier?" Ruby said, looking at him around Jane's shoulder.

He kept his smile in place, but lifted his chin in acknowledgment.

Ruby waited the briefest of moments for a ripple of panic to subside. "The answer is yes."

Ruby had the table set and a bouquet of blue asters in an ironstone pitcher in the center when the Parkers arrived.

"I'm John. This here's my wife, Maggie. That's Little John and Rosie."

Their clothing was clean, though wrinkled as though they'd recently unpacked it. The youngsters both appeared older than Claire.

"I'm Ruby, Nash's sister-in-law."

The couple darted glances at the others in the room, perhaps pondering the whereabouts of Nash's wife. "I brought you this," Maggie said, holding out a jar of light, clear honey. "We traded for a couple of jars yesterday."

"Thank you." Ruby took the honey. "I'm so glad you've come to join us for supper. It's nothing fancy. I'm still learning."

Nash introduced Silas and Dugger, as well as the children, and Ruby showed everyone where to sit while she brought the rest of the food to the table. She had prepared a beef roast, with potatoes and gravy, along with cooked turnips and pickled beets.

"Just wait till you try Ruby's biscuits," Nash said.

"I'll open the jar of honey." Ruby used a towel to loosen the lid. "This will be a treat."

"Tender beef is a treat, Mrs..." John paused awkwardly.

"It's Miss Dearing, but call me Ruby."

"You're a widower, Mr. Sommerton?" John asked.

"Yes."

"I'm sorry."

Ruby checked the tabletop, making sure everything was perfect before sitting between Jane and Claire. "You're headed for Sutton?"

John went on to explain how they were starting over after factory closings in Illinois. They'd
heard good reports from his brother already living in Nebraska.

Ruby enjoyed having the Parker family join
them. She made a second pot of coffee and
brewed tea for herself and Maggie. When the
others went out to sit on the porch, Silas took
over the dishes and shooed her from the kitchen.

The children played tag in the yard, and even
Jane joined their game. When Rose chased and
caught her, they both fell to the ground in a pile
of girlish giggles.

Ruby and Nash exchanged a look of surprise.
"I've never heard her laugh like that," Ruby said.

At Maggie's curious expression, Ruby explained how Jane had come to live with them.

"That's a heartwarming story." Maggie wiped
a finger under her eye. "We don't hear enough
about people's kindness. The both of you are gen-
erous. You're making a big commitment."

"I believe we're fortunate to be able to take
another child," Nash answered.

He was so right. As soon as Ruby had declared Jane wasn't going back to the Billingses',
welcoming her had never been a question. Ruby
wasn't entirely familiar with Nash's financial sta-
tus, but there was no lack in this home. They had

plenty to eat. The barn and the stable were filled with healthy stock—more born every day—and apparently he paid Silas and Dugger year-round. They were fortunate.

She had agreed to marry him, so talking about money was something they would need to do shortly.

"I just remembered something." Nash got up, headed around the corner of the house and returned a few minutes later with a pottery jug and a stack of short tumblers. "I had this tucked away for a special occasion. Who would like a drink of Kentucky whiskey?"

John accepted his offer. Maggie smiled and nodded.

"Ruby?" Nash asked, after he'd served their guests.

"I'll try a little, thanks."

He poured an inch into a glass and handed it to her.

"To new beginnings," he said, lifting his own drink.

"New beginnings," the Parkers echoed.

Ruby raised her glass, meeting Nash's gaze without missing his underlying meaning. The Parkers were starting over, yes, but she had only just agreed to become his wife.

She took a drink of the peppery liquid and it

heated her mouth and tongue, fiery all the way down her throat. "My mama would have chased us into the next county if she'd seen us drinking whiskey on her porch."

Nash grinned. "Why do you think I had this hidden in the stable for so long?"

John chuckled and held out his glass for a refill. "She sounds like my mama." He spoke of the factory closings in Illinois.

Maggie talked about the previous month's opening of the expansion bridge in New York, connecting the boroughs. "It was under construction for thirteen years," she said.

"I read about it." Ruby nodded. "The original designer died, and his son took over construction. His wife helped him oversee the work."

"I have a newspaper with photographs of the crowd and the ships in the bay the day the bridge opened," John told them.

Nash offered to show him the stable, and Flint in particular.

"Can I come see Flint, too?" Jane asked.

Nash glanced at Ruby, who nodded approvingly.

"Jane spends as much time with that horse as she can manage," Ruby told the other woman, when the others had left. "I suspect she will become quite a horsewoman, especially under Nash's training."

The women visited until Jane returned, the men following.

"I got my fiddle from the back of my saddle," John said, holding up a highly varnished violin.

"Play for our hosts," Maggie suggested.

"Do you mind if I bring a chair from the kitchen?" her husband asked.

Nash headed for the door. "I'll get one for you."

Once John was settled he spent a minute testing the sound, making sure the strings were in tune, and then, with nimble fingers, he drew the bow across them, coaxing forth a lively rendition of "My Grandfather's Clock."

Maggie added her voice to the music. "My grandfather's clock was too large for the shelf, so it stood ninety years on the floor. It was taller by half than the old man himself, though it weighed not a pennyweight more."

The children had come to the porch and gathered on the floor. Little John and Rose sang "Tick tock, tick tock," at the chorus, and by the third verse Claire and Jane joined in.

The song came to an end and everyone applauded.

"Aunt Ruby can sing, too!" Claire exclaimed. "Play something she can sing, please?"

"Yes, please," Maggie coaxed.

John suggested a few songs to Ruby, and together they agreed on a key. He adjusted his posture, raised the bow, and within moments mellow-toned notes flowed from the instrument. Ruby had listened to many musicians, and recognized John as an accomplished player.

"Beautiful dreamer," she began. "Wake unto me. Starlight and dewdrops are waiting for thee…"

The children listened, slack-jawed. Maggie clasped her hands together on her breast, and John gave Ruby a wink.

"Sounds of the rude world, heard in the day, lulled by the moonlight have all passed away."

Ever since he'd first heard about Ruby, Nash had known she'd left home to perform onstage. The first time he'd heard her speak, he'd been taken aback because she didn't have the smooth, melodic tone associated with a singer.

But she sang like nothing else he'd ever heard, the low, raspy quality of her voice provoking an emotional response. Though he'd heard the song many times, he'd never experienced anything like Ruby's seductive rendition of the words.

Her gift touched the listener. Touched Nash.

No wonder the Turkish woman had given Ruby her beloved horse. When she sang the sentimental words, his soul quieted, his heartbeat changed cadence. He hung on every nuance of the ballad-like melody.

John softly harmonized on the last words. "Gone are the cares of life's busy throng, beautiful dreamer, awake unto me."

Ruby's haunting voice and the notes of the fiddle faded into the night.

Nash finally took a breath, and the ragged sound sliced the silence.

"Land sakes, Ruby, that was beautiful," Maggie finally managed to sigh.

"Thank you." She brushed aside the compliment. "John is the true artist. You have a way with that violin, Mr. Parker. Would anyone care for another cup of coffee? Tea, Maggie?"

"Much obliged, but we'd better turn in," John replied. "Daybreak comes awfully early, and we'll be heading out at first light."

Like an old married couple, Nash and Ruby stood together under the stars and watched their guests ride out.

"I'm glad you invited them," she said, after the sound of the horses' hooves had faded.

"This makes me sound pretty dense, but I had no idea, Ruby. I've never heard anything as...as beautiful as your singing." He cocked his head. "You didn't sing in church."

"I wouldn't blend in," she said with a shrug.

"No, I don't suppose you would," he said from beside her.

"We should get the children in bed."

She had turned halfway around when he caught her arm. "Have you ever thought, Ruby, that maybe you're not intended to blend in?"

Slowly, she faced him. "What do you mean?"

He released his gentle hold and paused thoughtfully for a moment. "If a person looks into our corrals, they see a lot of brown horses. Some with black manes and tails, others with white markings, but they're all pretty much the same. Only a few stand out from the rest. Vivo. The Duchess. Individuality was bred into them."

"You're comparing me to a horse?"

He scratched his jaw with a thumb. "Not very flattering, is it?"

She shrugged.

"Okay." He took her hand and tugged her to stand right beside him. He tipped his head back. "Look up."

"Hadn't we better get the children ready for bed?"

"Look up."

She sighed. And tipped her head back to observe the star-studded expanse of night sky.

"What do you see?" he asked.

"A lot of stars."

"Yes. But really look now."

A bigger and brighter star caught her attention, and she focused on it. How could she have missed it? She pointed. "I see that one."

"Among all those millions of stars, one stands out."

"Doesn't that mean it's closer than all the rest?"

"For a dreamer, you're awfully logical."

She looked at him. "You think I'm a dreamer?"

He lowered his gaze to her face. "Nothing wrong with that. I'm saying you're a bright star."

He had changed so much she barely recognized the words coming from his mouth. "I don't want to be a star, Nash. Maybe you're the dreamer."

"Maybe I am."

The warmth and strength of his hand comforted and supported her, even if she didn't believe his words.

"Shall we plan a wedding?" he asked.

Chapter Twenty-Two

"Shall we get married in church?" Nash asked.

His question was unexpected. She'd agreed to marry him—she wanted to marry him—but she hadn't thought through how it would happen. "Were you and Pearl married at church?"

"This isn't about Pearl and me. This is about us, and I'm hoping to arrange something that pleases *you*. I could make arrangements at the courthouse and we could take our vows when we get the final papers for Jane's adoption. Or we could ask Reverend Colson to come to my parents' home."

Ruby considered his suggestions. It was likely he and Pearl had been married at the church in Crosby, with friends and family in attendance. Ruby didn't believe doing the same would be true to her own character, and even though the churchgoers she'd seen recently were nice enough, she didn't consider them her friends yet.

Ruby didn't want to take anything away from Jane by being married on the same day her adoption was finalized. They should plan a separate celebration for that occasion.

But being married at the Sommertons', with only family and perhaps Dugger and Silas present, sounded nice. "Could we have the ceremony outside at your folks'? Maybe on the lawn or under the shade trees?"

"That sounds perfect. We'll ride out and talk to my mother in the morning." He still didn't release her hand. "Ruby. I want to do things right."

"What do you mean?" she asked.

"I don't have regrets about the night we spent together, and it's not that I don't want to make love to you again. Because I do. But I want to honor you and our marriage. It might not be easy to wait, but I don't think we should let that happen again until we've been properly married."

She offered him an easy smile. "Let's get the sleepyheads to bed."

The following morning Nash set the brake on the buckboard and helped Ruby down before assisting Claire and Joel. Jane climbed over the side and used the spokes of the wheel to step to the ground. He led them to the back door, where Mrs. Gentry greeted them. "Come into the kitchen, young ones, and have some cinnamon buns fresh from the oven."

The warm kitchen smelled of yeast and spices.

"Your mother is upstairs. Seems your father didn't have a good night."

Nash took the stairs two at a time. He rapped on the beveled mahogany door, which sat ajar, before pushing it open. "Mother?"

Georgia sat on a chair beside the bed in the semidark room. The curtains were still drawn. "Miles?"

"No, it's me. What's wrong with him?" Nash crossed to the bed.

"He was in pain most of the night. Miles was concerned that perhaps it was his heart, and he's gone to see Dr. Morris to consult about medicine." She leaned toward her son. "I sent Winter to fetch Little Bird. She should have been here by now."

Nash rested a hand on his mother's shoulder. "She probably took time to pack her herbs."

"Stop whispering, the both of you, and open the curtains," Cosmo said, from where he lay against the pillows.

Nash hurried closer and lowered himself to sit on the bed, while Georgina complied and let in light. "Mother says you had a bad night."

"Your mother worries too much. Miles, too. He told me to lie here, when I have work to do."

The floorboards creaked as Ruby entered the room, and she went straight to Georgia and rested her arm around her shoulders. Nash was thankful for her supportive presence.

"Don't worry about the mill right now," he told Cosmo. "I'm sure Tucker will know how to handle anything that might come up. If he needs more help, I'll go."

"Thank you, son. You know, don't you, that I'm proud of you?"

"I know."

"I wasn't keen on the idea when you wanted to leave the mill behind and start your ranch. I always thought you'd be taking over the business one of these days. But I see how hard you've worked and everything you've sacrificed. You've done well."

"It means a lot for you to say that."

His mother sniffled behind him.

"Maybe one of these days, when you're ready to sit on the porch and take life easy, Tucker will take over. He's been at your side a long time."

"He's a good man, your sister's husband. He'll do a good job of it."

About twenty minutes later Miles returned.

"I was able to get a few doses of medicines

from Dr. Morris," he said. "I want to observe you today, though, before making a decision." At Cosmo's bedside, he turned the covers back and probed his father's ankle.

"What are you looking for?" Nash asked.

"Swelling."

Georgia stood beside Miles. "Would that be bad?"

"It would simply mean I'd need to give him something to remove the extra fluid."

Nash glanced at his mother, finding her concern evident. "Do you think it would be a good idea to have David Morris take a look at him himself?"

"I *am* a doctor, Nash," Miles pointed out.

"I know. But you're also close to the patient."

"That doesn't cloud my judgment."

"Nash," Ruby said softly.

He glanced toward her, thinking she meant to moderate his argument, but instead she gestured to where Little Bird stood just inside the room. The Cheyenne woman's movements had been soundless.

His mother hurried to greet her. "Little Bird. I'm so glad you're here. Thank you."

On moccasined feet Little Bird padded to Cosmo's bedside. She greeted Nash. "Boone said the wind brings change to your heart."

Nash had tethered the horse near the porch. "Boone knows things before I do sometimes," he replied with a wry grin.

She turned to his father. "Cosmo Sommerton," she said. "You did not expect yesterday's path to lead you where it has."

"I suppose that about sums it up," he replied.

She placed her palm against the front of his shirt. "Your spirit has always been content at your fire. The years have not changed that."

Miles laid a protective hand on his father's arm. "Who are you?"

"I'm sorry," Georgia said quickly. "Miles, this is Little Bird. Little Bird, this is—".

"The son of Cosmo Sommerton." Little Bird nodded.

"News travels fast in Crosby," he replied.

"I do not journey to Crosby," she told him.

"Little Bird is a friend of our family," Georgia said. "She has treated all of us at one time or another."

Miles raised his eyebrows. "You brought a medicine woman?"

"She's a healer," Nash said.

"He was in pain all night," Georgia interrupted.

"Place your hand on the pain," Little Bird instructed Cosmo.

"Let's leave them," Ruby said to Nash.

He met her at the door. Too many people probably added to his father's discomfort. She led him downstairs, where Miles immediately joined them on the back porch.

"Your Indian friend asked me to leave, too."

"My mother trusts Little Bird," Nash said. "There's no harm in seeing what she thinks. It's nothing against you, Miles. It's just that she's taken care of our family, the workers at the mill, even our neighbors, for a good many years."

Miles set his mouth in a firm line. "If the pain starts again, I want you to let me do what I need to."

Nash agreed. He glanced at Ruby. "I thought about going for Vivian, but maybe we should wait until we know more."

Mrs. Gentry carried out a tray with cups, poured coffee and then served cinnamon buns. "It's not my decision, but it seems there's no reason to upset your sister until you know whether or not there's a problem."

"What do you say we wait an hour?" Ruby suggested.

"You're both probably right," Nash said. "Mother didn't send for us. We just showed up."

His eyes met Ruby's and, remembering what they'd come for, she felt her cheeks warm. She wanted to tell him it would be all right if they needed to wait. They couldn't think about getting married while Cosmo's health was precarious.

After drinking her coffee, Ruby joined the children in the kitchen, where they sorted worn playing cards into stacks at the table.

"I've written down my cinnamon bun recipe for you," Mrs. Gentry told her.

Ruby smiled. "That was thoughtful. I had to buy a book with basic recipes, because even though I had quite a few that were my mother's, none of the ordinary dishes are explained."

"No one looks worse for the wear," the kindly woman assured her. "You must be doing very well."

"Is Grandpa going to be all right?" Claire asked.

"Your grandfather is going to be just fine." Georgia swept into the kitchen. "Little Bird would like some boiled water. Is there hot water in the reservoir?"

Mrs. Gentry scooped a panful into an iron-stone pitcher.

"She says it's merely indigestion," Georgia called to the men on the porch.

Miles loomed outside the screen door. "What's she planning to give him?"

"She's grinding peppermint leaves and ginger root right now. I have to get back with the water."

Through the screen, Ruby exchanged a look with Nash. He was obviously as relieved as Georgia had been. Miles had been raised in the city and had attended medical school. Trusting his father's health to Little Bird was probably the last thing he wanted to do. As another newcomer to this family, she felt her heart go out to him. He went upstairs twice within the following hour, checking on his father and the treatment.

Mrs. Gentry had taken the children out to pick berries when Little Bird and Georgia entered the kitchen. At the latter woman's smile, Ruby took a deep breath.

Nash stood from where he'd been sitting at the table with a cold cup of coffee. "He's doing all right?"

Miles turned from the open door.

"He's just fine," Georgia assured them. "Last night he ate quite a few of those peppers he's so fond of. I don't think he'll ask for them again."

"I am leaving your mother a supply of ginger root." Little Bird adjusted the leather bag she wore with a strap across her chest. "I showed her how to prepare it."

"I'll bring some beef by for you later in the week," Nash told her.

She offered him a warm smile. "I will make jerky for the winter."

Nash gestured toward the door with a thumb. "I'll get your horse. But please wait a few more minutes."

Ruby's pulse sped up. She sensed what he was about to say, and she understood that Little Bird was a close enough friend to be included in the announcement.

He surprised Ruby, though, by stepping near and taking her hand.

Georgia's palm went to her breast. She blinked, wide-eyed in anticipation.

Nash didn't waste any time. "Ruby and I are going to get married."

Georgia looked from one of them to the other. "Do the children know?"

"Yes, and I can't believe they didn't spill a word about it," Ruby answered. "The day didn't go how we'd planned. We came to tell you, and then everything spun in a different direction."

"Well—well…" Georgia stammered for a moment and then said, "That's wonderful news. I couldn't be happier for both of you."

Relieved, Ruby blinked away tears as Nash's mother embraced her. "I'm so thankful to hear you say that."

"Of course I'm happy."

Mrs. Gentry hugged Nash and then Ruby.

Miles stuck out a hand to congratulate Nash. He nodded at Ruby. "The surprises just keep coming."

"Ruby and I were hoping we could be married here," Nash told Georgia. "Outside, with Reverend Colson doing the ceremony."

"Yes, of course!" Georgia exclaimed. "When?"

"Soon," they said at the same time.

"If it's convenient, of course," Ruby added.

Georgia clasped her hands in front of her. "We have a lot of planning to do." She looked at Nash. "You will need to tell Vivian. She can help. Why don't you stay for supper? Your father is getting dressed now. I was too concerned about him today to plan food, but we'll figure out something and celebrate." She touched Little Bird's arm. "Please join us."

The Cheyenne woman seemed surprised at the invitation, but she accepted.

Georgia had always been accepting and gracious, but her ready pleasure over their announcement touched Ruby. Their upcoming union was practical in every way, and perhaps that's why Georgia hadn't been taken aback. Maybe she'd even been expecting it.

While Nash rode to invite Vivian and Tucker, Ruby pitched in, and the women prepared a meal, browning slices of ham in one skillet and frying potatoes in another.

Soon Vivian entered the kitchen, having already heard all the news from her brother. She hugged her mother, congratulated Ruby with heartfelt words, and hurried to check on her father.

Once everyone was seated around the table, Cosmo said a blessing and the platters were passed.

"We have two celebrations to plan," Georgia said to the children. "Your papa and Aunt Ruby told us they're going to get married, and we're going to have a party right here."

"With cake?" Joel asked.

"Oh, yes, with cake," Tucker answered with a grin. "That's almost the best part of a wedding."

Vivian elbowed him good-naturedly.

"What's the other party?" Claire asked.

"Soon after the wedding, we will go to the courthouse and sign the legal papers for Jane's adoption," Nash replied. "She will be your sister for good. We will have another party just for Jane."

Claire clapped.

Jane's gaze flitted from one face to the next, giving each person present a shy smile.

"Mama and Grandma Laura would be happy

to see our family now," Claire said, in her sweet and guileless manner. "Do you think they can see us from heaven?"

Ruby believed Pearl would approve of her marrying Nash. Possibly her mother, too, since she thought so much of him. They might simply be thankful the children were being well cared for.

"If they can see us, they are certainly smiling," Georgia assured her granddaughter. "I'm sure of it."

Ruby met Georgia's gaze.

"Can I see the papers when you get them?" Jane asked, surprising all of them by speaking in front of the gathering.

"Yes, of course," Nash told her.

"I want to read my name," she explained. "I can read some words now, so I want to read my name on the papers."

Ruby gave her a warm smile. "Jane has worked hard to learn her letters and numbers. She's a bright girl. She'll be ready for school when the session begins."

"I can read some of the words in the Hans Brinker book," Jane boasted. "And in Robin Hood's adventure book."

"I can, too!" Claire piped in.

"You're both clever girls," Ruby assured them.

While they cleaned up after the meal, Ruby said to Georgia, "I have been thinking about the quilt we've almost finished."

"What about it? It's going to be lovely."

"I'd like to give the first one to Jane on the day we sign the papers. It has scraps of everyone's clothing in it, and we can tell her about the pieces we remember so she understands she's a real member of the family."

"That's thoughtful, Ruby. She will treasure it, I'm sure. But we'd better work fast to finish it, because there are a lot of preparations to be done."

"Let's make a list." Excitement laced Vivian's voice. "I have a new brother, and now Claire and I are both getting new sisters."

Ruby hugged her, overflowing with plans and optimism.

But during the week that followed, a few nagging doubts plagued her as she did her daily chores, cared for the children and thought about the upcoming celebrations. She and Nash were getting married and adopting Jane for good reasons. But was doing the right thing enough to ensure their happiness? She couldn't forget he had loved and married Pearl first.

There were some concerns she simply had to put behind her. Nash's love for Pearl was one of them. Her own past was another. She'd put that behind her and proven she could fit in here. She could raise these children and make a home for this family. Nash was attracted to her. He wanted her in his life. She was worthy of his love. She was willing to fight for a place in his heart.

Georgia and Vivian would be coming to help finish Jane's quilt the following day, so Ruby cleaned house and put Joel down for his nap. While he rested, the girls played in Claire's room so Ruby could sort the last of the fabric. She and Georgia had cut and sewn what must have been hundreds of pieces, but she'd remembered some she'd run across that her mother had finished, and she wanted to use those as a border.

Ruby dug to the bottom of the basket of fabric squares, dividing them into piles of similar colors and setting aside several that were too faded. None of these fabrics were familiar to her, and possibilities swam in her head. Could they have been bits of her and Pearl's childhood dresses? Perhaps some of the scraps had come from clothing that had belonged to Laura's mother. Ruby would never know for certain, but she was confident they'd been important to her mother, because she'd saved them for so long, and so carefully cut and hemmed each piece.

Between two blue-and-green squares, something wrapped in a piece of paper touched her fingers. Ruby slid out the folded paper and turned it to see the writing. In her mother's handwriting, she read her own name: Ruby Gail.

It was obvious the packet held a small object. Though she was curious, her heart skittered with unease. Had her mother actually meant to leave something for her?

Ruby clasped the paper with both hands, closed her eyes and drew a slow breath, letting it out through pursed lips. Concern flitted through her, but she set the fear aside. Whatever she found was best dealt with now. Laying the packet on the nearest stack of quilt squares, she turned it over and unfolded it.

There, nestled in the letter, lay a gold locket on a chain. The same one she'd looked at in Laura's wedding portrait and in the photograph of Pearl on Nash's bureau. The same one Ruby remembered her mother wearing always. The necklace she'd wondered about.

Perhaps Mama had merely loaned it to Pearl for the portrait. Mama hadn't left the precious piece of jewelry lying in a drawer to be casually discovered. She'd wrapped it in this letter and deliberately written Ruby's name on the outside in hopes she'd find it.

The letters on the page were too blurred by her tears to read for several minutes. Ruby wiped her eyes on the hem of her skirt.

My Dearest Ruby,
Whenever I sit in my rocking chair, I remember holding you close and singing to you. I am not a particularly good singer, but you loved the songs, anyway. Before you could even talk, you sang along in your own precious baby language.

Ruby glanced at the rocking chair before continuing to read.

I understand it broke your heart when your father left. He loved you, don't ever doubt that. He loved us all, but the wandering spirit that drew him away was powerful. I pray he found what he wanted. I pray you do, too.
    I also pray this letter finds you one day, so you will understand how dearly I love you, and so these words can give you peace. I don't hold it against either one of you for leaving. You are young and there is much to be discovered about people, about love. I do hope you found love, Ruby Gail, because it's the only thing that truly matters—that

carries us forward. It's the only real thing in this world.

If you never look back, I know your tomorrows will be blessed. If you do look back, don't live with regrets. You have so many good qualities I admire. One of them is your courage.

You have my heart and my love always,
Mama

Her mother had mentioned nothing of the necklace in this note, though she had worn it always. Ruby clenched it and allowed her tears to flow freely. Mama had wanted her to have it, along with this letter. *"So you will understand how dearly I love you, and so these words can give you peace."*

How typically unselfish of her.

Ruby allowed the implication of her mother's words to sink in. It came as no surprise that Mama hadn't blamed Ruby's father for leaving them—and that she'd wished him only well. Laura Dearing hadn't wasted time on regrets or anger or blame—even though she must have suffered, and his leaving made her life more difficult.

She'd *hoped* Ruby had found love.

How ironic that Ruby had traveled the eastern states and had only a misguided interpretation of love, finding no one equal in character to those she'd left behind. She had carried her love of home and family within, well-hidden. And eventually it had brought her back to this place.

Ruby had agonized over her inability to apologize to her mother. She'd scolded herself again and again. Regret had eaten at her.

Mama didn't want an apology. Didn't expect one. Didn't need one. Mama hadn't blamed Ruby for leaving. She'd missed her, of course. But she'd wished her well. She'd considered Ruby *courageous*.

She'd *wanted* her daughter to find love.

Ruby had been so bent on leaving Dearing farm behind, on seeing places, meeting people, on living life without boundaries, that she'd run out on everyone who'd ever mattered.

The only person who needed to forgive Ruby was herself.

She walked to the mirror over the bureau and fastened the gold chain around her neck. The locket shone brightly in the stream of sunlight shining through the windowpane. How ironic that she'd worn one of her mother's shirtwaists today. Even so, she looked nothing like Laura Dearing. Mama's hair had been a lustrous shade of rich honey, and she'd always worn it in a smooth, neat knot on the back of her head.

Ruby had always felt so different from her gentle mother and her fair, sweet sister. She'd identified with her father, and when he'd left without speaking a word to her, the world had dropped out from under her. She'd been angry at him and she'd taken out the hurt on her mother.

Mama had understood. She'd been heartbroken, as well.

Ruby had been a child. A rebellious child, but a child nonetheless. Because she'd grown up so quickly after leaving the farm, she'd somehow forgotten that.

"I forgive you, Ruby," she said to her image in the mirror, and laid her fingers against the gold locket.

Maybe Mama had been right and God had been watching over them, taking care of them, but Ruby had been as belligerent toward any heavenly direction and protection as she had about her mother's.

"Thank you for the letter, Mama."

Her image in the mirror grew dark, and a gust of wind blew the curtains inward. Flecks of rain dotted the wood floor.

Ruby hurried to lower the window. Ominous dark clouds rolled across the sky, which to the north was completely black. A heavy wind had come out of nowhere and the tall trees along the windbreak bent under the force of the gale. This was no simple thundershower.

Ruby's heart chugged in panic, but her thoughts zeroed in on what she must do. She'd seen enough tornados to know she couldn't waste a second. She ran toward Joel's room, where he was sleeping. "Claire! Jane! Come into the hall immediately!"

Wide-eyed, the girls met her as she ran back with a startled Joel in her arms. Claire's face was white. "What's wrong, Aunt Ruby?"

"Down the stairs *now*. There's a storm, and we have to get to shelter."

"A tornado?" Claire screeched. She grabbed Jane's hand and pulled her forward. They hurried down the stairs as fast as was safely possible and darted through the house to the back door. As soon as they descended the stairs, cold raindrops stung their skin and the wind plastered their clothes against their bodies. The temperature had instantly dropped.

Dust mixed with dry grass blew in swirling eddies before skidding along the earth and disappearing into the murky gray air. A dented pail rolled past.

The mares entered Ruby's thoughts, but the

image fled as quickly as it had come. No time for that.

Jane burst into tears.

"Follow me!" Ruby shouted. Still carrying Joel, she ran across the dooryard.

Tugging a hysterical Jane behind her, Claire obeyed.

The wind sucked Nash's hat from his head, and he quickly finished loading his tools in the back of the wagon. There hadn't been a sign of a storm all morning while he'd been mending fences. He attempted to cover the tools with the tarp, but the wind tore it from his grasp. Cold pellets dotted his head and shirt, and he squinted at the darkening sky. Menacing black clouds skittered in his direction. This didn't look like a passing thunderstorm. His men were scattered across the land today. Ruby and the children were at the house alone.

After unharnessing Boone from the cumbersome wagon, Nash jumped on the horse's back without a saddle and lit out across the pasture, praying the horse's footing was sure and they came across no rabbit or snake holes. His heart pounded erratically.

They'd never talked about what to do if a tornado struck. Claire hadn't seen one since she was a baby, but he had showed her the storm cellar. How long ago had that been? Would she remember? He'd never told Jane about it. Or Ruby.

Of course Ruby would know. She had grown up here. She knew the dangers, and her father had dug that storm cellar.

Ruby knew what to do.

As long as she made it in time. Tornados were unpredictable and deadly.

He scanned the sky for dark clouds, a sick feeling in the pit of his stomach. If a funnel cloud hit the house it could be reduced to a pile of splinters within seconds. He prayed for his family's safety, prayed Ruby had had enough warning.

Nash rode as hard and as fast as Boone could carry him, fighting the wind. A tree branch blew across their path, and the horse spooked, rearing up and neighing. Nash held on to the reins, but gravity hauled him off to the side, where he found his footing in the wet grass and held on. Boone danced in a half circle. "Whoa, boy, whoa. There, boy. Whoa. Good boy, Boone."

Both of them were soaked from the biting rain, and Nash fought to get the horse under control and hoist himself back on top. When he managed it, Boone took a few steps to the side, but then lunged forward. The animal had enough sense to recognize they were heading toward the barn.

A few of the horses in the nearest pastures galloped about, while others stood along the fence
line. They were safest out here, where they could
run. It was the few mares still waiting to foal that
Nash was most concerned about, because they
were penned up in stalls in the barn.

When the house came into sight, he breathed
a sigh of relief. He rode across the dooryard, slid
from Boone's back and released him. The horse
ran to the corner of the barn and stood, nostrils
flaring, ears flattened back.

Nash bolted toward the sturdy wood door of
the underground shelter. It was unbolted from the
outside, which meant it had been bolted within.
Thank God. He banged on the wood. "Ruby!"

A metal sound grated, and he raised the door,
struggling to keep hold of it in the wind.

"Nash!" Ruby's voice. The most beautiful
voice he'd ever heard.

He lowered himself down the wooden stairs
and fastened the door securely above. A lantern
glowed in the dim safety of the underground
shelter, and his children sat on the benches, blan-
kets around their shoulders. Until that moment
he hadn't realized he was trembling.

Ruby stood facing him. "You're soaked."

She reached for a thin blanket and raised it
to his hair. He used it brusquely and hung the

fabric around his shoulders. "I knew you'd keep them safe."

He learned forward and kissed her, not caring that he dripped water on her face. She met his kiss and wrapped her arms around his neck, with the bulk of the blanket between them. She smelled so good. She was warm. She was his home.

Acknowledging the insistent tugs on his legs, he finally released her and knelt to embrace Joel and Claire.

"There's a big wind!" Joel exclaimed with a serious expression. "We run-ded so fast. Jane cried."

Jane remained on the bench, her eyes huge and fearful. Nash sat beside her. "You're safe in here. Ruby won't let anything happen to you. To any of you."

"But you weren't here." Jane's voice shook.

"I can't always be here," he answered. "But you're safe with Ruby. She won't leave you. And I'll always come home as quickly as I can. Always."

He looked up to read warm appreciation in Ruby's blue eyes.

"Aunt Ruby sang to us," Claire said.

"I'm sorry I missed that. Real sorry."

"She'll sing for you, too, Papa, and you won't

have to be scared or sad anymore. Won't you, Aunt Ruby?"

"Of course I will."

Above their heads the wood door shuddered under the threatening force of the wind, but the sturdy latch held it firmly in place. His men were smart enough to take shelter. The horses might run off, but he'd find them. His parents and sister knew how to survive a tornado, too.

Those who meant the most to him were right here. "Sing for me, Ruby."

She sat beside Claire, enfolded her and rubbed her back. "Oh Shenandoah, I long to hear you, away you rolling river. Oh Shenandoah, I long to hear you, away, I'm bound away, 'cross the wide Missouri…"

Less than an hour had passed when Nash pushed back the heavy bolt, raised the door and looked out at the clear sky. The clouds had all blown southward, where the distant sky was still dark, but the wind had disappeared. The ground was wet, and straw along with leaves and small branches littered the dooryard.

He propped the door open and led his family out. "Looks like we have chores to do."

Ruby studied their surroundings. The barn and stables stood firm. The house looked fine, though one side was plastered with wet leaves and the chairs had all slid to one end of the porch. A tattered basket was stuck in the blooming lilac bush beside the porch.

The children headed for the house, but Nash caught her wrist before she could follow them. "Ruby. There's something I need to say to you."

She looked up. His ebony hair had dried in unruly spikes, and his dark eyes were serious.

"I love you."

A tingle passed through her chest. Joy rose inside her, but she was hesitant to accept the emotion.

"When you showed up, I was afraid of how you made me feel. I didn't want to, but I liked everything about you. I wanted to be mad at you and stay mad. I didn't want to admit any failures on my part."

"Nash, you're not a failure. You've made a success of the ranch. You may have struggled with the kids, but you handled losing Pearl the best you could. You've done a good job. No one could have done better."

"That's not what I meant," he said.

She faced him squarely. "What then?"

"I mean Pearl."

"But you loved Pearl."

He nodded. "Yes, I loved her. She was sweet

and considerate, hardworking—all the things you already know about her. She was all those things." He swallowed and took his time preparing his next words. "But she wasn't passionate, Ruby. I loved her, but I didn't feel passionately about her. She didn't make my heart feel ready to explode when I looked at her. I didn't see her hair and want to hold her next to me and feel her body and the beat of her heart. I didn't look at her with the children and think my life was complete. I was not whole. *We* were not whole."

The ache of being less valuable, of being unimportant, lifted from Ruby's chest as she listened. She hadn't been prepared for this. Hadn't expected it. But she'd wanted it. Without admitting it to herself, she'd yearned for him to want and need her.

"I always thought there would be time to work that out. Time for us to get closer. I could have done more, but the desire to change it just wasn't in me, and I've felt bad about that ever since she died."

"We don't have to feel bad about our feelings," Ruby said. "I'm learning that, too. You loved her. You were good to her. She was happy."

He looked pained for a moment, but his expression softened. "She was happy."

Ruby framed his dear face with both hands.

How had she been so fortunate to find this man now? To have him love her? She had lost a lot, given up much on her own, but she'd gained so much more in Nash's love.

His voice was hoarse when he said, "I didn't love her the same way I love you."

"There are all kinds of love," Ruby answered. "We're both fortunate to have known a lot of them."

He kissed her. Life wasn't perfect and there were no guarantees. But there were promises. Nash had promised to always stay on this ranch and be her husband.

She wouldn't be simply a fill-in wife. She wasn't stepping into anyone's shoes, fitting into a mold or being like anyone else. She might not be like most women, but she was worthy of all the devotion he had for her. Nash Sommerton loved her.

Ruby was home.

Epilogue

❦

Three weeks later

Georgia walked toward the shade where Cosmo sat on a rattan chair, the big yellow dog at his feet. She seated herself on the recently mowed grass beside him and reached up for his hand. He leaned forward and kissed the backs of her fingers. "Thank you for this family," he murmured.

She glanced out at the gathering of family and friends who had come to celebrate Nash and Ruby's wedding. Tables draped with white linen and laden with food and desserts stood in a row. Another held pitchers of lemonade and a keg of beer.

The badminton racquets got a workout as children and adults laughed and batted the shuttlecocks back and forth. Jane frolicked in their midst, as much a part of the family now as anyone.

"I didn't make this family alone," Georgia answered. "It's come together rather like one of Laura's quilts."

"It might have been shattered except for your love and forgiveness," Cosmo said.

"Everything that's happened has made us stronger."

He kissed her fingers again. "I love you as much today as I did the day I married you. Probably more."

"Look at your son."

"Which one?"

"Well, there's the happily married one, kissing the beautiful woman in the white lace gown over there."

Nash and Ruby might have been the only two people there, for all the attention they paid to their guests at the moment. Ruby gazed up into her groom's eyes. He kissed her and then said something that made her laugh.

"But I meant the other one."

Cosmo's gaze moved as he searched for and found Miles, sitting on a blanket with Little Bird. The Cheyenne woman held something in her palm and he peered at it. Whatever tiny creature held him enchanted soon fluttered its wings and flitted away. An orange-and-black butterfly. Miles's expression of awe didn't change when he looked at Little Bird's face.

"I guess a few years' age difference means nothing," Cosmo said, pleasing Georgia. At the taxpayers association meeting he had introduced Miles as his son. There had been a few raised eyebrows, and Cosmo had answered questions matter-of-factly. Miles had accompanied the family to church after that, and Georgia had privately explained to her friends. With the truth about Miles in the open, there had been no fodder for gossip, so attention had quickly been diverted to the upcoming wedding.

Vivian and Tucker approached, hand in hand, and seated themselves close by. "This is the perfect day," Vivian said, joining them in their admiration of the gathering and the couples.

"You did a lot of the work," Georgia told her daughter.

"Just in time," Tucker added.

"Why is that?" Cosmo asked.

"She's going to be taking it easy for a while," he explained.

Vivian looked up at her mother.

Georgia's heart swelled and she flattened a palm against her breast. "Tell me."

"We're going to have a baby," Vivian said.

Georgia rose on her knees and hugged her daughter until she squealed. Cosmo got to his feet and pulled Tucker up for a sound handshake.

"What's going on?" Claire came running, out of breath, followed by Joel and Jane.

Their gathering attracted Nash and Ruby, and soon Miles and Little Bird joined them.

Georgia took Cosmo's hand and they looked at each other. Their family continued to grow, and their hearts were more than big enough to hold the love.

* * * * *

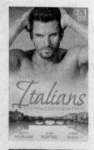